GRAND
PLANS

GRAND PLANS

REMKO JORRITSMA

Ambassador International
GREENVILLE, SOUTH CAROLINA & BELFAST, NORTHERN IRELAND

www.ambassador-international.com

Grand Plans
A novel based on Biblical Prophecy
©2019 by Remko Jorritsma

ISBN: 978-1-62020-722-2
eISBN: 978-1-62020-741-3

ebook Conversion by Anna Riebe Raats

Originally published as *Grootse Plannen*
Translation by Gert-Jan van Heugten

AMBASSADOR INTERNATIONAL
Emerald House
411 University Ridge, Suite B14
Greenville, SC 29601, USA
www.ambassador-international.com

AMBASSADOR BOOKS
The Mount
2 Woodstock Link
Belfast, BT6 8DD, Northern Ireland, UK
www.ambassadormedia.co.uk

The colophon is a trademark of Ambassador, a Christian publishing company.

Grand Plans covers the first half of the, widely recognized, Great Tribulation.

Recommendation: Feike ter Velde

MAIN CHARACTERS

Akhan and **Tarpi**: Banished inmates from Africa

Rita: joins Akhan and Tarpi

Scott, Order: Master and President of the Order

Kent, Order: Master responsible for the PRP

Tarik, Order: Master responsible of Muslim Affairs

Johnson, Wlascow, and **Rositioso**, Order: Rebellious Masters of the Order

Grandego: World leader, appointed by the Order

Molochi: false prophet and Grandego's right hand

Mnaba: Assassin

Jones and Bastian, Church: ministers

Frank, Church: Elder and dissident

Baris and **Zeri**: Heaven Group leaders

Stalnov: Russian tsar

Rekavit: Israeli prime minister

Goldstein: Israeli inventor of LaserDoom

1

AKHAN AND TARPI

THE FEARED PRISON WARDEN, BOMANI, looked threateningly and intensely at Akhan, the convict. "You don't have much of a choice. And if you don't agree soon, you can go back to the basement a little while longer . . . "

"Yes, of course, of course I'm in. But how are we going to get there?" Akhan answered carefully, in a tone that didn't reveal any fear.

Bomani said, "You're travelling with a group of refugees to Europe. One-way ticket . . . And if we ever see you back here again, you'll be executed on the spot. You should be glad your family was able to scrape together the six thousand dollars. God only knows what the poor sods had to do to get that kind of money. But the alternative was for you to sit out your sentence, all fifteen years of it. Tell me, did you enjoy the taste of cockroach?" Bomani smirked and looked provokingly at Akhan. He continued: "It's a good thing you're leaving this place. You wouldn't have lasted long under my regime anyway."

Akhan stood there in his prison rags. "I just want to see my children before I go . . . you can arrange that, can't you?"

Bomani looked up, feigning insult. "You can see your children once you're a European citizen. When you've finally got your residence permit your wife and children may come join you. But what's more important than reuniting the family is for you to announce yourself to our MM when you've been there, say, about six months. The MM will be watching you and will let you know when and where you're to report. Don't forget your journey to Europe is an alternative punishment. It doesn't mean you're free from your obligations. Fifteen years is fifteen years . . . you'll have to do odd jobs for us there, and if you cooperate, we'll leave you alone."

Bomani continued his monologue. "Your material wealth in Europe will increase once you've been there a while. When you get to Italy you must immediately see to it that you obtain some money. I don't care how you do it, but remember, we get a percentage. There have been people clever enough to get loans from banks, without collateral—incredible! It seems those idiots over there simply hand foreigners bags of money. They all know the myths about the Trojan horse, but they're blind as bats and actually finance their own downfall. Either that, or you steal it somewhere, because there's plenty of everything in Europe. You can even try to get friendly with a cute broad. Half the women there are dressed like harlots and are divorced or separating. A bit of friendly attention is all they long for, and they'll fall for you if you can give it to them." Bomani walked around Akhan, moving his hips seductively like a woman might do. "Their perfumed baths have made their skins soft. They all drive Alfas or Ferraris with park-assist and shock-absorbing seats. They won't mind having a good looking, friendly African in bed next to them."

Akhan shuddered with disgust. Suddenly Bomani held a fist up to Akhan's face, his voice and face darkening, and then Bomani caressed his hair.

"Or you get into drug dealing and destroy those arrogant Westerners. They don't see how their daughters and sons fall right into our traps. They have a bureaucratic watchdog for everything but finance their own cuckoo in the nest." Bomani's burst of laughter echoed through the concrete building.

Through the barred window behind Bomani's desk, Akhan saw a guard in a watchtower looking their way. Everyone feared Bomani's thundering bass voice. He could roar like a demon. At times like these a person had to be careful not to say the wrong thing or make a false move, because he could suddenly get violent and attack. Knowing this, Akhan practiced total self-control and nodded approvingly at the crazed prison warden.

"You leave with the next group—probably within a week," Bomani continued as he sat in his swivel chair behind his large, oak desk.

"Well, that's enough information for you. Guards!" The three black clothed men that had brought Akhan from his cell earlier that morning came back in to escort him back.

"Give me my food! It's been paid for!" Akhan shouted at Bomani as he was pushed out into the hallway.

Bomani shook his head.

* * *

"Oh, dumb people with their illusions and mirages, who will wake them up from their dreams?" Bomani said to himself as he pulled a file from his desk drawer. While he browsed through a pile of paperwork his mind went round and round. "I've done well for myself, getting this job . . . " he congratulated himself. "The common man, so naïve in his own little world, with his desire for paradise, he keeps dragging himself forward in his delusions with false hope. Eventually he'll see himself for what he really is and will die miserably without ever having enjoyed the riches this planet has to offer.

"And why? Because they held onto their morals, their so-called *conscience*. Or perhaps out of weakness, too weak to fight? Too afraid and too cowardly to use force to get what they deserve? If you want to break out of the downward spiral of poverty, you have to use brute force. That's how the world works."

Bomani was proud of his career. Although he had above average intelligence, Bomani had long ago found the limits of his social potential. His constantly repeating circles of reasoning were a defense mechanism to suppress the sense of frustration about those limits, and his violence was an outlet for his frustrations. His superiors didn't give him the slightest bit of power other than what he had already taken for himself. The region director, who paid regular visits to Bomani's prison, openly humiliated him by pointing out his weaknesses. The only thing he ever received from the director was a harsh reminder of everything that went even slightly wrong. There was never any reward nor even a compliment for all the things he did so well.

He suffered from the pecking order and small-mindedness of the system in which he was an intermediate, even a prisoner himself. There was never any rest for him.

Not for a moment could he ever be truly happy. A few times a month he was tortured by migraine headaches. Sex and torturing people were the only things that dulled his negative emotions for a moment. He had a tight leash on his three wives and had learned from his father how to control them. "With appropriate violence," had been his advice.

"All in all, I can't complain," he comforted himself once more as his thoughts wound down. "Yes, compared to many people I know I'm doing pretty well. I have more money, more power and a more luxurious life. I've done well for myself, better than most. Bomani, you're a step ahead compared to most others," he mused.

* * *

The guards threw Akhan back into his cell. Several of his fellow inmates looked at him to see if he had brought back any food. When they saw he hadn't, their interest disappeared. Tarpi, his friend, surveyed him. Akhan nodded to show his visit to Bomani, "the Beast," as he was called, hadn't been too bad. Tarpi was the only person he trusted and Akhan was fortunate enough to get a place to sleep next to his friend. There were about twenty convicts in each overcrowded prison cell and the lucky ones were able to sleep against the concrete wall, a place of relative coolness in the usually boiling hot cell. But a person had to pay for that privilege. He had to pay Sauda.

The other inmates called Sauda "the Dragon." Nobody dared defy him. The heavyset man and his two brothers dominated the cell, and everyone had to pay them protection money. They were also the only ones able to get commodities by obtaining them with the help of corrupt guards. This way, all the money that was smuggled in by the monthly family visits flowed to Sauda. He forced his cellmates to get as much money as they could from their visitors.

It wasn't a comfortable way of life for the inmates. The constant complaining, the smell of unwashed bodies, the aggression . . . but most of all that terrible corner where an overflowing steel bucket stood. The only sanitary installation, which was referred to as "the cesspit," was sickening. Every day an old woman, dressed in rags, came to empty the bucket and install a new roll of toilet paper, which was suspended on a rope at head height. After the old woman had left, Sauda was of course the first to defecate.

"What have you learned?" Tarpi asked Akhan when he was back next to his friend.

"We'll be going to Europe within a week." Akhan whispered excitedly. "We're going to be free!"

Tarpi looked at his friend. "That's good," he whispered, "but they say that only thirty people of the last group of a hundred survived the journey."

"Well, yes . . . but how does that compare to spending fifteen years as a member of this club?"

Tarpi smiled. "Whatever. Are you allowed to see your kids?"

Akhan stretched, lay down on his back, and sighed. "My children . . . "

Tarpi looked at him, waiting.

"My oldest son was good at languages, the teacher said. Probably even best in his class, and he might have gone to university. We had hoped to have at least one successful child, so that he could bring wealth to the family with a good job and improve the circumstances of the whole family." Akhan turned to Tarpi. "I've always warned them about criminal practices. 'Be a good Muslim, don't steal, don't befriend the wrong people . . . the criminals, the crooks . . . don't accept their loans or anything,' was my advice to my children.

"My brother had befriended crooks and was eventually found dead in the desert, with a bullet in his neck, but the change I had seen in my brother's eyes during those days had been worst of all. His friendly sparkling eyes had been extinguished by his criminal involvement.

"They became like dead lakes in a volcanic area because he had been forced to do things he hadn't wanted. And all that for a car, a modern cell phone, and a few coins in his pocket. Eventually he refused to be their messenger of misery. That's when they killed him. I wanted to keep the smile, the sparkle of love in my children's eyes, and enjoy it. I protected them from a fall into nothingness, from the hell of the damned, and from those who have no respect for man or beast."

Akhan felt the fire of his fighting spirit to protect his family kindled anew. But a jab of pain through in his shin robbed him of any hope for concrete actions. He looked around, confused. Perhaps he could escape during the journey with the refugees. But he knew people were often bound during the trip and shot if they caught you escaping. His toothache was getting worse.

"Give me another clove," he pointed to his painful tooth.

Tarpi looked at him with pity. "You've taught your kids well, my friend. We've only got one clove left, so I'll give you half," Tarpi replied with a warm voice.

"Thanks," Akhan said. In order to escape his precarious situation for a few hours, Akhan lay on his side and tried to fall asleep.

2

THE ORDER

MOST MEMBERS CAME BY PRIVATE jet to Busan's prestigious Cho Hotel in South Korea. The 40-meter-wide panoramic window in the luxurious conference room offered a view of the deep blue East Sea. Watching the foaming water wash up on the beach was a refreshment for any man's spirit. The green forested Kumjung mountain rose from the horizon on the left of the window. A breeze made the trees sway as seagulls adeptly crossed the skies.

In the evening, there was a trip for the members to the well-known university of Busan, where, in the central lecture room, famed historian, Yisi Bada, would hold a lecture on ancient Korean culture. Many members, however, were more interested in the extensive fish buffet at the moment. The Korean sushi drew particular attention. Its carefully guarded recipe consisted of special vegetables, soju, and peppers. Combined with traditional Korean gin, the sushi had a unique taste. Next morning there would be a trip to the famous Hwaseong fortress for those who were interested.

"Enjoy the sushi but watch out for the gin. We don't want intoxicated members at this important meeting," said Order President Master Scott coyly through the microphone, drawing the members' attention. He wanted to start the meeting. The happy sounds of people slowly died out as the members went to their places.

"The agenda and minutes of the last meeting and the announcements, gentlemen," Scott continued, as he gave a stack of papers to a member, who handed them out to attendees. The members immediately started to go through the agenda and notices. Although they had already received the agenda in an encrypted e-mail beforehand, they were curious to see if the president had made any last-minute changes.

Some members would want to see if their own propositions had been included in the agenda. Those proposals had to be submitted well before the meeting, but the president decided whether they were relevant enough to be included in the agenda.

"Dear High Members of the Order, welcome. As you know, time is like an hourglass. Most of the sand has already flowed through and there is but little time until, *pfft*, the last few grains have drained. Time, who can grab on to her?" Master Scott smiled with a philosophical look in his eyes at the present members. "Yet we shall see our goal realized within the foreseeable future. You will witness it, ladies and gentlemen! The culmination of what started several centuries ago in Scotland. Sam Bushio, our honored member and former president of the US, was the first to publicly announce some of our plans in the late 1980s. A New World Order will be revealed! Although he was a mere pawn who had to follow our Protocols, he was granted the privilege to openly speak of this. A New World Order, the One World Empire, will break through soon, friends!

"The minds of men have been made ready to accept the Number One, Grandego, the world leader who is in our service, and his world government. He will become more and more powerful and eventually subject everything! The total completion of our goals will be realized, and there will be a great feast in both the physical and the spiritual dimensions! It is my and your privilege, gentlemen, to fulfill a prominent role in these developments!"

This lovely introduction was greeted by a round of spontaneous applause, which Scott accepted with his arms raised high. "Thank you, thank you, ladies and gentlemen. But please sit down," the president waved them back into their seats. "Because of the time I will only read out the highlights," he continued. "An important item on the agenda we have to keep a close eye on, and I'm looking at you, Master Kent, is the PRP, the Population Reduction Program."

Master Kent immediately took the floor. "Yes, our policy to drastically reduce global population needs new incentive. We must keep up the pressure, because extensive birth control is simply against human nature. Encouraging euthanasia will meet resistance if it's implemented too quickly. You need time to nudge the mindset of the masses in the right direction. The influence of our media empires has mostly convinced the medical and political elite of our views. The US, Europe, and above all, Russia, show favorable statistics. Everything increases exponentially: euthanasia, easily accessible abortions, and end-of-life assistance, vaccination programs, AIDS and other sexually transmitted diseases, overdosing on morphine as painkillers for the elderly, et cetera. Hospices are opened everywhere. The elderly see themselves as financial burdens. Our pharmaceutical industry is showing large increases in revenue, which is a beneficial side effect. The knife cuts both ways," Kent snickered. "Medicines like Ritalin, methadone, anti-depressants, morphine, and steroids are delivered en masse. The bonuses we hand out to physicians are accepted gratefully. Although, I must say, their resistance is increasing. It seems people are starting to catch on. Groups of protesters, dissidents, activists, anti-globalists and whistle-blowers . . . You know how it goes: keep suppressing them.

"Except for those that have been initiated by us, of course. Our spies are everywhere, and the masses usually follow our lead. What can they do against big business? The anti-smoking campaigns are a setback. Increasing terrorism is a lucky break. I also see some countries aren't very cooperative. Regarding the Population Reduction Program, I want to point out the South American states, the Middle East, and North Africa. We need to exert more pressure on those countries."

Kent continued his discourse. "Most South American and African nations are indebted to our banks, hedge funds and the natural resources sector. Because of my recruitment campaigns, we now have many members amongst the captains of industry, military, elite, and politicians. Almost all are between the nineteenth and thirtieth degree. It cost us a fair bit, but the results speak for themselves." The other members nodded approvingly. "Yes, I can mark that down as a personal success," Kent went on. "I don't want to brag, but this nullifies the accusations of slowness and unimaginativeness I've received from certain members here."

Triumphantly, Kent noticed his fellow members' nods of approval. Kent delighted in these moments. In a flash, he saw his career path to the top before his mind's eye. He was standing strong because of the extensive media empire he had acquired in South America and

Africa during the past decades. The Leiman Bank had lent him many millions, and because the bank was nominated to be sacrificed, the account holders that would be duped by the bankruptcy would be the ones that had paid his bills. This clever contraption had been set up with the help of several other members.

Of course, this meant he had become a servant, bound to the Order. But Kent couldn't care less about that. It had all been worth his wile. His personal fortune was approaching the tenth billion. Kent felt on top of the world.

He could buy whatever he wanted. But the best part were the great feasts to attend and having a place in the exuberant world of the elite. The way one was announced at exclusive balls stroked his ego and reached into the very depths of his soul. Even a cocaine flash was nothing compared to that, although he didn't mind those either. His importance was honored because his unequalled capacities were mentioned extensively. The luxury that surrounded him, the feeling of freedom created by unlimited spending, and enjoying everything this world has to offer gave Kent a delightful feeling of power. A unique privilege that only a few people enjoyed. And if he had feelings of antipathy towards anyone, even if it were a member, he wouldn't have to hide them.

Those days were over and thinking back to them always filled him with disgust. The days he had to pretend. He had to dance to the tune of his superiors, and please them with humble servitude, which he abhorred. *No, it was probably a developmental stage you had to go through if you weren't just born into the loaded global elite. Once you had made it through, you were in. No more pretending. Up to a certain degree, at least.*

Recently, a sheikh had haughtily refused to shake his hand at the start of a meeting about selling the shares of one of his companies. The sheikh's abundance of wealth had made it impossible for Kent to undermine this deal. He had to submit to how he was treated. The refusal to shake his hand and the incapacity to abort the deal felt like a cut right into his heart. But the times he could afford to ignore those folk from the Middle East were permanently over.

Kent refocused his thought and continued without waiting for possible questions. "There is progress, but it's going too slowly. We're behind what was predicted. Several Christian groups are major opponents in these matters. I don't know what's gotten into those people, but they still think in terms of "the more, the merrier." You get what I mean, they're not up to the States' or Europe's level yet, where many churches are neatly following our ideas. But the Muslims are the worst. They don't even bother in the least about our population reduction strategies."

President Scott interrupted Master Kent in order to continue with the agenda. "Yes, we will talk about that later, especially when we're listening to Tarik's report.

"For now, I would like to reflect on how we could increase the pressure from the PRP. How are you going to do that, Kent? And please put forth some innovative ideas," President Scott suggested with a pout.

"Well, wait a minute," Kent responded. "Let's be honest and admit the Plan doesn't leave much room for the imagination. In the eighteenth century, the page of the Order's founder Master Weishaupt was struck down by lightning. That was the only supernatural event in the otherwise rational Plan of the arch-atheist." Kent burst into an impromptu fit of laughter at his own spontaneous but cynical remark. It was true that, a few centuries ago, Weishaupt's page was mortally struck by lightning as he was carrying top secret plans on his body about the Order's sinister plans. In those plans was a detailed description how the Order's strive for world domination should be executed. Monarchies, clerical powers, and similar institutions had to be overthrown. Nationalism had to be exorcised. The world population had to be reduced and humanity was to be controlled completely. The so-called "New World Order" had to be directed by the overlords of the world, a small, "enlightened," ultra-rich group of the elite.

One world government . . . The publication of these plans caused a lot of commotion amongst the established rulers in those days. Over time, some of what was said was forgotten, but the Order and her plans were alive and kicking. In fact, the powerful Order Members manipulated history in the desired direction. The end justified the means. And those were sometimes brutal. Wars, revolutions, and manipulating the financial world were a few of the things they initiated.

A soft murmur pulled him from his thoughts. Kent's cynical remark didn't sit well with many of those present. Full of disdain, they looked at Kent, then the president, and back again. They were rather proud of their founder, their titles, and their status within the Order. A derogatory comment about all that was despised.

When Kent saw that, he forced himself, with great difficulty, to produce an apology. "I'm sorry, I got carried away. Let it be clear that I hold Weishaupt, our founder, in high regard, as do we all. I meant to point out that the methods in this stage of the Plan are all in the spirit of death and destruction. I know these sacrifices need to be made to serve a higher purpose, but sometimes, it's difficult. And on top of that, I'm going through my third divorce . . . "

President Scott cut him short at this moment. "No sentiments, Master Kent, always keep your emotions in check. You have our respect. Continue your work and send regular e-mail updates concerning the progress and new initiatives of the PRPs. If there are any members," Scott looked at the members with a serious frown, "who have any good ideas, then please pass them on to Master Kent. In view of the time, we'll proceed to the next order of business . . . "

3
AKHAN AND TARPI

IN HIS SLEEP, AKHAN HEARD the scraping sound of metal gradually getting louder. It seemed as if he was raised up from the depths of the sea. He discerned the reflected light at the surface above him, which was rapidly coming closer. With a jolt, Akhan awoke and was aware again of the horrible reality of the prison cell. How marvelous to have been so far away from it all this night. It had been a long time since he'd enjoyed the sensation of a deep sleep. But now, hurried footsteps resounded through the hallway, and soon the commands of the guards echoed through the cell.

Protests and moans rose from the group of men who lay closely packed on the ground. Weary, fearful eyes looked at the barred cell door to see what was the matter and who would face the music. This wouldn't be the first time that convicts were dragged carelessly into the hallway to receive a caning in the middle of the night. Often without an identifiable reason.

"Akhan, get out into the hallway and turn with your back to the door!"

"You too, Tarpi. Hurry up!" a guard shouted through the cell while brandishing a cane.

Tarpi jolted wide awake.

No one else was called, so the fellow inmates sighed with relief. Akhan realized this meant the journey would start now.

Once outside the cell, Akhan, still dazed, was firmly grasped by two guards. He looked around and saw many other prisoners were also brought from their cells into the hallway.

Akhan was forcibly pressed with his nose against the cell door as his wrists were being bound with a tie wrap. Akhan looked meaningfully at Tarpi, who received the same treatment against the next cell door. Tarpi nodded. What was the worth of true friendship? Most don't have many soulmates in life. Tarpi was one such friend. They had often helped each other through a mental crisis within the walls of the cell. Speaking words of comfort and encouragement to each other, sharing bread, humor, and standing up for each other when other cellmates were getting aggressive. Akhan's faith in that he would survive the upcoming journey was largely based on the fact the two of them were going together.

A little while later they were in the courtyard, where they enjoyed a cool morning breeze. In the towers were guards—much earlier than usual.

Bomani walked up to them. He was eating a banana and looked disapprovingly at the prisoners. He halted about sixteen feet from them and looked at the group, silent but fierce.

"I hope I will never see you again, you understand?" the prison director said with his torturing booming voice.

"I will once again tell you a few things, and when I speak, you listen closely. I hate repeating myself. Be sure to let what I say get through your thick skulls! Know that your lives are bound to the Sickle Secret Service. You are allowed to taste the West, its riches and its women, your own car, and I don't know what else. But we see you. We know where you are. We keep an eye on you. You get your space, but it is limited. Keep in mind that you are always watched. You get a passport and your criminal past is wiped. But if you don't comply to our orders, we will recover your rap sheet and you'll be judged by us, wherever you are! We don't ask for much, only your life." He laughed before continuing. "When you arrive, I say, you will be very nice to the authorities. Tell them you were suppressed and tortured. You're pitiful and you want asylum, understand? The first half year in Italy, and then on to the Netherlands. You are the Dutch group.

"This conversation never happened, and you were never convicted of anything. You were a hardworking man who only wanted to provide for his family. But the rotten situation, the dictatorship, the suppression and poverty were too much for you. Feel free to scar your own body, it may speed up your access.

"But they will believe you anyway. They don't know anything; there's nothing for them to check. And they won't get any information from here, except that you are missing. Finally, you will be put amongst true refugees. That only makes it easier for you.

"All right, I'll hand you over to your travel guide Al. Do exactly what he and his men tell you, or you won't survive the crossing, I can assure you. Get in rows of three, to the gate and follow the instructions!"

The "refugees" marched across the courtyard and through the gate, where two trucks with idling engines stood waiting. Here and there were armed men. A cloud of diesel fumes wafted over them.

Akhan liked the smell of diesel and took it in. This unlocked a stream of memories. His father had worked in transportation, so Akhan was used to the penetrating smell of diesel from an early age.

He often got to go along to help his father. Akhan's father was stern, but just. He didn't make much, but it was usually enough to feed the whole family. In the afternoon, they would stop for lunch. He'd bake an egg on the boiling hot hood. He often knew where to find cactus fruit beside the road through the dry wilderness. Occasionally, he even caught a lizard. Akhan sometimes had to laugh when they ran after the animal together.

Flour and water were kneaded into dough which he flattened to bake a cake. So, lunch then consisted of an egg sandwich, adorned with fruit. And sometimes with meat, which made a deliciously satisfying meal. Akhan, the eldest son, knew he was loved by his father.

"Hurry up!" somebody yelled. Akhan felt someone pull on his sleeve. It was Tarpi.

"Come," he said, "loiterers get beat up."

Immediately, Akhan was back in reality and hurried to the truck, where he climbed onto the bed. About fifteen people were seated on the benches that had been assembled lengthwise.

Through the open back end, they saw a big man, standing in the middle of a group of heavily armed men. They all carried automatic rifles and a holstered pistol was on their belts.

"I am Al, and I am all over!" Al shouted out at his thirty-strong audience. "These here are my brothers. We control the roads. And— never lay a hand upon my family members, because vengeance is certain and fatal," he added.

Al clicked on a bright floodlight and aimed the blinding beam at his passengers.

"In a few hours, we'll lose the tie wraps. By then, we'll be in the middle of the desert. Escape is futile. There is nowhere to go.

"The scorpions and snakes also obey me, and they will find you. If someone's missing, the heat sensor on my chopper will definitely discover you. I'll enjoy feeding you to the vermin. It's been a while since someone wanted to play hide-and-seek with me in the desert, so I secretly hope that at least one of you will try to escape . . . All right, let's go then."

The last phrase was directed at the drivers. They saluted and the caravan jolted forward, leaving thick clouds of dust in their wake.

4

THE CHURCH

"PRAISE THE LORD!" PASTOR BASTIAN shouted from the stage. The service was going rather well this Sunday morning. Everyone participated.

"Hallelujah, amen! We know He lives, so give Him all the glory! God is good. Marvelous." Each song seamlessly blended into the next. Many people were standing. At the front, a couple of worshippers were waving colored flags. The band really gave it their all.

"Glory! Marvelous!" the pastor repeated a couple of times through the microphone. "Hallelujah! Let it flow through you," he encouraged. "If there are people in need of prayer, feel free to come forward. Don't be embarrassed."

Several people went forward, as did the pastoral team. This went on for another fifteen minutes, after which the pastor called upon the band to slowly wrap up. The music's volume went down and the people who had come forward returned to their seats. "Let's give the Lord an offering of applause," the pastor directed, and he put his words into action. The crowd of three hundred to four hundred clapped their hands. "Thank you. Let us conclude this marvelous service. Please do not go home yet. You are invited to a cup of coffee in the meeting room! We're all family, so please be mindful of each other. Brother Frank, could you please finish in prayer?" the pastor asked.

"Of course," Brother Frank said. "Heavenly Father," he began, "help us to be good to people this coming week and to conquer our bad habits. We bless this upcoming week in Jesus' Name. Amen."

Pastor Bastian took over again. "Thank you, Brother Frank. People, please don't forget to take home a bulletin with this month's activities, and to send us your offerings, because you know the needs. Give generously. Have a nice week."

Pastor Bastian's tasks weren't limited to leading the Sunday services. Besides preaching, he had to lead the board and manage the assistant pastors. He also had to spend time paying house calls to church members. For internal affairs, the Council of Brothers was the most important consultative body. This was the council of church elders. They came together for one evening a month to talk about the problems, vision, and mission of the church. Today's meeting was exceptionally important.

"Historic changes in the church's course," the special invitation had read. All elders were expected to be present.

"Let's open the Council of Brothers in prayer," Pastor Bastian said.

After prayer, coffee was poured, and the ambience was joyful. Eventually, Pastor Bastian asked for everyone's attention again and invited the brothers to sit down.

"Brothers," he said as he looked around. Only when all attendees gave him their full attention, did he continue.

"Listen, this gentleman is Brother Jones from Florida. He leads several congregations with over four thousand members combined.

He's had a long career in the charismatic movement which has led to his authoritative position."

The men looked upon a lightly bronzed man with a broad smile and a dignified blue suit. His hair was combed back, and his big brown eyes were amidst the wrinkles of the fifty-year-old. His nose was flat, a characteristic shared with some boxers. This gave him a tough demeanor.

"Thank you, Brother Bastian, thank you. Now, don't exaggerate, it was all God's doing." The brothers smiled because of the usual humility and nodded approvingly.

Brother Bastian continued. "Important changes are happening in our churches," he said with a tone that was clearly soberer. "You know that there have been many divisions throughout the church's history. Protestantism has become a delta of many streams, with countless denominations. But Protestantism evolves. The enmity between the Roman church and Protestants, that has on occasion led to horrible events, is over. Tolerance and mutual respect have grown. This movement has brought us closer together. This is very good, as there is also a commandment to pursue peace.

"Brother Jones' church has started a formal collaboration with the Roman Catholic Church in Florida and his congregation sees this as an enrichment for their thoughts and experiences. In times of secularization, this is one of the answers the church can offer. As a bonus, many of the beautiful Catholic churches have become available for evangelical congregations. But I'll let Brother Jones have the floor now. After his explanation, he'll take any questions you may have."

"Amen, thank you, Brother Bastian," Jones said. "Very impressive service. I really enjoyed it last Sunday. I was sitting in the back, incognito, and I was pleasantly surprised by the participation of the congregation. Together, you have built something beautiful. Because of this, I feel especially inspired to tell you of my mission: the church and her future. We know generations are like grass, and her flower is her glory. But the sun rises, the grass withers and the flower wilts. What I am saying, brothers, is that we have to think ahead. We need to create goals for the next generation to grow towards. We know a people without vision runs wild. And I am not talking about greying," Jones snickered at his own joke. Aging was a serious problem. He only had to look at the faces around him to see that. Jones continued.

"In Florida, we have long feared a cooperation with the Roman Catholic Church. But after we once again carefully examined the theological essence of the Gospel and compared that to what the pope teaches, we saw the differences were minor. We have the same Bible, the same mission, the same longing for peace. Unity makes us more powerful and influential. Which is exactly what we need to reach the masses. After a retreat at Saint Catherine's Monastery on Mount Sinai, where we studied John chapter seventeen, about unity, we've made our decision.

"That was three years ago, and boy, that worked out better than expected, in all respects. Sharing accommodations, holding joint services and cooperation of leadership. Where there were once walls of prejudice, there is openness. We've summarized our experiences in our booklet 'Better together, better man, and a better world'. The World Council of Churches is very excited about the initiative. They have made available a large budget to be shared amongst the first twenty-five church chains that formally join this movement, which we dubbed One World Faith.

"It was truly great that the Islamic grand mufti of Egypt visited us at the monastery. He even said he was willing to contribute to a movement with a name like ours, if it brings world peace a little closer. Incredible, right? I see it as a higher calling. Now I can use my years of experience to realize this grand plan: One World Faith as the instrument of world peace." Jones looked around with a big smile, realizing he was dealing with many older brothers who might need a new challenge. Jones continued, "From politics as well, there have been agreeing and stimulating voices, both from the right and left end of the political spectrum. This is a global movement that, like a rolling snowball, quickly grows! It would be nice if you would join."

Brother Dant, one of the eldest, seemed to be so fired up by Brother Jones' speech he could no longer contain himself.

"Fantastic!" he exclaimed. "Amen, marvelous, brother!"

Another elder agreed. "An eye-opener, a true eye-opener. So good of you to have gone through all this trouble to involve us. As you were speaking, all kinds of ideas came up. I can see us holding services together with the Church of St. Mary. I say amen!"

Some others clearly needed more time to let all that was said sink in. A couple of the elders had listened skeptically.

"Let us move to the questions, then. Are there any?" Pastor Bastian asked as he invitingly looked around.

"If I may offer some first thoughts on the matter?" Brother Frank asked. He waited for President Bastian's nod of permission. "Our church constitutes a fine number of people. Our teachings are true to the Bible and we are blessed. So why should we suddenly allow different teachings? My concerns are tied to Biblical principles. For example, the Catholic customs of worshiping Mary and post-mortem

sanctification, churches filled with graven images, celibacy, the rejection of Israel, praying together with believers of other religions, even
though they have a very different view of God—?"

Brother Dant interrupted Frank. "Frank! This isn't the time to
start talking about differences in opinion. You don't want to revert
to the Middle Ages, do you?" he sneered.

"To me, those differences are very important," Frank answered.
"I'd have a difficult time praying together with a Buddhist who be-
lieves in reincarnation, amongst other things. I'm all for freedom of
religion, but not for blending them. Then you'd get a religion where
God is saying opposite things. This seems wrong to me."

Brother Jones joined the discussion. "You must be willing to
compromise. That's how conflict resolution goes. All parties need
to show some flexibility in order to get things done. What's not important to you might be important for the other. All you need to
do is take those small differences for granted. If you're striving for
world peace, you have to keep the contents of your faith in the background. Everyone has his own truth, but collectively, you cherish
peace, so that must be in the foreground."

These remarks didn't seem to sit well with Brother Frank.
"Each his own truth? There is only one truth. So, if I believe my
jacket is brown while everyone can see it's blue, you wouldn't say
it was 'my truth', would you? I'm sorry, but this is madness. I don't
want anything to do with religion, I want the Gospel. Legally
speaking, isn't there but one way to God, the cross of Calvary?
Wasn't the punishment for our sins against the perfect Law of
God carried by the sinless Son of God, Jesus, and no one else?
This is why God can grant forgiveness and access to heaven to all

who sincerely ask for it. He remains righteous, because the Law's demand for punishment has been fulfilled through Jesus' substitutionary suffering. God doesn't adapt to our needs, brothers, but we must adapt to Him—"

"Take it easy," Brother Dant urged. "In this same manner people start talking too exclusively about promises for Israel, while there are also promises for Egypt and Iran in the Bible. You have to see all these things in a broader perspective, Frank."

Brother Bastian interrupted again. "Men, don't go into too much detail in this meeting, please! We have to stick to the big picture instead of accentuating the differences, especially when you're recruiting," he said, a bit impatiently.

"Recruitment?" Brother Frank said in amazement. "I thought we were talking about some sort of merger."

"Yes, of course, but one thing leads to another, brother," Bastian replied. "We've lost touch with the larger public a long while ago. Secularization is still increasing. Working together and forming a broad-based world religion will bring more peace than competitive religions. To me, One World Faith seems the most suitable for that job."

"I'm sorry, but I've got some problems with that," Brother Frank said. "You won't be able to see large parts of the Bible in the proper context if this development continues."

Brother Robert, who sat next to Frank, nodded approvingly. There were others present who sympathized with Brother Frank's remarks.

When he noticed this, President Bastian decided to end the Q&A. "Enough has been said for now. Please take these ideas into consideration, and we will speak about them again at the next meeting," he said. "But remember we're living in a time where we can no longer afford to distance ourselves from global developments. The time of non-committal approach is over. We have to jump on the bandwagon."

5

AKHAN AND TARPI

AFTER A TERRIBLE WEEK'S TRAVEL through the desert, rumor
had it the refugees would soon arrive at the last waystation. At least,
the final waystation on African soil. Afterwards, they would head out
to Europe by sea.

The men were exhausted by the journey. The terrain was rough,
even the sparse paved roads were full of potholes, and the trucks'
benches weren't very comfortable. Water and food were distributed,
but it was no excess. They were forbidden to talk during the ride. And
even if they had been allowed, conversations would have been short.
It was difficult to talk, after all, with a swollen tongue that stuck to
the roof of one's mouth and the never-ending hum of the diesel engines overhead.

They slept each night in hastily erected tents. All day long, no
matter where they were, they were tormented by insects. By now, the
travelers had gotten used to sleeping on nothing but a thin roll-up
mattress between themselves and the hard ground. But they only
slept when they were truly exhausted. Then they dozed off and escaped the deplorable living conditions for a little while.

The hubbub of sounds, the stench, and the touch of sweaty bodies eventually wore them out completely. To escape reality, Akhan

tried to think as many happy thoughts as he could. In his mind, he could be with his loved ones, feel his wife's caress, feel her lovely smile warm his soul. He could hear the joyous sound of kids playing and sipping fresh tea in cool evenings.

The journey through the North African desert didn't take the most direct route. The trucks went from town to town and from watering hole to watering hole. On several locations, people were added to the company. Altogether there were over a hundred people now.

"Out! Everybody out!" the hoarse but penetrating voice of Al shouted, pulling everyone back into the uncomfortable present.

The stiff-legged refugees clambered out of the trucks. Akhan clumsily jumped off the bed and only regained his balance after three steps. He rubbed some life back into his cramped muscles and looked around.

Akhan saw three old warehouses. Those were erratically surrounded by a wide and high cactus fence. The only way in and out of the compound was through the well-guarded gate, which, at the moment, was still open. Around them was a rugged landscape dotted with cacti. The grating of the gate itself was overgrown with vines. This place was well-camouflaged.

Akhan and Tarpi were driven through the gate along with the others. Once inside the warehouse, their eyes had to adjust to the darkness. Eventually, they saw Al, standing with arms crossed on an upturned coffee box. When everyone was inside the stifling warehouse and the doors had shut with a dull thud, Al started speaking.

He had the body of a sportsman, but his control of the language showed he had had above-average schooling. "Salam, he who has ears must listen, because I will say things only once. Know that you are blessed to be part of a larger plan without you even realizing this. The full moon is coming. But that power is born on the shoulders of the masses. You are the masses, and without the masses, there is no victory. Sacrifices are stones on the road. You may well be part of that. Blessed the mother who gave birth to you, for she can be proud of you. Tomorrow, you will go out to see and are in the hands of heavenly guidance. We have prevented you from listening to the devilish news of the world media or reading newspapers. Believe nothing but that which I say to you and what you see with your own eyes. Don't accept anything from anyone but your fellow warriors. Great steps have been taken last week. Refugee camps are our barracks, if you will. You'll be surprised about the western world but keep looking upon the light of the crescent moon. The West is money-hungry and haughty. She wants to dominate the rest of the world. But that which has been foretold and longed for will be realized in your generation. It is possible you will end up in houses that strangers have unknowingly built for you. We will take over the world!" Al's eyes gleamed at that last sentence. With a broad smile, he looked at his audience.

Tarpi carefully leaned towards Akhan and whispered. "What's he talking about?"

Akhan shrugged. He was just as clueless.

"Let yourself be waited upon by the wife and child of the conquered," Al continued. "Just a short battle which asks for your full effort, perhaps even your life. But it has a purpose . . . But now, to business."

Al's tone of voice changed immediately.

"Tomorrow, your route will take you through Lampedusa, Sicily, and then the Italian mainland. From there, you're on your own, but our eyes are upon you, so make sure you're available."

Although Akhan and Tarpi didn't understand much of Al's message and what was waiting for them, one thing was clear: there was no way back.

The next morning, Akhan woke early. Scattered beams of sunlight shone through cracks in the warehouse's roof, where mosquitoes performed their aerial acrobatics. Before long, Tarpi and the rest of the group awoke as well. The rusty sliding-gate of the warehouse was opened with a penetratingly rusty sound.

Several of Al's heavily-armed companions entered.

"Get up and take everything that's yours, then get into the trucks!" they shouted throughout the warehouse. At once, everyone hurriedly followed the order. The guards didn't have to tell them to move along. Al's shady henchmen weren't the type to invite to a tea party. They had shown little interest in their well-paying passengers during the trip, and the weapons they carried weren't just for show.

When the group was seated, the trucks drove downhill, as always covered in a cloud of dust and exhaust. Tarpi nudged Akhan and pointed at the sky. Seagulls! They hadn't seen those before. Akhan was pleasantly surprised by a whiff of fresh sea air that suddenly blew through the trucks. The refugees breathed in the salty air and many looked at each other with delight. The sea, the gateway to a new and better future, got closer!

Many came from the inlands and had never seen the sea. This was exciting, despite the circumstances.

The trucks soon entered a fishing port. Ships in all sizes were everywhere; rusty barges in clear, blue water that lay awaiting their next trip.

The trucks stopped and the usual commanding shouts began once more. "Everybody out!"

This time, the refugees had to stand in line while they were counted. Some men came walking down the gangplank of a fishing boat.

The boat had an oddly shaped upper deck that was clearly a later addition. The parts were crudely welded together. The stern was unnaturally deep in the water, causing the bow to rise too much. Between the ships, Akhan could see the breakwater.

Beyond the breakwater, the white crests of the waves shimmered in the burning sun. The fresh blue air seemed to bear the dream of freedom. The screeching of the gulls sounded like singing, the call of a better life, far away, at the other side of the lively, blue sea.

In the distance, a fat man in a green shirt was talking to Al's henchmen. They seemed to be arguing and waved their arms. The fat man, who turned out to be the captain, pointed at his improvised upper deck.

Akhan looked at Tarpi and they could guess each other's thoughts— if a hundred people were going to be stuffed on that boat, the dream of a free life in Europe might soon change into a watery nightmare.

A small crane lifted some large boxes on board. Akhan hoped they'd be carrying water for the journey.

"We stay as close together as possible, my friend, and we try to get a place on the lower deck," Akhan said. Tarpi gave the boat another look and nodded. There, at least, they'd be sitting in the shade.

The negotiations had apparently finished, because the captain's assistants urged the group to go up the gangplank and find a seat. When the last line, Akhan and Tarpi's, was going aboard, the boat was already full, and everyone was forced to move closer together. Al's henchmen were watching from a distance, weapons ready. Whoever looked at them saw the weapons going up to urge the refugees to board faster and do what was said. The captain went to his wheelhouse. He closed it off with a grate, so the passengers had no access.

The people muttered and complained and cursed under their breath, but they had no choice. Was this what they'd paid for so lavishly?

Akhan and Tarpi had been unsuccessful at finding a place on the lower deck.

They were in the burning sun and following the example of some of the other passengers—they tied their dirty shirts around their heads to protect them from the sun. Bottles were doled out as the rickety boat crossed the small harbor with a throbbing engine and a thick cloud of black exhaust gas. A meager but welcome comfort. The excitement of seeing the harbor that morning had quickly turned to grumbling and complaining.

The refugees were glad to be underway and found strength in the thought that their suffering would soon be over, but on the open sea the wailing soon became louder. The beating of the waves precariously rocked the rusty barge. Several people became seasick. Akhan clung to the railing of the upper deck as if it was his lifeline. The rocking motion of the boat deprived him of any possibility of finding a comfortable position.

A man who was barely able to hold on got red-faced and vomited his entire stomach's contents over Tarpi's legs.

"Thank you very much!" the startled Tarpi cried out and gave the man a firm shove. The man groaned and looked at Tarpi with shame and remorse in his eyes.

"I'm sorry," Tarpi stammered. "Scumbags!" he shouted at the wheelhouse.

The captain, of course, couldn't hear him over the drone of the engine. And even if he had heard, he'd have ignored the comment. This was everyday business for him. He just had to drop off his cargo, and then he'd have his money.

After a couple of hours of sailing, half the refugees were sick or getting sick. Their nostrils picked up whiffs of the nauseating stench of vomit and sweat in the fresh sea air.

"Focus on the horizon," Akhan shouted at Tarpi. "It helps you fight seasickness. After the boat trip, the worst will be behind us."

Suddenly, panicked shouting sounded from the lower deck.

"No, no!" they heard. A splash followed, and cries for help came from the water.

Akhan and Tarpi looked bewilderingly at the waves through the bars of the railing. They saw a panicking man with a bloodied face thrash around in the water.

"Help!" he yelled, right before his head disappeared. He came up coughing. "Help! Please help me!" he screamed over the drone of the engine.

A compassionate fellow passenger dove after the drowning man to try and save him. He shouldn't have done that. The rescuer grabbed the drowning man, but he couldn't swim back to the boat against the current. The captain didn't show any signs of slowing down or turning around to help the men come aboard. He kept the boat at full throttle, and a large plume of black diesel smoke obscured the sight of the two men.

Several people cried out at the wheelhouse in an attempt to draw attention to the two men in the water. But the captain sounded the ship's horn and a deafening sound filled the air. One of his assistants fired a few shots in the air with his Kalashnikov.

"Everybody quiet!" he thundered through a megaphone from the railing near the wheelhouse. "Quiet, or more will go overboard!" Immediately, the shouting became a quiet muttering.

The death-threat couldn't cure the passengers' seasickness. Some were hanging over the railing. Others moaned as they tried to find a posture that allowed them to keep the last bit of water they'd drank in their bodies. More water needed to be doled out, and soon, otherwise some would die of dehydration. But after the display of power from the wheelhouse, nobody dared pointing this out to the cruel crew.

The wind had died. This made the waves less rough, and it was easier to find a good posture. The boat now seemed to make good headway and the trip was a lot calmer.

Hours passed. Akhan thought back to the man who had fallen overboard and his unfortunate rescuer. They'd have drowned by now. The chance a passing ship had spotted them was zero. Akhan had once heard people could survive at most a few hours in the water before they succumbed to exhaustion or hypothermia. A feeling of powerlessness gnawed at him. There was nothing he could do, so in silence, he prayed for mercy for these poor souls.

When the evening sky began to turn red, Akhan's thoughts were drawn away from the misery on board and the events of that afternoon. He was always impressed by nature's beauty. This world could be so beautiful.

He looked at a school of silvery fish that had been following the boat for a while now. They frolicked and jumped out of the deep blue sea and had been feasting on the vomit the seasick passengers had barfed overboard.

For hours, they sailed in a monotone cadence, straight through the splashing water. The screeching of the gulls was constantly interrupted by the sobbing and moaning of the refugees.

Akhan and Tarpi tried to close their eyes for a bit while sitting in the lotus position in order to give their bodies some rest. Then, a buzz rose amongst the people. Those with keen eyes could see land on the horizon, and the boat was heading straight for it. Dusk was setting in, but the silhouette of the land became more defined, which brought hope back to the passengers.

"We're here," was the mumbled message.

The closer the boat approached, the more details could be distinguished. On the horizon, two dots grew rapidly larger. Were those ships, closing in on them? On land, red tongues of fire lit up the dusk. The phenomenon drew all attention of those who could see it from their position in the boat. Akhan looked at the wheelhouse and saw fear in the captain's face.

"I've got a bad feeling about this," he said to Tarpi, who now also realized this wasn't the usual course of events.

Even over the noise of the engine the passengers could hear some dull explosions in the distance. Terror took hold of Akhan. He knew what it was he was seeing, up there in the hills: bomb strikes.

"What—" Akhan faltered.

One of the ships was clearly heading their way. It fired! Akhan heard a high-pitched whistling and a few seconds later, an explosion shattered the bow. People panicked and screams filled the air. Many were instantly dazed and moaning. Others started calling out names and looking around in panic. Several people clambered over others in their attempts to abandon ship. The explosion had blown Akhan and Tarpi several feet away. They were lying in a heap of people, some of whom were wholly wedged between the bars of the railing, which had been bent every which way as a result of the impact. A few had been killed outright, but many were wounded and screaming in pain.

Disoriented, his ears ringing heavily as a result of the explosion, Akhan saw Tarpi's face loom before him. His mouth moved, and it took Akhan a while to register what his friend was saying.

"Get into the water! Jump!"

Akhan and Tarpi struggled to free themselves of the jumble of people and crawled several feet before they could fling themselves overboard. Several people were swimming between the wreckage, making for the shore.

The coastline was visible, but the distance was considerable.

Tarpi was able to grab a plank and waited for Akhan. They could now conserve precious energy they'd need to reach the shore by paddling their legs.

Akhan turned around to look at the ship. The deck was completely twisted near the bow, but if the captain would calmly go on, they'd probably reach the shore, Akhan estimated. As the thought crossed Akhan's mind, another high-pitched whistling cleaved the sky.

"Under water!" Akhan yelled.

The two friends immediately dove under and stayed there as long as their lungs held out. The water muted the bang and the pressure wave of the explosion, but Akhan still felt it. The water pressure pushed them in the right direction. Loudly coughing, they emerged.

The fishing vessel had been hit dead center. Fire and smoke billowed up high into the sky. The fishing boat was quickly taking on water, and before long, it sank loudly into the depths.

"Incredible," Akhan said, amazed. "What's going on here?"

Tarpi took in the scene with big eyes. The waves were fairly high, so they couldn't see very far, but they heard panicked shouts all around. Everywhere, people were calling for help as they sank away.

"Forward, now. Don't look back. We can't help these people now," Akhan said to Tarpi.

With heavy hearts, they paddled as hard as they could, pushing the wooden plank before them, further and further away from the disaster area.

Suddenly, Akhan remembered what that human trafficker Al had said in the warehouse during his little speech. That in a few weeks, a lot had changed. Akhan turned his head towards the warship in the distance. With a furrowed brow, he focused his gaze on the ship and spotted the Italian flag. The Italians? Weren't they the helpers of the refugees? At least, that's what he had been told. The Italian navy shooting fishing vessels on their own land? Were they even heading for Italy, or had they drifted? All kinds of questions roamed inside his head.

"Swim, man!" Tarpi called him back from his thoughts.

For a minute, Akhan was afraid the warship would come back to finish the job. But that fear proved unfounded. Dusk soon turned into night, but the water wasn't cold, so their muscles didn't cramp.

Akhan and Tarpi struggled to keep up the tempo against the current. Despite their efforts, the land didn't seem to get closer. Eventually, the sun set, yet the moon didn't rise. It was impossible to estimate the distance to the coast in the pitch black night.

More stars disappeared behind the dark landmass before them. Was that the sound of breaking waves in the distance? Akhan was nearly exhausted when he suddenly felt land under his feet.

"We've made it!" he yelled at Tarpi, who was shorter and couldn't feel the bottom yet. "Can you stand now?" Akhan asked.

Tarpi nodded, looking relieved to feel the bottom. Soon both waded into the shallows.

The sea floor was littered with sharp stones and shells that hurt Akhan's feet. Panting heavily, they made headway and could eventually heave themselves fully onto dry land.

"Ouch!" Tarpi exclaimed and Akhan looked up, perplexed. Tarpi had sat down and was waving his arms around forcefully, splashing around the water his legs were still in. A crab! A crab had caught hold of his foot. He eventually shook it off. It hit the water a few yards away.

"Blast!" Tarpi shouted and rubbed his wounded foot. But he quickly got up and climbed on hands and knees to higher—and dryer—ground.

The coarse pebbles turned into boulders, and finally they were fully out of the water. They climbed over the ever-larger boulders and at last could finally lie down on their backs on a large slab of rock to catch their breath. The waves crashed against the rocky plateau and sprayed saltwater over them.

They lay there, exhausted, and were even able to catch some sleep. Daybreak, however, was very welcomed. The increasing temperature speeded up their recovery. Akhan stood up and after some stretching exercises, he started exploring his surroundings. To his dismay, he saw several bodies bumping against the rock formations—fellow passengers who hadn't survived. A little further along, he saw a small beach between the rocks. A small boat carelessly bobbed against the beach.

A closer inspection revealed it was the fishing vessel's only lifeboat. There was nobody on the beach, however. Further inland, the beach was surrounded by forest. The view was idyllic. Very different from the sandy environment he had called his home. There was vegetation in his homeland, but not as dense and lush as here. The moist air combined with the pleasant temperature felt refreshing. So, this was the heavenly Europe of which he had heard so much! When he returned, Tarpi woke up.

"It's beautiful here," he said, echoing Akhan's thoughts, as he held a hand over his thigh and moaned.

"Tarpi!" Akhan yelled happily, drawing a smile on his friend's face.

"We survived, Akhan. We've been so lucky!" he said. But a sadness returned to his eyes when he saw the bodies.

"Creepy, those traffickers. May Allah punish them!" he said angrily. The morning sun had risen, and it was quickly getting warmer.

"Come on." Akhan walked towards another rock formation.

Climbing and clambering, they eventually reached the beach. Once again, they let themselves lie down on their backs in the soft sand to give their muscles time to recover. A tingling feeling surged through Akhan's body as the tiredness flowed away. This was marvelous, he wouldn't have minded if they could just lay here for a week, just enjoying the sun, sea, and relaxation. But they couldn't fully relax.

There was a sense of alarm Akhan couldn't shake. There was a threat in the air, a tenseness that couldn't be ignored. The uncertainty of their immediate future didn't instill fear, they were used to that. But the unknown surroundings and the knowledge the captain and his companions were somewhere near made him feel uneasy. They got up and Tarpi pointed out the footprints in the sand near the rickety lifeboat.

They headed for the forest, which was dense, but accessible. They were amazed by the size and variety of plants and trees.

As they cautiously headed into the forest, birds filled the air with their happy whistling. Further along they saw some blackened craters between upturned trees. Were those the bomb craters of last night's shelling?

"What's going on here?" Akhan wondered again. "We should have been in a refugee camp by now . . . "

They walked, cautiously but curious, deeper into the unknown forest, keeping an eye open for something to eat.

6

THE ORDER

"WELCOME, MEMBERS OF THE MOST-HIGH Order," President Scott raised his hands out to the side.

The attendees, who until now had been having discussions amongst themselves, gave him their full attention for the formal meeting.

"I'm glad to meet you here in Rio de Janeiro. Do try to free up some time this week for the pretty ladies on the Copacabana." He winked at his audience. "Enjoy this bustling city. And for those of you who'd rather enjoy air conditioning and a good book, our exquisite library has more than nine million volumes at your disposal."

With another generous gesture, the president turned their attention to the thirty-foot-high walls where ancient, bound books were invitingly displayed.

"As you know, my friends," the president said with pride in his voice, "five hundred years of colonization has not only brought riches to the West's elite, but it has also aided in resurrecting the Roman Empire. The Roman knowledge and art to build an empire, combined with industrialization, technological innovations, and modern weaponry, allowed every western European country to erect its own Roman Empire. The colonies, which are the rest of the world, were subjected to the West. The American continents are the impressive phoenixes that revived the lost Roman Empire. Just look at the White House, the Senate, and the military superiority! The West is Rome, friends, and this impressive library in Rio, where our meeting is, is a unique symbol of that fact. But our plans will surpass this modern Roman Empire. We're heading for a total world domination to which all peoples, yes, the entire planet even, will be subjected!"

The proud tone had turned President Scott's voice downright arrogant. "We're heading there. We're not there yet, but we're approaching our goal!"

The others yelled euphorically during this introduction. To his pleasure, his oration had been accepted favorably. He now turned his attention to the documents before him. He leafed through the stack and drew out the minutes of the last meeting, which he held up.

"Here they are," he said. "Were there any questions? Otherwise, I'd like to move on to the two main items of this meeting."

One of the attendees raised his hand. "Not so much a question," Master Hugh said, "but more of an announcement, nonetheless one of the utmost import." It was clear Hugh tried to sound as formal as possible. "The Youth Anti-Poverty Movement in Southeast Asia is on the fast track. We've initiated that through our media. This has resulted in the formation of many militant youth groups. From the densely-populated slums they call their homes they execute terrorist attacks on other districts, destroying many luxury cars and other property. As we foresaw, the conservative governments responded violently to these attacks.

"The Youths, as they call themselves, retaliated with bloody acts of revenge. The situation has escalated quickly, leaving many dead in its wake. The destruction of cars is good for our economic interests, and the many dead are a new advantage for the Population Reduction Program," Hugh said.

"On top of that, the governments use this situation to draw more power to themselves by offering the population a choice—security or privacy. They always choose security, which means they create a police state. The Youths are targeting the last rich royal houses of that region. They serve our purpose to dismantle every monarchy in the world, thus reducing, and ideally eradicating, national sentiment. We need world citizens, not small-minded nationalists. A textbook case of how several aims of our protocols can be developed simultaneously," Hugh concluded.

"Thank you, Hugh, for the update of the situation over there. The developments are in our favor, and with that," Scott continued, "we reach item *numero uno* of the agenda. This item, gentlemen, requires an objective discussion. And I'm looking at you, Master Tarik."

The master stared patiently and unmoving. He knew what was coming.

"I'll ask you some critical questions in a moment," Scott said, "but first I want to put words to the feelings of many of us."

Tarik nodded briefly, a sign of consent. His dark, penetrating brown eyes always commanded respect. He represented an extraordinary number of people. And not the most compliant group of earthlings at that, the Muslims. There was something inscrutable about Tarik, but when he smiled, he seemed to be the friendliest person alive. Then he looked very approachable. He could be very jovial and charming, especially to the ladies, such as at a gala. A man of his status was highly honored and very powerful in the Muslim world. While Westerners could openly joke about their elite, a prominent

Muslim was proudly considered a hero by the masses. He had followers who, without a second thought, would walk through fire for him.

"You know, gentlemen," President Scott said, "that we had decided in the fifties to allow a certain portion of the Muslim population to integrate into Western society. We knew the Muslims' character would mean there'd be no assimilation. But a sufficient presence of Islam would at the very least counter the power of the Church. We had not foreseen the huge windfalls this would bring in the fight against traditional Christianity concerning morals and family values, materialistic benefits, the sexual revolution, extreme emancipation, etc. We have of course stimulated these things. We undermined family ties and the family as the cornerstone of society by encouraging individualism. Television, internet, and cell phones were all big breaks for us. Simply incredible! Everyone started living for themselves and with the increase of immoral lawlessness, social intolerance also increased. People became self-centered consumers with a disposable lifestyle. Hordes of people started online gaming, online shopping, online sex, and narcissistic comments on social media. A bit of drugs on the side or some sort of medicinal cannabis—everybody just boards the train to hell. Secularization and the church's grand apostasy are a fact. We were able to replace the Genesis-theology with the atheistic theory of evolution, which has been drilled into the minds of the masses. Universities and the media have done an excellent job. Secularization among caregivers has nullified their knowledge of the Christian origins of health care. The Muslim migration has helped question the Christian identity of the West. Because of confrontations with Islam, public expressions of religion were banished.

"We forced the Church, or what was left of it, to compromise concerning their delusion of exclusiveness. They had to share everything and were forced to fuse into a single global religion. They had to accept Muhammad as equal to Biblical prophets like Moses and Elijah and add him to the list as the final prophet. Only those ever-growing evangelicals and other free groups have always been difficult to get a hold on. This is cause for concern, and the force behind the growth of these groups is difficult to rationalize. But terrorism helped us prepare the people to give up their extensive privacy, to a level even Hitler would have been jealous of. Thanks to modern communication, we can track people anywhere and anytime through their cell phones, internet usage, and money transfers. The smuggling pipelines for drugs from Afghanistan and Colombia—protected by us, of course—aid in the increase of drug fatalities. Especially cocaine use has increased exponentially. How I love that misleading term, 'elite drugs'. Drug abusers can identify with this term, narcissistic as they are. In the meantime, statistics keep showing a similar exponential increase in drug-related deaths." The president snickered.

"But you all know this. As for the agenda item, and now I'm putting words to the thoughts and feelings of many members, I'd like to hear Master Tarik's opinion in a moment—" The president broke off his sentence to swallow and frowned at Master Tarik, who was calmly listening to what Scott had to say. Tarik's casual demeanor went down the wrong way and a heat rose up his neck.

President Scott could no longer hold in his anger and cried out loudly, "My daughter was, when she was walking in my own town, ordered to wear a headscarf or leave the neighborhood, because it was now under Sharia law!" He jumped up in his fit of rage and now stood looking around, the knuckles of his clenched hands white and bent forward. His anger startled many members. Even Tarik looked slightly uncomfortable. A long, tense silence ensued. Nobody dared to break it. All eyes were fixed on him. Eventually, Scott let himself slump back into his chair and did what had to be done.

"I apologize for shouting." Scott took a sip of water. The tension created by him was lifted and a buzz filled the room.

"Master Tarik," Scott said, "don't take this personally, but the initiative from the fifties has gotten out of hand. The Muslims have become too numerous and money flows too readily to the Middle East. The oil revenues have been invested cleverly and the mainstream means of production have come into the hands of the sheiks and the Saudi's. For the West, only advanced production techniques and related market shares remain. Of course, Muslims are an important group in the global communion, but it's desirable they comply a bit more with the general directives. Each population group has its own sub-cultures with extremists, but the self-declared caliphates, which have sprung up everywhere in the world and are causing veritable civil wars, are excesses that have not been planned by us. They are bad for business, since many outlets for the usual trade have been lost, because the caliphates tend to only do business with their own. This has gone too far and is not serving our cause . . . Tarik, these things are your responsibility. But that is not all, if the rumors can be believed. You're planning a coup to overthrow the central power within our own Order!"

"Nonsense!" Tarik exclaimed loudly as he jumped up. "Complete hogwash, this fear. You're going too far with such accusations! There is an agreement, and the covenants will not be broken! That would be dishonorable. And with all due respect, Mister President, don't you dare call me dishonorable. The influential members within the Muslim governments are loyal to the Order. It's true the Middle East has been surprised by how fast their capital, and the accompanying power, have increased during these past decades." Tarik was now also looking at his fellow Order Members in the room. He paused before continuing.

"This area, that around the 1950s still mostly lived in the Middle Ages, has developed into a serious world power with incomparable speed. Of course, Islamic rulers realize this new demographic distribution can lead to a position of power. Of course, there are those who think world domination is within their grasp. Of course, there are those who, judging by the distribution of funds, see Islamic countries have come to possess a large share of the planet's riches. There are those who proclaim Death's scythe should be run through the immoral West. Of course, we also could start to think like imperialistic Westerners. Yes, many Muslims find it strange the bankrupt West is still the most powerful player in the world. There are Muslims who are saying, 'We should take over . . . ' But Mister President, we are not Westerners, and that's the difference. We think and act different than you would.

"Members, I know the hearts of the Muslim elite. Those who know the Order has helped them to power will not betray her. The image of traitors like Brute and Judas is always in the mindset of Westerners, which is why there is always distrust in their hearts. We have Mecca, beautiful lands, from the deserts in Arabia to the jungles of Indonesia, and we're content with what we have. The current wealth is converted into never before seen luxury and prosperity.

That's a fact. Take it from me they're not waiting to squander that by starting a war against world powers that are armed with highly destructive nuclear missile systems. The womb shall have the final word. 'The more, the merrier' is our motto. And well, if we're having children and others don't, then eventually we'll be populating the entire globe . . . "

Tarik was quiet for a moment to let this last argument sink in. Then he concluded with a final declaration of his loyalties. "Extremists erecting caliphates are not our allies. We fight them as much as anyone. Nobody benefits if the planet is destroyed. Regional power, luxury, and comfort, my friends, are what motivates the Muslim elite to prevent escalations. Take that from me."

When Tarik was arguing his case, the thoughts of President Scott slid away into a state of self-reflection. He discovered classical images of enemies were still rooted within him. They had been able to use the Crisis, the Germans, the Japanese, and later the Soviets for their goals, safely from their own comfort zone, before eventually destroying them. But with the powers from the Middle East, bursting out of bounds, he had lost most feeling of control.

They were everywhere and part of everything . . .

In his imagination, he saw, because of Tarik's words on nuclear weapons systems, missiles flying for Moscow, Peking, and yes, Mecca . . . boom! Just one push of a button. Boom! Bye bye, obstructive powers . . .

Scott smiled, but had to correct himself. The guidelines of the Order prohibited him from cherishing nationalist or racist ideas. On the other hand, he would not hesitate to apply such satanic methods if it led to the final victory. But, he realized, because of the multicultural society a war on two fronts was no longer a realistic option.

Scott briefly shook his head. Why was he always tormented by and preoccupied with endless trains of thought?

Shaking his head didn't help in the slightest. A next thought had already flowed into his mind. Satan walked different paths than he had imagined, say, about fifty years ago. And with this thought, an even more terrible question appeared: was Satan, the bearer of light, whom he had always served so faithfully, trustworthy? Had he bet his money on the right horse . . . ?

His daydreaming ended abruptly when one of the members coughed loudly to draw Scott's attention back to the matter at hand.

"Uhm, yes, yes, of course, Tarik, you have a point," Scott responded, and he changed his expression instantly from dreamy to an attentive frown.

7

PROJECT MOMENTUM

THERE WAS AN AGITATED ATMOSPHERE in the Knesset, the Israeli parliament. Decisions about the threat of neighboring countries and provinces were an everyday occurrence for the government, but this time, it was different.

"Mister President," Secretary Lauff said with a frown, "the budget for Project Momentum has to be increased because of the international acceleration of events which we have to deal with. Do you wish me to explain to you again that even the United States is no longer going to support us? You keep putting your faith in our lobby over there. They have done an excellent job for many decades. They held their ground, despite wars and crises. Our glorious army has written history, miraculously and because of smart leadership, partly thanks to the US's support. But the tides have turned. The ruling elite in Washington are being blackmailed. They bow to the economic pressure of renegade states and the internationally growing anti-Semitism. Once we were revered in the White House, but now we are openly insulted. They feel quite safe and untouchable, between the Atlantic and Pacific oceans.

"The anarchy in our neighboring nations, fed by civil wars, suppression, shortage of drinking water and other primary necessities of life, can escalate to unexpected attacks on our soil. It's very likely that in this situation, professional soldiers will defect and join terrorist organizations. But we must also consider a large-scale attack by a hostile alliance. And I wish to make it clear—they're not coming yet, Mister President, not yet. You know the reports of the secret service. It's not a matter of *if* they're coming, but *when*. They've been getting more nervous since we've begun exploiting our oil and gas reserves. Thanks to our oil well Leviathan we've procured a global market share of seventeen percent. Because of that, the OPEC has lost its means of manipulating the oil market."

Joachim Lauff's smile at his own remark was answered by snickering from others.

"Please continue, Mister Lauff," the president said. "What is it you wish to say?"

"The Psalm 2 scenario . . . " Joachim began.

"I protest!" came a loud cry from the left wing of the congressmen. "We have agreed to leave religious influences, or manipulations as I like to call them, out of the debate!"

Senator Joshi was standing and looked as if stung by a bee. The president had to agree with Joshi.

"No religious talk, Lauff," the president said, looking reproachfully at Joachim Lauff.

"Mister President," Lauff continued, "it's about Project Momentum. The project is based on the text of this Psalm, so it is imperative to mention it. It says in that Psalm there will be a time when the whole world, or literally, 'the kings of the earth', will turn against us. How many absurd resolutions against us have already been passed by the United Nations—"

Senator Joshi, who kept standing after his first interruption, now walked down and rudely took hold of the microphone, causing a short but ear-splitting squeak to ring from the speakers.

"Gentlemen, this is all well and good, but I have always had my doubts concerning this project. It's absurd to base our modern politics on a three-thousand-year-old line of poetry! When push came to shove, we always got help from the States and other countries that, at heart, supported us. I agree much has changed and that there is an increase in negative criticism against us. But I'm sure everything will be fine. Humanity would never agree with a total destruction of our state, as reported in the critical media, would they? Fear is a bad counsellor, Mister President," he concluded his contribution.

The hubbub in the parliament once again became loud enough for the president to draw a few firm blows from his gavel.

"That's enough. The project has been passed, so the ultimate plan will be fulfilled."

"And the budget for that plan needs to be increased!" Joachim Lauff cried out. "The only trustworthy land in the region that won't attack us is Egypt. They know we'll blow up the Aswan Dam if they'd participate in an alliance against us. The whole Nile Delta would be washed away in a few hours by the water mass of the reservoir. People say they won't attack us. But I say the Egyptian elite has built its ivory tower well away from the Delta, in the shape of the new underground city of Khufu. That city is built in the shape of an inverse pyramid. It's a huge, nuclear bomb proof system of catacombs that provides all the comfort you could imagine. Voices are saying those elite are willing to sacrifice everything if there's going to be an infallible offensive against us. The Egyptian people suffer heavily from the ambitions of the political leaders, but they don't seem to care. The story is getting more and more bizarre, people, and I insist we should prepare against the most bizarre weapons that can be forged against us."

Joachim Lauff looked grave. The members of parliament had settled down and let Joachim's words sink in. Most members of the Knesset knew Psalm 2 by heart. Perhaps they had even prayed to the Eternal One to spare them these events during their lifetimes. But the course of events forced them to doubt if God would answer that prayer. Many of the senators had nuclear bunkers and escape plans in place for themselves and their families, in case a deadly war would break out.

Many senators were grandfathers, with lots of grandchildren. What would the future hold for them? The ancient demonic shadow of massacres and holocaust regularly crossed their minds. Many senators had heard first-hand accounts from their own grandparents.

It seemed that, if one was born a Jew, one was cursed. The oftentimes unfounded and irrational hate speech about the Jews was not something that was easily ignored.

It was noteworthy that fear was often transformed into courage and fighting spirit. That's also what had happened with the fear of new persecutions and the extermination of the Jewish people.

Project Momentum was born because Israel, as a small country, had no chance whatsoever of winning against the greater force of her surrounding enemies. This plan was founded on the bloodcurdling pressure of the reality that a driving force was working in the minds of people to destroy the Jewish nation. The World War II death camps were a low-point, but the terrible persecutions throughout the centuries had been beyond count.

That courage and fighting spirit, which rose time and time again like a phoenix from the ashes left behind by this destructive force, became clear in the attitude of the Jews who would fight until the last drop of blood to keep the State they had gotten in 1948. They expressed their fighting spirit by building an ultra-modern military device, but also by excelling intellectually. Israeli companies produced a higher number of relevant high-tech patents than Russia and China combined. They had invented drip irrigation, that could make deserts bloom. Many innovations and applications of computer chip technology had come from the Promised Land. The number of physicians and engineers per capita had become the highest in the world. Israeli scientists were discovering a large amount of relevant pharmaceuticals.

Over one third of the Nobel prize winners were Jewish. How is it possible this insignificant people could measure up to the absolute best of the world?

The world should admire Israel and the Jews for this. But it seemed they weren't admired, but envied and despised. That jealousy could put their enemies to terrible things, and that realization made it necessary to develop an effective defense strategy. That had become Project Momentum. Momentum was actually a collective term for several projects that all served the same goal: to ensure the continuation of the state of Israel and the Jewish people. The most important sub-projects were in the areas of laser technology and genetics and developing those into weapons. The genetics part of the project was curious, because it concerned a "Weapon of Revenge."

"The costs are going to be a bit higher than expected," Joachim Lauff reported to the parliament, interrupting the president's thoughts. "Especially the genetics project is going over budget, but the results are promising. I would not ask for more money for Project Momentum if there wasn't evidence there's a crucial genetic difference between Jewish and non-Jewish DNA. People of Jewish decent have so-called 'genetic markers' non-Jews lack, and the other way around. By the way, it seemed there were more identifiable groups, Mister President."

The president furrowed his brow. Joachim saw his look and tried to explain himself clearer.

"It appears the East Asian groups can also be distinguished from the other human races by these genetic markers. This can be applied, but details and further exposition of the practical applications will be discussed only between the closed Momentum committees for security reasons. So, I will not say any more on that now. The budgets indicate its necessary funds are increased."

"Cut to the chase, Lauff," the president said. "How much do you need?"

"Another fourteen billion shekels," Joachim said with a slight blush.

The hubbub became louder again.

8

AKHAN AND TARPI

AFTER SEVERAL HOURS OF WALKING through the woods, Akhan and Tarpi reached a glade. Along the way they had stood in awe of nature's overwhelming green. The glade was surrounded by forested hills. There were many traces of human activity. Utility poles, trails, and dirt roads crossed the glade. But the poles were partially destroyed, and the power lines were scattered on the ground.

Just as Akhan was considering staying in the concealment of the forest, they heard a strange buzzing noise quickly becoming louder.

"Get down!" Akhan shouted to Tarpi, and he pulled him to the ground by his sleeve. From behind the relative cover of the bushes the men looked around for the source of the noise. Akhan was the first to spot the flying object. It acted like some kind of helicopter, but it was much smaller.

Akhan raised his head and saw it was indeed a drone. The drone got closer, and the friends pressed themselves against the ground in an attempt to remain invisible. The device moved more slowly now and at one point hung stationary in the air, a dozen feet above the ground and less than sixty feet from where the men were.

Cameras started turning around like prying eyes. Suddenly, a metallic-sounding voice sounded from a speaker in clear English, Italian, and Arab. "Stay where you are. You have been detected. We're coming to get you and help you on your way. Wait until the jeep arrives."

Akhan stared at Tarpi in surprise.

"What the heck?" Akhan whispered.

He nodded at Tarpi and pointed to the edge of the forest. Tarpi understood. They jumped up simultaneously and ran as quick as they could through the tall grass, dodging shrubs, towards the close-packed forest.

They heard the buzz of the drone somewhere above them, but the noise grew dimmer as they ran deeper into the woods. They kept on running for many more minutes, even after the sound had completely died out. Akhan stopped for a second to listen and motioned Tarpi to do the same. Panting, they tried to listen for sounds of pursuit. The whistle of a bird and the rustling of the leaves were the only noises in the otherwise quiet forest.

Relieved, they continued at a normal walking pace and over time, their anxiety ebbed away.

Akhan had no idea where they were. He saw no clues as to their location and couldn't orient himself in the forest, which looked the same in all directions. On top of that, they had fled in a zigzag pattern. Where in heaven's name should they go? And what was the meaning of all this?

A hundred questions went through his mind. There was nothing else to do but walk, and hope they'd reach a place where they could gather some information.

Akhan saw brambles bearing ripe fruits. A lucky break!

Now they could replenish their exhausted energy reserves a bit. They feasted on the sweet fruits.

Here, the forest was a little less dense. In the distance, Akhan and Tarpi heard the sound of an engine, which seemed to be coming closer and closer.

Suddenly, a jeep was visible between the trees, and before they could react, it was upon them.

In the car were some soldiers with Arabic-looking faces, armed with machine guns.

"On the ground!" one of the men commanded them in English. This time, Akhan and Tarpi saw no way out. They did as ordered, somewhat crestfallen at how fast this had taken place and the help-lessness of the situation.

Akhan and Tarpi were roughly forced onto their backs by a man with the body of a professional wrestler. The men from the jeep were busy talking and paid no attention to their prisoners. Just as in prison, it seemed so long ago, their wrists were bound with tie wraps.

"Who are you?" Akhan asked. "We've done nothing wrong! Why are you doing this?"

"Take it easy, you'll find out," one of the men answered.

They were forcefully put onto the bed of the vehicle.

As the car raced easily through the woods, Akhan and Tarpi now saw there were many car tracks crisscrossing the forest. The driver apparently knew the route well, because at crossings and side-roads, he turned without hesitation. The jeep drove over jutting roots and rocks at full speed. The guards were able to brace themselves, but Akhan and Tarpi bounced painfully across the bed at times, sending jolts of pain through their tired bodies.

After a while, Akhan saw an improvised barrier with groups of black-clothed soldiers around it. It was the entrance to some sort of encampment. Beyond the barrier, it was a short drive until they reached the barracks. There were groups of men everywhere. Some of them cast curious glances at the jeep, which stopped at a barrack with a gold-painted door.

Akhan and Tarpi were taken out of the truck. One of their captors cut the tie wraps. He shoved them towards the golden door, a sign they were expected to enter.

Once inside, they saw a dozen men, smugly lounging in comfortable recliners. Here and there stood ornate tables with china and pots of steaming tea, cups with roasted sunflower seeds and nuts. Beautiful Persian carpets gave the interior a sense of status. Several visibly armed men, probably bodyguards, stood behind a man who appeared to be in control. He sat behind a large, hand-carved wooden desk and looked up when the prisoners were brought in.

"Come in and kneel down," he said, as he got up to take a good look at Akhan and Tarpi.

"Hmm, I don't know you. Kneel down," he said once again. Tarpi and Akhan were forced onto their knees by the men who had led them into the barrack. The man who stood before them had a skinny face with a large, sharp nose, wide mouth and intelligent, dark brown eyes.

"You must have come from the refugee boat?" he asked.

Tarpi nodded to confirm his statement.

"And you were with the group from Mali?" he continued.

Tarpi nodded again.

"Oh, well, it doesn't really matter whence you came. You've arrived at a crossroads in your life. Your highest calling has become a reality."

The man looked at them threateningly. Suddenly, seemingly without reason, a smile split his face.

"But don't be afraid," the man said. "I'm not forcing anyone, because then I can't trust you. And misplaced trust leads directly to a dishonorable grave. I don't like eyes in my back, and I don't like people who gossip, you understand?"

Akhan opened his mouth to respond, but he didn't get the chance.

"No, you don't need to answer, because I know what you're going to ask. I know what you're thinking: rebellion. But I don't know what you're going to choose. I hope submission.

"Sacrificing your life for the higher goal, which is nothing less than founding our world domination, is what counts. Do you understand? Only under our rule can we force everyone into the right direction. Then everything will work out. Willingly or not, either way. And you should be thankful you're being offered the opportunity to contribute to that.

"Make no mistake—the rewards in paradise are plenty. Beautiful virgins await your arrival. But should you work against us, torture in hell will be the consequence."

The man looked at them sternly and gave a shout, which apparently was a command, because immediately a few soldiers ran towards him.

"One week. You get one week to make your choice. And let it be the good one."

He turned to his soldiers.

"Give them the pamphlet and move out!"

The soldiers poked Akhan and Tarpi in the back with some sort of baton. The meaning was clear: they got up and followed the men outside.

Once outside, they were blindfolded. After at least a quarter of an hour's walk, they were led through another door. The blindfold was taken off.

"No tricks," one of the soldiers said. "Here, read this. There are a few loaves of bread in the corner."

Akhan and Tarpi each received a pamphlet and the soldiers left them alone in the barrack. The door closed, and Akhan heard a latch slide into place. Imprisoned!

"What is going on here?" Tarpi sighed. He quickly strode to the loaves of bread. They were hungry enough to enjoy even the taste of stale bread. Eventually, they laid down on the floor. Their tired bodies welcomed this position. The blind walk had not been easy.

Tarpi sighed deeply a couple of times.

Near the ceiling were several narrow, barred windows, through which bundles of light came shining in. The barrack was pretty deep, but empty. The walls looked solid. The roof was made of corrugated iron and was at least eight feet high. Akhan held up the pamphlet in the light to read the text.

"Your choice, Muslim," the cover said, in both Arab and English. It was only a few pages thick.

"What is it?" Tarpi asked. He didn't take the trouble of looking at his own pamphlet. Akhan looked at him.

"One guess, my friend," he said.

"If this is what I think it is, we've just been taken prisoner by a militant Islamic group," Tarpi said.

Akhan quickly leafed through the pamphlet and drew the same conclusion.

"Yes, extremism," Tarpi said. "Participate or die. It's always the same—"

"Wait, be quiet!" Akhan interrupted him.

In the silence, Akhan heard a noise that sounded like a woman's sobbing. He rose and held his ear to the rugged wall nearest the sounds.

"Yes, a woman crying," he confirmed. The sad sobs continued for a while and then became silent.

It wasn't long before nightfall. Their tiredness caused the men quickly to fall into a deep sleep, even if it was on the hard floor of a barrack.

* * *

They were sore and stiff when they woke up the next day. Akhan moaned as he stretched his muscles.

"Good morning, friend," Tarpi said.

"I sure hope it's going to be good," Akhan replied.

"At least it's good we're still together." Tarpi smiled.

"Let's do gymnastics," Akhan suggested. "I'll lead, you follow."

"Let your muscles work for Mecca," Tarpi joked in a voice that realistically mimicked the camp leader's.

Together, they did some refreshing stretching exercises.

"They could have given us some cheese and jelly, don't you think?" Tarpi said after their morning exercises. Akhan looked at the high windows and didn't respond.

"Stand against the wall over there, would you?" Akhan asked his friend. "And give me a leg-up, so I can stand on your shoulder to see what's outside."

"You're taller, logic dictates I should climb onto your shoulders," Tarpi protested.

"It was my idea, so my call," Akhan roguishly replied. Tarpi sighed and did what was asked.

Akhan put his foot into Tarpi's hands, and then climbed onto his shoulders. Once he was high enough to look outside, he saw another barrack, like the one they were held captive in. There was about fifteen feet between the two buildings, enough space to drive a vehicle between them. A ten feet high fence marked the edge of the complex. The fence was topped off with large amounts of barbed wire. Directly behind the fence was the edge of a forest.

"How much do you weigh?" Tarpi asked.

"If we keep up the meager meals we've had of late, it won't be long before you'll find me light enough," Akhan replied. But he also understood it wasn't a walk in the park for Tarpi to have his friend standing on his shoulders.

Akhan was just about to climb down when they heard footsteps.

"Wait, just a little bit longer," Akhan whispered.

Three men walked past Akhan and Tarpi's barrack, deep in conversation. Because of the high, narrow window, they soon disappeared from Akhan's view. They stopped at the building next to theirs. Akhan heard the sound of chains rattling.

The men snarled something. Then they heard the broken voice of a woman. She said something, but they couldn't understand it because of the distance and the walls.

Then Akhan got a shock. He saw the men drag the woman by her arms. She was slender, with long, black hair, and clothed in a dirty gown. She protested and tried to struggle free, but it was useless.

"Filthy scum," Akhan hissed. He jumped down from Tarpi's shoulders and hurried to the door. Once again, he put his ear against the wood to listen. Tarpi followed suit. But all they heard were the subsiding snaps of the men and a single, soft cry of protest from the woman.

They didn't hear anything else as the day wore on. Nobody came to replenish their bread or anything. Akhan and Tarpi were upset about the whole situation, but they couldn't do anything about it except resting their bodies as much as they could.

Throughout the morning, Tarpi had scoured every inch of the barrack for a possible exit, but found escaping was out of the question.

When dusk set, they heard the woman being returned to her barrack. This time, Akhan let Tarpi stand on his shoulders to look outside.

Tarpi reported the woman wasn't protesting anymore, but walked compliantly, sad and defeated between the men.

When they were convinced the men were out of earshot, they quietly called out to the woman.

"Hello, who are you?"

The woman responded immediately.

"Who's there?" she asked in broken English.

"We're imprisoned here, too. How long have you been here?" Akhan asked.

The woman started crying loudly.

"Three miserable months," she said when she had regained her composure. "You have to do what they say, or they'll shoot or behead you. They say you'll get used to everything, once you cooperate. Then you'll become like them.

"I am—" Her voice choked and seemed to have great difficulty resuming, "the emir's sex slave."

She started crying again.

Akhan and Tarpi looked at each other in shock.

"What a twisted bunch!" Tarpi hissed angrily.

The friends were silent. What was there to say? What could they do?

After a while, in which they each thought through the situation, Akhan spoke again.

"Tarpi," he said, "we're going to have to try our luck."

"What did you have in mind?"

"When they're coming to get an answer from us, there'll be, I think, two or three men. At least, that's what I hope. When they open the door, we act very enthusiastically and tell them right away we wish to join them. We'll say we want to fight for the good cause, and we wish to tell the boss immediately.

"Perhaps the men will be pleasantly surprised, and no longer see us as enemies. Perhaps they'll let their guard down for a moment. That's when we overpower them. We neutralize them and take their weapons and everything else we can use, and then we dig a hole underneath the fence.

"After that, we disappear into the forest."

Akhan looked at his friend expectantly. Tarpi seemed doubtful.

"I hear a lot of 'maybe' in your plan, but I couldn't think of anything better myself. Let's hope those men will act as 'pleasantly surprised' as you say. I don't think we can expect that, but hey, I'm up for a fight." Tarpi took a ridiculous fighting stance.

Akhan laughed and was relieved his plan was met with approval.

"Either way, we'll take them down. I feel primordial powers rising up in me." He snickered.

"Keep in mind those guys have had a good night's sleep and a good breakfast, friend," Tarpi said somberly. A little concern crept into his voice. "We don't know what else is in the forest. Maybe this prison camp is just an enclave in a larger part of the camp. Then we're both dead by nightfall. We could try to cooperate, and sneak out when we're in the field," he said pensively.

Akhan frowned at him.

"No, you're right," Tarpi said. "I'm not doing anything to help these extremists. I'd rather die than be used by them. My family wouldn't fall for it either. We've never given in to terror and murder. We'll get those guys as soon as they come, that's the best plan."

Tarpi now began to pace up and down the limited space of the barrack. "We'll kick them to death, we'll hit them where it hurts. I can already see them squirming," he grunted.

But the guards didn't visit that night. Nor the next day. A bit of rain at the end of the afternoon supplied them with fresh water, that seeped in through the leaky roof. All they had to do was hold their mouth underneath the streams. The water was a blessing. They could freshen up and felt their strength return. They had rationed their bread and used water to soften it.

Yet another night passed without any sign of life.

The next morning, they heard footsteps and there was a muddling at the barrack's door. This was the moment they had been waiting for!

Akhan was right. Three men in black outfits were standing in the opening. They each had a green girdle on with a dagger. Those were mostly for ceremonial purposes, Akhan knew, but no less sharp for that matter. Usually, the name of the family or tribe was engraved into the blade. Each had a pistol in a holster at his hip, and an AK-47 around the shoulder.

"Here's water," one of the men said with a dead voice.

Akhan took the little jerrycan with water. The man immediately went to close the door again.

"Wait, listen," Akhan said hurriedly, and pushed the door back open. One of the men immediately aimed his gun at Akhan.

"Why is this taking so long?" Akhan asked with an insulted look on his face. "To let your brothers hunger and thirst, is that what the Compassionate asks of you? Of course, we wish to join you. We want food, drink, and a woman," Akhan said resolutely. "Tell that to your boss."

The men were confused and blinked their eyes.

"He wants a woman?" the one standing in front said and caught the gaze of his companions. All three of them burst into laughter.

"He wants a woman!" he shouted and laughed pointing at Akhan. It seemed as if this was the first joke the men had ever heard. They couldn't stop laughing.

"He wants a woman," another laughed as he, too, pointed at Akhan, which made them laugh only harder.

Akhan and Tarpi looked at the three men in amazement because of this unexpected response. Akhan turned towards Tarpi, who also started to smile. His friend's smile and the hearty roars of the men caused Akhan to start laughing himself.

At that same moment, Tarpi stepped forward, within reach of the first man.

Suddenly, he stretched his leg and kicked the first man square in the face with his heel. The force of the unexpected blow caused him to topple backwards into the man behind him.

Akhan reacted immediately. He jumped past the door and wrapped his arms around the arms and chest of the third man. Akhan, filled with hatred, gave him a directed headbutt.

The man's nose broke and blood spurted in all directions.

They fell together, but Akhan had the advantage of lying on top. He managed to land several hard blows on the man's head, after which he lay unconscious.

Meanwhile, Tarpi had been busy with the other two men. The one who had received his kick to the face stayed down. Tarpi had jumped the other one, but he was exceptionally strong. Tarpi couldn't get the upper hand. The man used one hand to hold Tarpi under control as he tried with the other to get his gun from the holster.

Akhan saw Tarpi's struggle and ran towards the man to help his friend. The man shifted his grip on Tarpi and tossed him away, towards Akhan.

Akhan dodged Tarpi and in the blink of an eye grabbed a handful of sand and tossed it into the eyes of their opponent. The man rubbed his eyes to get the sand out, but also realized the danger of his vulnerable position and started shooting at random. Bullets flew in all directions, but because of his action, Akhan had bought enough time to grab the dagger off one of the others. A self-assured rest came over him. Akhan held the dagger at the tip, squeezed his eyes to focus on the target, and threw the dagger. It flew through the air, and in less than a second penetrated the clothing and chest of the extremist. For a moment, the man just stood there, fixed on the spot with an expression of unbelief and amazement.

Then he slumped down.

"Quickly!" Akhan shouted at Tarpi, who was getting up and had looked at Akhan's masterstroke in amazement.

"I need a moment," Tarpi said, panting from the fight.

Akhan looked at Tarpi and saw something was going on.

Blood! Tarpi held his hand to his side, and quite a lot of blood was flowing between his fingers. Akhan jumped into action and tore a piece of cloth off the gown of one of the guards.

He knelt in front of Tarpi and bandaged his body where it bled.

"Can you walk?" Akhan asked.

"I'm going to try. Staying here doesn't seem like a good option." Tarpi grimaced at Akhan. "Wait. We're taking that woman." He pointed at the barrack in which they had locked her up.

Akhan sighed and looked Tarpi deep into his eyes. The delay of traveling with a woman might become the death of them. And if they were caught, all three of them would be killed, what good would that do?

"You're right, she's coming along," Akhan heard himself say, to his amazement, as he picked up an AK-47. He walked over to the door of the next barrack and told the woman to take cover. Without waiting for a reply, he shot the lock. Akhan kicked open the door and saw the woman sitting on the ground. Big, brown eyes stared at him in surprise.

"Come on, we're going," was all he could say. With slight diffi-culty, the woman got up and walked towards him. Once outside, she looked at the three motionless bodies in amazement.

When she realized this was a rescue, she seemed to gain renewed energy. She walked over to her former guards and looked at them full of disgust. Immediately, she started to fiddle with the belt and holster. Tarpi and Akhan followed suit.

"How are you?" Akhan asked, pointing at the red stain on Tarpi's shirt.

"No vital areas were hit, I think," he answered with a bit of triumph in his voice.

"Come," said the woman, as she started walking between the barracks, slightly dragging one leg, as she was still getting the belt with the holster on.

Akhan took the jerrycan with water and slaked his thirst with great gulps. Then it was Tarpi's turn to do the same. The water was lukewarm, but because of their thirst, it tasted like honey to them, and their insides soaked it up like sponges. It gave them the renewed energy they so sorely needed in these circumstances.

Off in the distance, they heard men shouting—the gunshots had been heard!

Quickly, they followed the woman between the barracks. At the end of the row of barracks, they turned the corner. The woman stood at a metal door in the fence.

She didn't wait for the men but started shooting at the lock. Akhan and Tarpi hurried towards her, as well as they could with Tarpi's wound.

A well-aimed bullet caused the iron gate to jump open.

Near a barrack some distance away, a few men stopped running. Some of them knelt to help them aim, two others had machine guns.

Akhan and his company didn't hesitate and disappeared into the neighboring forest, between the high trees and bushes.

In spite of her effort, the woman made little progress.

Akhan worried when he saw it. He didn't just fear for the fate of this woman, but also for themselves. Delays. Just what they didn't need. The bushes that surrounded them concealed them. But they were very vulnerable, outgunned and outmatched.

Tarpi rested with his arm against a tree trunk. From the looks of his grimace, he was fighting jabs of pain.

The woman constantly looked around in fear. They didn't know where they were going. But at least they were out of the enemy camp. Perhaps they should find a secluded space and wait for their pursuers, trying to shoot at them from an ambush?

Akhan scanned the terrain as they moved as fast as possible. Perhaps he would see something that could give him an idea or point them into the right direction.

It was at that time they heard a swelling, high-pitched hum. It soon filled the sky. It was unmistakably fighter jets! Several fighters flew over them. A moment later, hard, penetrating explosions rattled the forest, causing their ears to ring.

Tarpi, Akhan, and the woman flung themselves on the ground, hands covering their ears. Birds flew from between the branches of the trees in panic. The ground shook as in an earthquake. The explosions lasted at least fifteen minutes. In the brief moments of silence between them, they could hear the shouts and screams of people. Dull thuds and cracking rushes echoed through the forest, and the wind blew clouds of smoke their way. They crawled closer together. Tarpi pointed at some dense bushes near their position.

"Perhaps we'd better hide for now, instead of fleeing," he shouted. In order to leave as few traces as possible, they crawled through the bushes on hands and feet.

The bushes contained plants with sharp thorns but were otherwise an ideal hiding spot under these circumstances. After a while, the silence returned. The fighters hadn't returned, and the racket caused by the bombing mostly died away. Only a scorching smell reminded them of the bombardment.

There were no sounds of men in hot pursuit. However, they remained in their hiding place in silence, too tired to continue.

For now, they just had to trust they were relatively safe, and that the people in the camp had other things on their mind than pursuing them. Akhan relaxed a bit at this thought, while his body ached for rest and a good bed.

He lay on his back and looked at the sky. The smoke thinned, and blue dominated the sky once again. That's how it was with life in this world, he mused. Full of natural beauty, but all too often disturbed by the filthy smoke of evil . . . a sickened world. Akhan had to be careful not to be overwhelmed with depressing melancholy. He was sensitive to that, he knew. That had given him many difficult days and nights. He was a pessimist at heart, formed by the disappointments of grownup life.

As a kid, he had been joyous, life had been a challenge. But as he grew older and came across more and more misery, he started to see how misery kept the world together. He had become disillusioned.

But perhaps the worst was the realization that the reality of this world had always been and would always be this way. That had broken something in him. He wanted to live, do nice things, have a happy family and intimate moments with his loved ones. Sports, work, and building something good with others. But it had all been made impossible.

Akhan wasn't the only one who felt that way. He had seen many secretly take their refuge in booze and drugs. Others joined violent organizations, that all wanted to fight against injustice, but ironically only served injustice and deepened the spiral of violence. Some way or another, Akhan could understand these things, but he had never felt drawn to it. Violence wasn't the answer. But just being a passive victim didn't satisfy him either.

This journey had given him the hope of discovering a world in which someone could follow their ideals. What he was going through now was very confusing. This was Europe, wasn't it? The streets were paved with gold, it was said. Everyone lived in a palace. There were no worries about food, drink, and other primary needs. Everyone had a car, computer, and every weekend, parties everywhere.

What was going on? Or were the stories, TV shows, and films about the beautiful cities in America and Europe, with all anyone could wish for, fake? Made-up stories and nothing more than movie sets and décor, actors and play?

Even the moon landings in the 1960s weren't real, but scripted, he had once read. People on the moon, that did indeed sound like a dumb joke. Akhan smiled at that thought. Was it all madness?

"Are you daydreaming again, Akhan?" a pleasant voice interrupted his thoughts, which quickly faded.

Akhan took a deep breath of oxygen-rich forest air.

"Hmm, yes, I'm back again." He turned on his side to look at his friend's smiling face. Next, he looked at the woman they brought. She was still laying there but reacted to the friends' chatting and rose to a comfortable sitting position.

"Are you all right?" Akhan asked.

"I'm all right, glad to be here," she answered. She rubbed her knee with her hand and moaned. When she saw Akhan's look of concern, the woman said it was nothing.

"It's all right. Thanks for bringing me along," she said with a hint of emotion in her voice. "I wouldn't have held out much longer."

She cast down her eyes and held a hand to her face. She bent forward and softly started crying. Tarpi, who was closer to her than Akhan, put his hand on her shoulder. Neither he nor Tarpi knew what to do with this woman. At least, she had stood her ground when they escaped. That gave Akhan the confidence they had made the right choice, that she wasn't going to weigh them down as he had thought at first.

She had hit a soft spot with him and Tarpi. A spot of endearment. He was struck with an angry feeling. Anger and aversion against the violence he had to endure the past few months.

This emotion became mixed with battle lust and a deeper conviction that justice would one day reign on this earth. But how, and when? These questions captivated him.

When he saw this woman's sorrows, he wanted to take her under his protection. He wanted to show her there were still trustworthy men. He wanted to help her recover her self-esteem. Akhan was glad there was a way now to put these emotions into action. And that made her a great moral addition to the company.

Tarpi touched the wound in his side, and Akhan asked his friend how he was doing.

"It stopped bleeding. I think it was just a graze," Tarpi said.

"As soon as it's light, I'll look at it," the woman said, looking at Tarpi. "It needs to be cleaned. I used to be a nurse," she added, seeing the questioning looks of the men.

"I used to be able to handle other people's pain very well, but in the past few years, I have these emotional episodes. I need to cry on a regular basis, and I just can't hold it back. For years, I could, but not anymore," she said with mild trepidation.

Akhan looked at Tarpi. This was quite touching.

"It's no problem, just let it out," he said compassionately. He saw the woman rub her leg again.

"Can you walk, or are you also hurt?" Akhan asked.

"It's just muscle pain, I think, but I'm all right," she said.

"By the way, I'm Tarpi, and this is Akhan. What's your name?"

"Fati," she replied, as she repositioned herself and looked at the men. Her pretty eyes were just as brown as the hair that hung down the side of her face to her shoulders. With her lightly bronzed skin, she was an attractive woman who seemed to be around thirty.

"Well, actually, my name is Rita, to be honest. I received a new name because I've become a Muslim. It wasn't what I wanted, but there was no other way. I'm from Spain, but a lot has happened."

Rita paused. Akhan looked at her with understanding. She took this as a sign, so she continued her story.

Their interest revived her a bit, and her voice was a little less sad when she continued.

"I was born in San Roque and have worked for years for an English shipping company in Gibraltar." The woman swallowed and continued.

"My husband left me and my kids." A silence that said more than words ensued. "My kids have disappeared. The police didn't have time to do anything for me, because they had been drafted into the army and were preparing for battle. I fled to Italy with friends. I went to my sister to contemplate life. I didn't know what to do any more, and I miss my children."

Rita now looked at her folded hands.

"Then, that horrible nightmare also broke out over there. It all happened so fast. The village where we were staying was hit during the night. There were noises and screams everywhere, gunshots and what not. Our door was broken open, and a few men in black robes forced themselves into the room. They grabbed us by the hair without even a single explanation."

She sighed deep and put her head in her hands.

"We were forcefully put into different cars. It was terrible. Everything hurt, and the car drove over bumps and through holes, with nothing for me to hold on to. We reached our destination, were dragged out of the car and put into one of those barracks. That was the camp we just fled.

"I'm a Catholic but had to denounce that. Then, a stranger married me, and I could do nothing about it." Rita once again broke down crying. "My life is just ruined. It was terrible."

Once more, Tarpi put his hand on her shoulder and let her cry, without saying anything.

Meanwhile, night had fallen, and the forest became pitch-black.

Rita sought a position that would allow her to rest and hopefully sleep.

"Rest, Rita, rest," Tarpi said softly.

Akhan and Tarpi were silent and tried to lie down as comfortably as possible, in the hope sleep would find them and renew their strength. They felt tired, but also satisfaction because of the escape from the cruel extremists and the air raid. That they had been able to save a victim from the claws of those monsters filled them with pride.

Akhan was plagued by questions. What was going on in the world, for heaven's sake? What did Rita mean when she said the nightmare also broke out over there?

9

THE CHURCH

MANY MEMBERS OF THE CONGREGATION had made it known they wouldn't become part of the One World Faith movement.

However, this was pushed through the hierarchy from above, and membership of the world movement was a fact. For many churchgoers, this was a reason to leave. But most stayed, trusting in their leaders who said it was good for the church and for world peace. Others stayed, simply because they'd been going to church for years, but had never been deeply interested in what church was really about. They came for an appealing service and to be sociable. This Sunday, the affiliation would be celebrated officially.

For months, the Council of Brothers had been preparing.

One month ago, they had declared symbols of other world religions should be placed in the church. Pastor Bastian now had to study not only his Bible, but also the Hindu Vedas and the Quran, amongst several other holy books.

Brother Jones had come all the way from Florida to the Netherlands to be part of this unification service. He had brought a couple of friends, amongst which was Brother Ganesh from northern India. As representative of Hinduism Ganesh was to light a *diya*, an oil lamp, during the singing of a psalm.

Brother Dant was appointed to lead the service, because these past few weeks, Bastian had been busy studying the other religions that were part of the one world faith, so he could weave them into his sermon.

And then it was Sunday. The doors opened. Brother Dant and Pastor Bastian welcomed people at the church doors and reveled in their looks of amazement. Bastian had to smile. It would take a while before most churchgoers would get used to the new look. The church was now filled with elements of other religions, to emphasize unity. Near the entrance, a statue of Buddha was placed on a pillar. On the wall to the right hung a large, beautiful painting of the Virgin Mary, beneath which an altar was placed for burning candles. To the left near the front of the church, a model of a mosque had been put on a standard. A golden statue from India of the dancing god Shiva inside the circular arch of flames, a dream catcher, an all-seeing eye, and numerous other statuettes and talismans now adorned the building.

All objects that were already present had been polished. During the preparations, Brother Mark had almost fallen down a ladder when he replaced some broken lightbulbs in a high, graceful chandelier. When he had narrowly regained his balance, thus preventing a deadly fall, that "blessing" was ascribed to the "combined spiritual forces" that had been created inside the church because of all the objects of worship.

"Good morning and welcome; glad you are here, sister."

The visitors came in, first one by one and in small groups, but later on, it became a veritable stream of people. There weren't only old acquaintances, but a lot of new faces as well. Hindus, Muslims, new agers, spiritualists. As he was greeting people, Bastian's thoughts turned to the past week. Everyone had been busy with the preparations. Only Brother Frank worked against them, along with some of his sympathizers. He had remained a member to be—in Brother Frank's own words—a beacon of light. Because of this, he had refused to sign for and accept the crate containing the Buddha statue that a mailman brought to the church. This meant Brother Bastian had to go to the post office himself, which cut into his valuable study time. Eventually, he had dismissed Brother Frank. If he wasn't going to cooperate, he might as well stay at home.

As they were welcoming people into the church, Brother Frank suddenly appeared in front of them.

"Good morning, Bastian and Dant," Brother Frank said as he shook out his umbrella. "Nasty weather today," he remarked.

His coming surprised Pastor Bastian. Perhaps his recalcitrant phase has passed, and he had decided to join them.

"Welcome, Brother Frank, come in, find a seat."

As usual, the service started off with Christian songs.

The Brothers had decided on this, in order to let the congregation become accustomed to the new system. When Brother Dant opened with prayer, it was clear not everyone was willing to get used to it.

"We thank you, God, Yahweh, Allah, and the gods, for this Sunday. We thank you, Mother Mary and angels and saints, for your protection . . . that we can gather like this in peace."

Some churchgoers had to swallow for a minute; they hadn't expected praying to Mary from the very beginning. But Dant hardly noticed the shuffling in the pews and continued with his prayer.

Bastian had composed this prayer, together with Brother Jones, after the model they used in his church. But the Americans were clearly further along the path to unity than the Dutch.

Dant read the prayer from a sheet of paper. A whole list of gods was called upon and praised to incorporate visitors from different backgrounds.

"The gods have made men equal to gods, we thank you and praise you for that," Brother Dant said.

At this point, he noticed the congregation got a bit restless. Because even though there were a number of new faces, the majority were the ones who had been coming to church for years to worship the Christian God.

After singing a song of unity—the pop classic "We Are the World"—it was time for a creed. This would also be expressed by Brother Dant. The Apostles' Creed would no longer be used. A new creed had been composed by the leaders of the world religions. The text was projected on a screen, so the congregation could, while standing, say it aloud together.

"I believe all ways lead to God, that all people are one and that all religions are expressions of One World Faith.

"I believe in respect and solidarity. I believe in one world religion, one world order and one world leader. In the message of the prophets, of Moses, Jesus, Mary, Muhammad, Buddha; a message of love and brotherhood—"

And then, three things happened at once. The lights of the chandeliers went out. Someone on the second row had taken a raw egg from his pocket. A well-aimed toss made it splat apart against Brother Dant's head. But the real disturber of the peace was Brother Frank, who had jumped up from his seat and ran forward, shouting at the top of his lungs. He held his umbrella at the tip, with the curved handle above his head, as if he was storming the enemy lines brandishing a sword. However, his target wasn't his egg-faced fellow Brother, but the life-size painting of Mary.

"Out with idolatry!" Brother Frank shouted. With a wild swing of his umbrella, he was able to hit the edge of the frame, which caused the painting to fall from the wall. The gilded, baroque frame shattered loudly on the red marble floor.

Frank raised his umbrella to further mutilate the damaged painting. One of Brother Jones' assistants prevented that by felling Frank with a firm right hook.

The chaos was complete. Some churchgoers hurried forward to support Brother Frank, others to help Brother Dant. Still others tried to get outside as quickly as possible. Children started crying, and everyone was shouting simultaneously.

Brother Frank was removed from the church by an external security company, and Pastor Bastian and the Brothers needed at least half an hour to calm down the congregation and to get those still present back in line.

In all the ruckus, someone hurled the statue of Shiva onto the floor. When Brother Ganesh from India saw that, he took his stuff and, outraged, left the church without saying a word.

Red-faced, Bastian decided to end the service and instead continue with the reception.

* * *

That afternoon, an emergency meeting was held in which the Council of Brothers would assess the disrupted church service.

"Quiet, quiet!" Pastor Bastian shouted above all the noise.

The outraged Council of Brothers discussed the desecrating events of that morning, followed up by emotional reactions.

"Quiet!" Bastian shouted again and waved at those assembled with outstretched arms to physically underline his call. Slowly but surely, silence returned, until only Brother Dant was still audibly weeping.

"I feel so insulted," Dant sobbed. He had clearly not recovered from the egg that was tossed at his head.

"This is unbelievable, friend. Such a beautiful, collective, reconciliation service. And what Brother Frank did to the painting of Mother Mary. I don't understand it anymore, I'm very upset and I don't know what to do next. How must we carry on?"

Pastor Bastian took the floor.

"It's all very embarrassing. I've learned Brother Frank has broken his jaw. I'm not going to visit him in the hospital. As far as I'm concerned, there will be no sacrament of healing administered. The motivations of Brother Frank and his sympathizers must be investigated, if we can even call him a Brother anymore. That man is so annoyingly dogmatic. I, too, am but a human being, and not above the power of frustrations. But there have been many incidents the past few years on the miraculous road to reunite with the Roman Catholic mother church. It pains me to even consider it, but I think we should probably excommunicate certain people. I know it sounds medieval, but the word 'heretics' applies to a situation like this. We cannot allow the unification of humanity through the development of a composite world religion to stagnate just because some individuals cannot cope with this progress. Those who place themselves outside the gates are, because of that very deed, a threat to unification, in my humble opinion. We'll need a private meeting with Brother Jones and the representatives of One World Faith, Saints of the New Endowment."

At that point, Bastian was filled with an enormous anger. The evil spirit filled the pastor with a strong feeling to take radical actions against the rebels. Bastian assumed a very pious pose. He raised his arms in blessing over those present and took a few steps forward.

"Brothers," he commenced gravely, "open thine hands to receive."

The Brothers, impressed with Bastian's sudden forceful demeanor, stood up and opened their hands. Some closed their eyes.

"Receive the justice and the willingness to get rid of them who would disturb the rising of the Sun of the New World Order. That they may inhabit the prison camps and suffer, to repent or to die! That death penalty shall be the proof of their erring. Their deaths testify we are the living who, in these turbulent times, keep a steady course! This way, we can spiritually lift people to the higher Plan. The stars have predicted it, the runestones that had been cast pointed towards chaos, but from which the bundled light of the ecumenical togetherness of the world church of religions will finally lead humanity to unity. This will allow us to overcome great challenges. The world, which seems about to collapse, will, with the help of the supporting arm in the form of the true prophet Molochi and the great leader Grandego, help to carry out what seemed impossible!

"Because to God, nothing is impossible, amen?"

The Brothers had gotten euphoric during these inspiring words. Several had sunk to their knees to give glory to God. Others had become ecstatic, and still others simply nodded in agreement with clenched fists.

"Let us purify them from our midst and make them dissolve into nothingness to clear the way! Let nothing stand in our way to be seated in the highest! Let us . . . "

The gathering went on. A buffet had been made ready, and the room was refreshingly rich with oxygen and pleasantly warmed by a modern climate control system.

Outside, the autumn weather was chilly. Shadows of beggars and starving people moved through the streets of the big city.

10

PROJECT MOMENTUM

WITH A STROKE OF HIS gavel, President Eli opened the seventh meeting of the twelve-strong committee named Project Momentum.

"Ladies and gentlemen, protocol demands that I announce to you that strict secrecy concerning everything mentioned in this committee is crucial. No minutes will be written down to ensure confidentiality, and because of our members' genius everything will be kept in our collective memories.

"Let us start by memorizing the contents of the sixth meeting. Participant Cohen, if you please?"

"Certainly, President," Cohen said. He recounted the conclusions and main points of the previous meeting with literal precision. Half an hour later, when Cohen had finished, the president checked with the other members to confirm Cohen's account had been without mistakes. There were no remarks.

"Due to the fact that all committee members agree with Cohen's text, I now give the floor to Professor Goldstein. He will update us on the development regarding the weapon options to give Project Momentum some contents."

Goldstein was a man of at least eighty. His grey beard reached to his knees. Combined with his bushy eyebrows, he could perfectly well be cast as a wizard in a fairy tale movie.

President Eli knew that Goldstein hadn't grown facial hair because he liked dressing up as a wizard for comic book conventions. He had served in the last Arab-Israeli war, in which he lost his best friend. From that moment on, he hadn't shaved, to keep the memory of his friend alive.

The old scientist was known for his innovative thinking. He wasn't truly an inventor, that he left to others. No, Goldstein was a master in converting, applying, and adapting new, functional techniques. He made connections nobody else could.

He had made a huge name this way, as of late mostly through the development of drones. The VI Stealth drone was of his making. It could automatically change its design and color pattern, which made it invisible to the human eye. This sixteen-foot-long UAV had an array of electronic gadgets to remain undetectable to even the most advanced radar equipment, which made it unique in its kind. Not only was this drone a great weapon for espionage, but it could also be used for precision bombardments. The VIs had been used several times to neutralize Iranian nuclear facilities.

Goldstein had many drone related patents to his name. He had contracts with all the world's major drone manufacturers and developers.

And that was where Goldstein derived his power from. He had all those companies build his drones. Patent keepers could use his designs and freely apply their own innovations for commercial gain. But there was one small condition, namely that the essential parts were bought only from his own company. What those manufacturers

didn't know, was that those essential parts were equipped with remote controlled nanochips. These chips allowed the Israeli army to
track the drones.

One push of the button could individually disable every drone
that was manufactured with this Goldstein chip. This encompassed
almost eighty percent of all war-drones around the world. Goldstein
had built in this safety mechanism in case the drones would be deployed against Israel.

"Gentlemen," Goldstein began, "I believe in Psalm 2 and I believe
in Project Momentum. I believe, based on Zechariah twelve verse six,
we're the fulfillment, the executing force of this prophetic word."

The elderly gentleman spoke calmly, in a low, soothing voice.
His old eyes, half covered by his drooping eyelids, kept staring at
his hands.

"These hands," Goldstein said as he raised his head to look at the
assembly, "these old hands have probably made an essential contribution to the fulfillment of the prophecy. The Middle East will burn
when we're attacked. That is why, fellow scientists, I now and then
lift these hands to the blue sky and pray, 'Rather not, God, rather not.
If they refrain from hostility, it doesn't have to come to pass.'

"I wondered, has peace ever truly come through destructive weapons? And still, I have made them. I didn't want to, but an irresistible,
driving force kept me going. Long nights have I spent in my labora-
tory. For months, I have scoured the horizon of modern science, until
I had found the solution to my problem. The solution, in the form of
all-destructive forces.

"An incredible invention has come to me. Regarding Momentum,
I think I have found the instrument that allows us to reach our

goal—the Nanolaser. This is mounted on my Type-A drone and can, with a pulse of a few seconds, permanently disable any human being that carries something of metal in an area of several square miles."

The eleven other committee members looked at each other in disbelief.

"That's amazing," Raplov said, putting everyone's feelings into words.

"Yes," Goldstein answered, "it is, I'm still amazed myself." For a moment, everyone was quiet.

President Eli let the excitement of the impressive announcements run its course. Eventually, he spoke again. "In lieu of the precarious pressure of time and in view of our national security, it's quite extraordinary that technical inventions give us the tools from which we can draw hope. About that, I would like to invite the next speaker to share his views with us. Dayan, you've also requested speaking time. Please explain your ideas clearly."

Dayan cleared his throat.

"Of course, President," he said, "But I doubt I can outdo Professor Goldstein, and I don't know if I can make the DNA story understandable. What I do know, is that with the new weapons, moral dilemmas rear their heads, for which we have to be accountable in case we should deploy them."

Dayan looked around. Once all eyes rested on him with a certain gravity, he started his report.

"DNA markers, ladies and gentlemen. Fifteen years ago, we started this complex research with pain in our hearts. We spoke about a cynical plan, that doesn't reflect our character. The scenario we feared is that the United Nations in New York might accept a binding resolution, that implies the state of Israel may be legitimately annihilated if, in their eyes, it proves to be an obstacle on the road to world peace. We know from experience how, in the past, resolutions have been accepted against our country on irrational grounds. Now that the US has also turned its back against us, our support in the world has become very thin. Add our prosperity to that, which is an eyesore for many countries that are struggling with failing economies. Our feedstock and industrial potentials have turned Israel into a player of global proportions. Other countries can hardly crawl out of the debts they were themselves responsible for, while our riches are piled high.

"Common jealousy, combined with the temptation of apparently easy spoils, can lead to sneaky war plans against us.

"Russia looks at us with the eyes of a snake. Anti-Israel rhetoric is commonplace in Moscow. The former Soviet states in the Caucasus and Turkey want the Russians, because of their technical advantage, to be their big brothers and lead them in this matter. The strenuous relations, remnants of their past, are wiped away. A common enemy reconciles, after all, and now that the Russians have less to fear from the Americans, they become bolder. They've built sturdy strongholds in Syria, Egypt, and other countries. But those are not the only places where there've been rumblings.

"Rabbi Zebulun of Jerusalem was talking about the dangerous Gog and Magog coalition. The fictitious work about the forged *Protocols of the Elders of Zion* sells like hot cakes. Even variations of *Mein Kampf* have become popular in large parts of the world!"

Disgust and indignation was written on the faces of the Committee members. They all knew how, in the *Protocols*, the Jews were accused of planning world domination, and how Hitler's book had poisoned the thoughts of many Europeans by painting the Jews as a "lower species of human." Millions had been murdered because of this.

That these books had been gaining popularity for a long while made the Committee fear the history of pogroms and the Holocaust would be repeated, this time on a global level.

Dayan continued his speech.

"But that is not all. The ancient hatred of the Jews in many of our neighboring countries has reached a dangerous high due to the continued preaching of hatred. It seems deeply embedded in their DNA. Ironically, this is also where we can find the solution to our problem . . .

"The instructions were to develop a technique to find a biological agent, through which we could win a war, yes, your ears do not deceive you, even against the entire world. That agent has now been found, thanks to so-called 'unique DNA markers'! With this weapon, even a collective war of the nations against us can be won!

"Based on certain DNA markers, three groups can be distinguished: Jewish, East Asian, and the rest. For the first time in history it's possible to develop a deadly biological deterrent that targets DNA structures and can distinguish between these three groups. We can deploy this agent in such a way it's very effective against a group with one of the DNA markers."

All Committee members started talking at the same time when Dayan ended his report. Most had no background in genetics and asked their companions to explain things.

President Eli called everyone back to order.

"Dayan, is it possible to give any understandable details?"

"Of course," Dayan said. "It's as simple as it is complex."

Dayan took a flash drive from the inside pocket of his jacket and asked one of the Committee members to dim the lights, while he beamed his presentation on a screen.

"It works like this. In each of our cells, we have almost ten feet of DNA. Over three billion bits of information. Letters, if you will. Those letters aren't random—they contain a code. Some pieces of the DNA code for proteins, those pieces are called genes."

Dayan saw a few of his listeners' eyes were starting to glaze over, so he quickly went to the next slide.

"Proteins are like little machines that perform all kinds of tasks within a cell. The situation is that only a small percentage of our DNA encodes for proteins. The rest, they thought, is 'junk DNA', garbage, evolutionary waste.

"But that doesn't seem to be the case. Much of that so-called junk DNA appears to be functional. That's what ENCODE-2 concluded, an extensive DNA research project.

"There are at least four million genetic switches. These switches determine whether a gene is to become activated more or less frequently. You can compare it to the dimmer on a lamp. The system of genetic switches turns out to be incredibly complex.

"The computer calculations that analyzed the data lasted over three hundred years, combined. This is the scientific basis on which we built.

"We sort of zoomed in on those switches and discovered all the markers I mentioned earlier. We discovered there was less junk DNA in the Jewish and East Asian races than in others. That's the key to our project. Our weapon triggers a piece of junk DNA that's absent in

Jewish and East Asian races but is present in the rest. It shuts down that piece of DNA, causing paralysis."

Despite the technical jargon, the message started to get through to the Committee.

"If I understand it correctly," Eli said, "it's possible to exterminate the world population by causing paralysis?"

"Exactly," Dayan replied, relieved his message had come across. "Exclusion from contamination can be guaranteed based on certain DNA markers. The paralysis will be so severe and complete that those affected will be unable to function and eventually die."

"Terrible," a dazed Committee member exclaimed.

"Yes," Dayan said, "our technology is the last resort in case the Jewish nation is attacked. We may use it only if all else fails, in a life or death situation, if we have to choose between the lives of our citizens and those of our enemies. I hope we'll never need it."

"I think some of our citizens would rather die than be responsible for billions of deaths," one of the Committee members mumbled.

"You may turn the lights back on. This was the general information I also use for my classes, but my further explanation is not on the slides, as per our sworn secrecy."

Dayan ejected his flash drive from the laptop and put it safely back in his jacket, while he continued his report.

"To make the weapon effective, we'll have to spread microscopically small dust particles that trigger the paralysis throughout the entire planet's atmosphere. For that, we need the air force. They can eject the dust high in the air at strategic places, so that wind circulation can take care of the rest. The process takes two months."

The members remained silent for a minute. One of them broke the silence with a question.

"When you say two months . . . do you mean the incubation period is two months, or does the paralysis become effective immediately after contact with the contaminant, and is two months the period until starvation?"

"The paralysis takes place immediately after contact with the contaminant," Dayan replied resolutely, "but it takes two months to spread the agent."

This time, it was professor Joshua who broke the painful silence.

"I know this Committee is a very elite group, who apparently must hold the fate of the world in their hands. We're discussing the fate of billions of people here. As we progress, I find that increasingly difficult. I don't know about you, but I find myself in need of pastoral care. I haven't slept for months. It seems as if I'm tormented by millions of souls. The crying voices of children, women and men. Sometimes, I have to gasp for air out of anxiety. I always sought help with the Eternal One in my pleas, but I cannot rid myself of these oppressive thoughts. I find it difficult to say, but my study of the Tanakh was open one morning at Isaiah fifty-three, the suffering servant. You know, the part about torture, suffering and sorrow. He was pierced and killed, so others could be delivered and receive the gift of life. I find it difficult to say, but I still want to do it. I got the strong impression that we still have another option. An option that's at the heart of humanity, in my opinion. Namely, the option to sacrifice ourselves, so others can live. By that, I mean it's within our power to choose for ourselves to be annihilated. That we receive death from our enemies and discard worldly possessions, to let our enemies be. We die so they may live."

Red-faced, he looked at the other Committee members, whose faces had looked more and more crestfallen.

"Self-sacrifice?" Dayan asked, who had not yet considered this idea.

"Yes," Joshua said. "Self-sacrifice here on earth, to inhabit heaven, worthy and crowned with honor."

Joshua ended his reflection by raising up his tanned hands. He looked at his fellow Committee members with a look that seemed to call upon them to take the Most High into account.

Silence again ensued.

"Members of the Committee," President Eli eventually broke the silence. "I hereby end this turbulent meeting. You will receive the date and location of the next meeting through the normal procedure. Be careful, shalom, and Godspeed."

11

THE CHURCH

THE ECCLESIASTICAL TITLES HAD BEEN changed to reflect the new spiritual reality. Within the new church order, Pastor Bastian had been promoted and was now officially His Eminence Grand Minister Bastian.

That title also meant many new responsibilities. Often, Bastian was asked to lead the continental council of the One World Faith movement.

Such was also the case today. The leaders of the churches, mosques and Hindu temples—who were now allowed to call themselves Bishop—were all gravely waiting in their baroque armchairs. A kind of bellhop who was standing near the high, ornate doors of the classical meeting room, opened the door with a bow and announced Bastian.

"His Eminence Grand Minister Bastian of Europe!"

The Bishops, dressed in newly designed robes, rose and nodded in submission to their spiritual leader.

Bastian wore a green robe, decorated with gold, that reached to the floor. It was elegantly designed, but in such a way the Grand Minister could move freely. Colorful lotus blossom patterns adorned the robe impressively.

His Eminence sat down in his seat in front of the forum with a dignified movement.

"Be seated." He invited the Bishops with a gesture of his hand.

"Brother Bishops," the Grand Minister said. He was purposely silent for a moment.

"Brothers, first I want to say, our church—and I mean One World Faith, which is a merger of all the world's religions—is immeasurably popular. After long periods of secularization, our churches are packed once again!

"Personally, I think music has been our greatest weapon in the reuniting of Protestants with Catholics and the approach of Hindus, Muslims, and Buddhists. The pop bands, playing rhythmic rock tunes and supported by light shows in the ambience of gothic cathedrals, bring people into a devout trance that can last for hours. By leaving dry rationality and making room for emotions, the services have become very popular once more. That, combined with charismatic speakers who focus on the talents of men and make promises that correspond to the ambitions of the public, are the reason our church services draw massive audiences. Churchgoers are encouraged, Brothers, by stimulating them to work on their self-realization and make a career for themselves, to express themselves as central, valuable creatures. It's become a spiritual soul show, comparable to that hit by George Harrison of The Beatles, where 'Hallelujah' turned into 'hare Krishna'.

"The cross is a symbol of the two arms that welcome you unconditionally. The strenuous and humiliating confession, just as those useless karma philosophies, has faded and has been replaced by what really matters—feel good, my brother. The only obligation people have, is to bow for the idol composed by us and declare there is no other.

"We have to admit the charismatic and evangelical churches have helped us by turning the service into a swirling show, that's attractive and draws many people, but without losing the religious feeling. Masterful.

"You couldn't imagine a dancing pope in classical Catholicism . . . and now look at High Priest Molochi. He's swinging during a service. That's what I call having feeling with the layman. The religious cult is developing and flowering like a rose in the desert! We see people united. All in all, we're hugely successful, and that's why now is the time."

The Bishops looked at him enthusiastically, significantly, and curiously.

"Isn't it so that bitter blood must first flow, before the sweet honey can be tasted?" Grand Minister Bastian said. "Was it not that Samson from the Bible, who had killed a lion, later came upon that same location and discovered bees had built a hive of sweet honey in the cadaver? That he could relieve his weariness with honey . . . that's the case, Brothers. The old church had to die to have the honey built into that cadaver. It gives us new strength and revival."

Bastian looked triumphantly at the bishops as he said that eloquently.

"The old lion and its cubs had to die. The anti-ecumenical splinter groups, who have gathered under the name HG, Heaven Groups, and seemed to pop up all over the world, who counteracted our supporters and sabotaged our chosen course, have been largely defeated. They wanted to stop progress. They had no prophetic insight and would thus never get to taste the honey. They, who confused the people, the sects that suddenly appeared on the streets all over the world and proclaimed the intolerant, false teaching of the One Way Jesus, we've literally decapitated them.

"These evangelistic groups said they based themselves upon the Bible and claimed Jesus was the only way to God, which directly opposed the teachings of One World Faith—that all ways lead to God. We've been allowed to bless the troops of the One World Defense Force and be a part of the extermination of the rebels," Bastian heatedly continued. "World Emperor Grandego and the Prophet Molochi went before us in a rite of dedication. The first one hundred enemies were sacrificed by them personally with the golden cyanide awl. And it's just that only they could enter and become a Bishop, only they who were willing to take part in the killing of the enemies. You are Bishops, Brothers. Ye have killed the lions and may now eat of the honey; you will have the power in this world and will be honored globally in our religion shows. You were anointed in blood by the Prophet Molochi. You are privileged to witness the dedication of World Emperor Grandego in Jerusalem!"

Cheers arose and echoed through the room.

Bishop Vandergreen winced uncomfortably at these words. He had known Bastian for a long time. A little while ago, he had been in the Brother Council of the church in the Netherlands where Bastian was a pastor. Bastian's rise to power had been quite lucrative for Vandergreen. He had Bastian to thank for his appointment as Bishop. But despite the fact he agreed with the ideology of Bastian and the One World Faith, he had had some internal struggles. He didn't like some aspects: anointing with blood and dedication—disgusting. He thought it was just criminals that had to be sacrificed. But when he arrived at the place where it would all happen on that exciting day, he saw many former colleagues. Although these Brothers had refused to belong to the One World Faith movement, which wasn't smart, they were good people.

He was shocked to recognize the black-eyed face of Brother Frank, who was standing between the others. Brother Frank had indeed been out on the street with all those others and preached the forbidden gospel. What was hostile about their message was that arrogant exclusiveness: there was only one Way and one Truth, namely Jesus, without Whom no-one could come to the Father. Yet, Vandergreen always had sympathy and great admiration for Brother Frank. Frank was always very diligent. He helped everyone and prayed with power, so that people sometimes were healed and delivered. He also helped the poor and was a board member of a Christian rehab center.

With his eyes squeezed tight and disgust in his heart he had administered the poisonous cyanide awl to his former church fellow. A shudder of doubt ran over his back when the memory of that moment crossed his mind.

"Join the HG," Frank had said at the very last moment. The penetrating voice of His Eminence brutally disrupted Bishop Vandergreen's train of thought.

"Yes, it is time. An exalted era dawns. The eon, the epoch, has come upon us. The white light, that unites all hues in itself, will be crowned. The incarnated Krishna, the Mahdi, and the Christ the Savior that was prophesied by all faiths, is coming! It's the World High Priest Prophet Molochi. He will execute the inauguration and coronation of World Emperor Grandego. We will go to Jerusalem together!"

Excited cheers filled the room once more at these words and the invitation for the inauguration. This was a once in a lifetime event; a privilege to witness.

"Excellent! Congratulations! Yes, to Jerusalem!"

The Bishops looked at each other with glee.

"Marvelous to travel together, with such an exalted purpose, glory!"

* * *

Grand Minister Bastian let the euphoria run wild for a moment.

He let his eyes wander through the gothic room. Where once hung paintings of the ten stations of Christ's suffering, there were now ten modernistic watercolor paintings of Molochi and Grandego. On these representations, the two great leaders fed hungry people, laid the first stone of a World Faith Temple, and revealed the talking Image, to which everyone must bow. All historic moments. Bastian, who was well-versed in history, couldn't deny a comparison between the stations of Grandego with the images of Stalin and Mao in the former communistic power blocks. When the assembly had calmed down a bit, the Grand Minister went on to explain the plan.

"Filled with joy from these events in Jerusalem, we will continue to Mecca and then Delhi. Between us, who had dared dream such a thing? That we would get this far in our lifetimes. One world religion, one world government! World peace is at hand."

Grand Minister Bastian gestured to the waiters, who came in with bowls of fruit, different kinds of meat, breads, wine, and other delicacies.

The Bishops' good moods only increased.

There were even those who gave each other a spontaneous hug.

"Take, eat, drink," His Eminence Bastian encouraged them. The Bishops didn't need to be told that twice and started greedily with their favorite hobby: eating. The swollen bellies of most Bishops stood testimony to that fact.

During the meal, His Eminence Bastian's cell phone vibrated.

"Lord High Priest Molochi!" Bastian said joyously, after he had seen the caller ID.

The Bishops sitting near Bastian heard Molochi's name and immediately were all ears.

Bastian listened to Molochi say, "Two men have appeared in Jerusalem and attracted the media's attention by loudly proclaiming things and call themselves prophets. Loudly, they have declared World Emperor Grandego is a deceiver, a God-hater, and servant of Satan, and that he has a short time before he'll be judged, things like that; and all that in front of the cameras while the press were doing live shows. The entire world has heard those disturbing words and seen those men. You have to take them down through prayer!" Molochi ordered.

The high pitch of Bastian's voice betrayed His Eminence's nervousness.

"Pray them away?" His Eminence Bastian repeated.

The phone call had become the center of attention and all Bishops had gathered around Bastian.

"Can't he send soldiers to those two psychopaths?" Bastian replied outright, while he looked at the Bishops around him for support. He neglected the fact that this conversation was supposed to be confidential. Bastian fell silent because of the response. The by-standers couldn't hear every single word, but Bastian was sure they did hear a lot of swear words coming from the other end of the line. Molochi continued on, explaining more of the situation.

"I don't care how, just fix it or otherwise you'll be in trouble." The call was cut from the other side.

His Eminence Bastian looked at the Bishops in astonishment, concern, and disbelief. The fearful voice of His Eminence didn't sound too promising. Bastian wasn't easily taken aback, but this conversation was a major buzzkill. After a while, Bastian lowered his cell phone.

"We've gotten an assignment," he said eventually.

"An assignment, what kind of assignment?" the Bishops asked.

"We have to kill those camel hair wearing false prophets to prove our spiritual powers."

The Bishops looked at each other, surprised. Bastian clarified the situation.

"Apparently, two self-proclaimed prophets have appeared in Jerusalem, who prompt people not to join our One World Faith movement. Their message is that people should accept Jesus the Nazarene.

"The worst is that Grandego was holding a live interview on the Intercontinental Network for a viewership of four billion people. Those two madmen mysteriously gained access to the location where the interview was held and disturbed the broadcast with all kinds of statements. Deeply offended, Grandego ordered his security to remove those two immediately.

"But apparently, they couldn't: the security guards were killed by lightning strikes.

"In his function as supreme commander of the World Defense Forces, Grandego commanded several platoons of heavily armed soldiers to immediately kill those two idiots. However, before they could do this, fire fell from the sky which devoured them while they were still on their feet. A squadron of Apache helicopters that was supposed to take them down from a distance befell the same fate. Grandego even sent in fighter jets and tanks, but nothing helped.

"This situation has caused enormous chaos and confusion in Jerusalem. Grandego accused those two prophets of witchcraft. Later, in an explanatory speech on the World Network, he said the two were members of the highest satanic order of witches and that a convergence of occult forces had been invoked by the two wizards, which had temporarily enabled them to unleash their demonic display of power against them.

"Terrible, all this, because the authority of Grandego and Molochi has received a huge bashing.

"The inauguration has even been pushed back because of this, and Grandego has now given us the responsibility and ordered we, the highest clerical power of the One World Faith, should fix this case by permanently taking down those two fools. He calls it a religious matter, and because we handle the domain of religion, it's up to us to solve it."

A cold shiver ran across Grand Minister Bastian's back, because he knew full well he possessed no magic powers whatsoever. Bastian was good with words, that's where his talent lay. Talking, mesmerizing, impressing, intriguing. He knew all the impressing poses and rhetoric a man needed to captivate the audience.

The combination of his university degree and elite background had given him the career many spiritual leaders were jealous of.

But wizardry? He hadn't the faintest idea.

"We must take those two down. And we must do it in front of the cameras. High Priest Molochi says this is at the same time a test of the authenticity of our faith. If we refuse or if we fail, we'll be 'replaced' and banished to prison camps as hypocritical imposters. That's the same as being put to death!"

His Eminence Bastian recoiled a little at his own words. High-pitched, he continued. "Molochi straight-out called me names. He compared us to the bishops of the past. He called us pedophiles and money-hungry opportunists . . . " Bastian realized the total power-lessness of his position.

He felt this moment of total loss into the deepest depths of his soul.

"Your Eminence, would you like an aspirin?" a nearby Bishop asked him.

"No thanks, that's all right," the Grand Minister said. He was a master of self-control during speeches and important meetings and knew how to take every pose that seemed relevant, but most of all natural, at that time.

But the dead feeling deep inside almost always, as an aftertaste, kept spoiling the full experience of things. He had encountered that before in an extreme form, with difficult setbacks. A deep, dead feeling of loss and abandonment. Even during his speeches, as he preferred to call his sermon, it happened from time to time. Professionally, he had met High Priest Molochi a couple of times, and he was indeed a very dominant person. One could hardly get a word in edgewise and there wasn't a grain of sympathy to be found in his monologues. One always went home with a deep sense of rejection.

Bastian remembered how he left Rome after that first meeting with mixed feelings of, on the one hand, incredible awe for Molochi's display of power, and on the other hand a humiliating feeling of rejection and realization of his own puniness.

Bastian knew his position was fully dependent on the high priest, a man who could overturn anyone without compassion or even permanently remove someone. And yet, the total power he had felt with Molochi still intrigued him. He was jealous. And Grand Minister Bastian had become a powerful man in his business himself.

Everything that was placed beneath him just had to bow. The realization his position was that weak after all, which Molochi had so clearly insinuated, yielded a very depressing undertone to everything they enthusiastically wanted to work on just a while ago.

12

THE ORDER

"GENTLEMEN, QUIET, QUIET PLEASE!" THE pompously clothed registrar said on Master Scott's cue. The smartly dressed men quieted down and took their places in luxurious armchairs. Hardwood tables with small TV screens, a microphone, and a set of in-ear headphones were set up near their chairs, so they could listen to the live translation. Each table was adorned with an array of refreshments and bottles of the most diverse drinks.

"Welcome, World Masters. It's a privilege to lead this Order. Let's give our Chinese hosts a grateful round of applause!"

The applause that followed reflected the respect for the hosts. The large room was completely decorated in classical Chinese ornamental style. In the four corners, near the ceiling, red dragon heads stared threateningly into the room. Technically ingenious light effects made forked tongues in the form of flames flash from their mouths. The walls were covered with a warm velvet wallpaper, with abstract patterns in light hues.

The lower part of the wall was covered by a high, traditionally carved wooden paneling, with representations of farmers harvesting, oxen drawing ploughs, and women carrying baskets on their heads.

Against the wall, behind Master Scott's rostrum, hung a huge, masterfully executed painting featuring the Chinese Wall. The Wall snaked from the distant mountains in the background towards the front of the painting, where happy-faced workers were busy building it. To the right, a royal entourage was depicted. The emperor, in all his glory, seated in a carriage, encircled by architects with building plans and worshipful concubines, was inspecting the builders' progress.

To the right of the rostrum sat three prominent Chinese men, who were honored to accept the applause.

"Especially for you, our hosts have ordered golden sweet and sour chicken to be cooked for you. It's made after an old and secret recipe. In this form, the dish used to be prepared only for the great Mao. It signified the exaltedness of Chinese culture. Mao loved it."

Master Scott picked up a chicken leg, dipped it in the sweet and sour sauce, and took a bite with a satisfied expression. The Masters followed his example and the assembly enjoyed the delicacy.

"Pour yourself something and drink; it's a spicy dish."

Master Scott looked a bit mischievously at his audience.

It was always a good idea to start a meeting with a meal or delicacy. It made the atmosphere less tense.

And it was clear there were tensions. A lot had happened the past few years. The events on the world's stage had accelerated. Good things, that were in line with the Plan, but also things to worry about, that caused sleepless nights, even for those at the highest level. Which was saying something, because this Order of the super-rich wasn't easily disturbed. These people held the world in their power. They decided the policy the national political errand-boys had to adhere to. To those errand-boys, it was imperative to master the art of communicating this premade policy to the people. The Order Members could make or break economies. They controlled the capital. *Das Kapital*. They had eliminated Marx. They had, without major confrontation, brought down the power blocks of the Soviet Union and China.

How did they do this? With money, lots of money.

These two power blocks had been fully absorbed by the world economy and had become dependent on that. China itself had become a prominent capitalist stronghold.

Although they formally adhered to communism, they had developed themselves into the Scrooge McDucks of capitalism. The big money was in the hands of people who in name were still communists.

But also, in Beijing they were bound by and dependent upon the global economy and foreign capital. The Order, who controlled many multinationals and banks, was above it all in the end. One snap of the fingers was enough to drive the sea of peoples into a certain direction. A single telephone call with a president or ruler, anywhere on this planet, was enough to determine the course of something.

"Gentlemen, how great is it that our Grand Master Grandego, as UN President General, head of the IMF and commander of the World Defense Force, has almost reached the status of Total Ruler!" Scott opened.

Noises of agreement were heard from the room, and even some spontaneous cries of joy.

"Hurray, hurray, hurray!"

"More steps need to be taken, friends, and that is why I declare," Scott took the large president's gavel, raised it high above his head and slammed it down on the lectern, "our meeting opened!"

The men who had stood up, sat down again.

"You have received the present agenda, but I don't know if we can treat everything today," Master Scott said. "Grandego still needs to win some electorate amongst the common man. Of course, we don't necessarily need it, but to get this and that done, a larger majority comes in handy.

"There are a few points we need Grandego to press. So, let your media machine get to work on that.

"Through the judicial power, especially in the West, we have tormented people for decades by boosting crime. We did that by giving ridiculously mild sentences. I must say, our thinktank has done a good job by introducing the phenomenon of 'community service'."

One of the Masters in the room took the microphone. "There were drug dealers who made millions with the blood of their victims. After extensive detective work, they were dragged in front of the judge and got away with a couple hundred hours of community service." His laugh echoed in the chamber.

"Yes, I know, spare me the details." President Scott scowled. They were allowed to laugh about those kinds of details, but not during official meetings. It was a good topic for an informal meeting, over a drink.

The Master who had made the comment now noticed the looks of disapproval from his colleagues and quickly sat down.

"We hereby propose to allow Grandego to impose the death sentence to drug dealers and addicts in all his territories," Scott continued.

Scott looked around the room to see the reactions. The realization that this affected a large number of people had to dawn. Several members were heavily addicted to cocaine themselves. What did the

Master mean by this? One of the members, Master Rashid, now stood up and asked if he could give some details concerning this proposal.

Master Scott knew what went on in the minds of those present. "Don't be afraid, gentlemen, it's about street junkies. Since the nineteen-sixties, drug abuse has increased exponentially. It's become a pandemic. This was also effective regarding the Population Reduction Program. In the meantime, people are terrorized by addicts and drug gangs.

"So, I'm referring to criminals, drug addicts, and dealers on the street level. Grandego will gain enormous popularity if he can rigorously and permanently deal with this menace.

"He can do that by implementing capital punishment for these kinds of crimes. He must do it very theatrically—like during the middle ages—in the stocks and public executions! The old-fashioned way, as far as I'm concerned, with an executioner who roughly sentences them."

Scott made no attempt to hide a grin because of this statement. In his rich imagination, he already saw the executioner, a morbid looking hangman, with a black leather mask on and wristbands with steel spikes, dressed in long, black robes and holding a torture device, ready to strike mercilessly. A good executioner would make the audience cover their faces because of the fear and pain he could bring upon his victim.

Now that those present understood this wouldn't endanger their own interests, they once again responded, relieved and agreeably. This genius proposition could expect full approval.

"Since there's still an opportunity to raise objections at the end of the meeting, I'll continue to the next topic."

With these words, Master Scott closed this item.

"The next item is rather sensitive. It has been discussed here before. It concerns the contents of the secret meeting of the AG, the Arabic Group. We've heard before from our eminent and respected Master Tarik that the Middle East remains loyal to the Order, and that they keep using their increased power to preserve their luxurious lives.

"He told us they respect the nations who hold nuclear power over them. We don't have to fear the AG will turn against us. In the end, we've created and even partly financed their growth options.

"Yet, I read a spy report about this AG meeting, which painted a different picture than this communicated loyalty. This report implies the Arabic Group aims for absolute power within our Order."

An unprecedented tumult filled the richly decorated room.

Several Masters got to their feet and started to shout.

"We have to do something; this is unheard of!"

Master Tarik stayed remarkably calm through it all.

A moderate Master took the microphone and called the room to order. The ruckus finally died down after a few failed attempts.

President Scott gestured for this Master, Lars Nord, to address the assembly.

"Hear, Masters of the World," Lars Nord began. "Perhaps similar words have been heard in the AG, and if not, there are always some groups and factions who indeed think that way. But—and I emphasize *but*—isn't it so that all factions represented in the Order have thought that way once in a while? Double agendas, deliberations, probability calculations, and dubious initiatives that are directed only towards power gain for their own faction? Even detailed plans for a coup have been discovered once. The point is, that no single faction has the power to change the mainstream goals of our Order. They must comply, willingly or otherwise. An equilibrium between the different power houses has already been established. A singular assumption of power that leads to a dictatorship of one of the factions is virtually impossible. People are economically woven together, and everything is dependent upon everything else. It's a dynamic equilibrium, in which only trivial accents can shift. Accents that will never have enough impact to be decisive for one faction to dominate. The continental division of the earth in ten territories, as we have in our plan, has largely been realized. All we need is a formal confirmation. This division and the interrelations will allow us to keep ruling. 'Divide and conquer' is the driving force that keeps us in control. Our capital will always be enough to manipulate the parties in such a way that relationships will remain intact. I'm not afraid of undercurrents within the ten territories. One way or another, we rule supreme, and we will keep doing so. Even the AG cannot change that. It's up to Grandego to execute our plans in detail, and he will."

Many of the attendees embraced these words with an applause for the speaker. President Scott thanked Master Lars Nord extensively for his contribution. Still, he couldn't help himself warning the assembly the Arab forces shouldn't be underestimated.

Master Tarik took the word and declared he fully agreed with Master Lars. Some more remarks were made by other speakers, but because the arguments kept turning in circles and nothing new was presented, Scott decided to end the discussion.

"Then, we have one more point before we end the plenary meeting and divide ourselves into groups to develop detailed proposals for the specialized subjects. Master Johnson," Scott said, as he looked at the Englishman.

All faces now turned to the man who was always dressed in a black three-piece suit. His tie, which had a standard blue color, left no doubt about his political preferences, a classical liberal, who had no problem seeing the common man as pawns to serve in the military or in factories. But he was also a democrat, who didn't refrain from heavy, cynical critique of his own party. As a modern Shakespeare, he could use his academic speech to play a high-blown devil's advocate. One should not have a heated argument with him, because loss was certain.

"Masters of the World," Johnson opened flatteringly. "My item is that our Number One, Grandego himself, commanded me in an email to send two billion dollars to one of his friends, an emergent industrialist in India, within a week. The day after I had explicitly refused, my villa in Florida was bombed, supposedly by Muslim extremists. However, a thorough investigation I instigated led me straight to the address of our 'honored' leader!"

Hubbub rose in the room. "A little while later, I received a visit from some Canadian diplomats," Johnson continued. "At least, that's how they presented themselves. At the start of the conversation, they started to openly threaten me.

"From now on, I must go along with the plans of World Emperor Grandego without complaint. With no further ado, I thusly received the threat to quickly wire the requested amount, or else. I've had these two men followed and have made them disappear from the world. I'm sorry, but I'm not letting anyone intimidate me or force me to do things I see no use for. I call upon President Scott to call our honored World Emperor Grandego to order and put him diligently in his place!"

Near the end of his speech, Johnson had greatly increased the number of decibels and his words rang piercingly through the room.

Another master took his microphone and shouted he'd had a similar experience with Grandego. The meeting now derailed into a hubbub of responses. Here and there, fierce debates arose. Someone stood up emotionally to express his anger. This was something they had never experienced before. That a leader had arisen, appointed by themselves, no less, who afforded himself such a bold, egoistic move, through which he intimidated and even threatened his fellow members!

"Who does he think he is!" one of the members now loudly shouted through the room.

"He must immediately be corrected or be deposed!" another cried.

To restore order, Scott hammered a couple of times loudly with his gavel on the block.

Scott had listened with horror. This was something he had feared. It was certain that Grandego was a strategic mastermind who was capable of using the most influential people for his own goals and to help the Order reach theirs, but he had also developed a fear for this unscrupulous man. This was mostly to do with his unyielding and haughty attitude. There wasn't a single grain of empathy in that man.

The thought he had to go and correct Grandego gave him the shivers, but he stood with his back against the wall.

The Order justly obliged him to do so.

It was an unwritten law that if a member obtained a collective correction from the order, he should openly declare accepting that correction in the next meeting. This, of course, was seen as something humiliating. That's why a correction was seen as an abomination by the members. Grandego was secretly hated by many and they reveled in the fact that this would concern Grandego himself. They looked forward to it.

The assembly had been brought to order and Johnson once again took the microphone.

"Mister President, all due respect for the assets Grandego has acquired, but we as Upper Ten must ensure we keep ourselves firmly positioned in this planet's driver's seat. Grandego is our Number One, and our Order has chosen him as such. Weishaubt, our honored founder, started back in the eighteenth century to draw up the protocols that led to this ultimate moment and to this man. However, it's never been the intention our man should become the sole ruler. Even he, the Number One, must follow the policy guidelines and decisions that are made in these meetings."

Sounds of agreement filled the room.

"We cannot tolerate this Hitleresque tendency to self-elevation over his own party," Johnson continued. "Grandego has gone too far. When someone uses the power given by us against the interests of the members, that could mean the end of our carefully constructed Pyramid. We need a capstone with global power, a personification of our identity, and not of his own self. That's the last thing we need! Power is our highest goal. We've made cruel sacrifices to obtain it. Once more, we demand an open declaration by him, in which he promises to comply with our decisions!"

President Scott knew he had to face the facts, and it stifled him.

"Yes, yes, you repeat yourself," he agitatedly said. "I will personally confront High Master Grandego with this and correct him."

This announcement was met with approval from all sides. If there was one who could redirect High Master Grandego, it was Master Scott. Scott had become so authoritative that no one could ignore him anymore. It was a good plan to confront Grandego with his mischief and the correction would place everything back in the correct order, and everything would go along as planned.

Scott needed rest and fresh air. "We'll take a break and continue this afternoon in subgroups. Enjoy the Chinese lunch. And don't forget to freely fill out the objection forms and mail them as feedback about agenda items." And with that he ended the charged meeting. Heavy-hearted, Scott left the conference room. A cheap thought that "it would work out for the best" couldn't remove his fear about this matter. Scott had left "best," and even "good," a long time ago. Confronting and correcting Grandego was on his mind—a terrifying thought.

* * *

After the subgroups had finished their meetings early in the evening and the members got ready to leave for home, Master Johnson sent texts to several of the members, requesting to meet soon to exchange thoughts about the negative developments concerning Grandego.

* * *

That same week, Johnson, the Russian Master Dimitri Wlascow, and the South African Master Pablo Rositioso met on the highest floor of the pretentious office building of the renowned weekly magazine *TimeNow*, which Johnson owned.

"Friends, enjoy the champagne, and if you want something to eat, just let me know. There are all kinds of things in the cupboards here.

"Speak freely, because on this floor, it's technically impossible to get outside espionage equipment to function. Let me get straight to the point: I'm very concerned about that big-head Grandego. He's the wrong man," Johnson said. "Not only has he extorted me out of forty percent of my working capital, he has also humiliated me to the bone and draws all power toward himself."

Rositioso cast a friendly look at Johnson with his big, brown eyes as he lit a big Havana.

"Uhmm, not the wrong man, but the wrong development within the man," Rositioso answered as he blew the good-smelling cigar smoke into the luxurious room.

Wlascow, the Russian Master, smirked.

"Yep, that's a lot of money . . . forty percent," he sneered. "But it was predictable Grandego would turn out this way. He has always been immeasurably arrogant, our grand ego," Wlascow added to the conversation.

Wlascow had an impressive physique. Every week, he went ice-swimming in an ice-hole in Siberia. He theorized vodka tasted best immediately after an icy bath.

He had been a feared member of the St. Petersburg mob. By acting as an informant for the KGB, he had been able to launder his money through their connections, which he used to set up a legal liquor supermarket. His liquor store imperium had grown to serve thousands of franchise companies.

"He needs to be taken out as quickly as possible," Johnson said.

"That would be the best, but who will we put forward in his place?" Wlascow wondered aloud, as if the deed had already been done.

"Perhaps you should replace Grandego, Wlascow," Rositioso said.

"No, I don't like publicity. Perhaps we should let Scott handle that."

"Next week, Grandego will visit Kenya for a charm offensive," Johnson said. "Mnaba is in Nairobi. He could take care of it."

"He could, but that man costs at least a million. Don't you think that's a bit steep?" Rositioso said.

"He's expensive, but he doesn't leave a trace and he's been tried and tested. He has never disappointed an employer," Johnson pointed out.

"He is indeed the best," Wlascow said, and thus the decision had been made.

* * *

In Saudi Arabia, Grandego and Molochi went to, as they called it, the Dark Room. Grandego's white marble palace near Mecca had many secret rooms and escape routes. The Dark Room, fully isolated from the outside world, was their room where they went to analyze current events and, if necessary, adjust plans. Carefully, Molochi closed the enormous oak door behind him. The only light came from a flickering candle. The black walls showed moving shadows in the dancing candle-light. A pentagram, several yards across, was depicted on the black floor.

After they sat down on a stool and sighed deeply a couple of times, Grandego said, "Abyllon, is that you?" A deep, dreary voice, that seemed to be coming from nowhere, answered this question affirmingly.

"It is I, Master."

"It must be very important, for you to have the guts to show up here," Grandego said.

"Yes, Master, they want to kill you," the demon answered.

When he heard this, Grandego looked at Molochi's face, distorted by the flickering flame of the candle.

"Well, great prophet," Grandego said to Molochi. "Had you fore-seen this?"

"Yes," was the curt reply. "It is written."

Molochi now turned to the demon. "When and where?"

"Kenya, and the assassin is the famous Mnaba," Abyllon said. "He will attempt to kill you when you're in the streets of Nairobi in the honorary parade."

"Hmm, smart move, and Mnaba is indeed one of the best snipers," Grandego said. "I've seen many souls fall into the realm of the dead because of his bullets. Funny those Masters still don't know who they're dealing with," he smirked. "All right, make sure Mnaba gets paid five million dollars to come to our side, and see to it he fires a plastic bullet, which will hit my head, but won't penetrate my skull. I don't want to become deaf on one side, so pick a neutral spot. Make sure our medics are already in the hospital, because it needs to seem lethal. My resurrection will amaze the world and give me even more authority than I already have! Excellent!" Grandego began to get ex-cited about what was to come.

"Which members are they?" Grandego asked Abyllon.

"Johnson, Rositioso, and Wlascow," the demon answered, making a humble nod.

"Hmm, that doesn't surprise me. I did squeeze them pretty hard, those playboys." Grandego smirked. "They're goners. Let them know the sender before you kill them. The name's Lucifer." He laughed before continuing, "and tell them I will personally dunk them into hell's lava, my 'faithful' servants." Grandego laughed even harder.

Molochi grinned. Yes, that was always a good time, when they could confront their human servants after their physical deaths with the realization of who had tricked them. Always that same surprised dismay on those faces—priceless. And to let them feel the full hate and pain they felt for them . . . Yes, the many pop artists, businessmen, criminals, mediums, politicians, and so many more, who had sold their souls for temporary worldly success. Well, they could have it, Molochi sneered to himself.

The final result was a deeper place in hell. And what to think of those amateur Satanists with their stupid and pointless fiddling with rituals, human sacrifice, and abominable deeds—they thought they would get an abundant and primary position in the realm of evil by serving evil. As if there even where such kinds of positions!

They only condemned themselves to more painful depths in the terrible atrocity of the realm of the dead. But those blind fools didn't know that.

All these murky thoughts crossed Molochi's mind. Of course the information about those things had been well concealed for their followers by him and his demons—especially that Gospel of the Crucified, that could have saved them. He smirked.

No, there is no day of judgment—of course not . . .

13

AKHAN AND TARPI

AKHAN WOKE FIRST. HIS BODY felt better, but in some places, the pain became worse the longer he was awake. He took a few moments to stretch his muscles. As he rose, he saw his company was starting to wake as well.

"Good morning!" Akhan said to start the day.

"Good morning," Tarpi moaned.

"Hello," Rita said. Waking up in the great outdoors was a nice experience, especially for Rita, who had been held captive for so long. But their stomachs growled, longing for food.

"I'd kill for a hot cup of coffee." Akhan looked around to see if something edible was growing in the trees. But no, there was nothing they could declare "breakfast."

"We should get going," Tarpi said. "If we stay in one place too long, we might get discovered by those extremists."

"Do you know the surroundings?" Akhan asked Rita.

"No, I'm sorry. I have no idea where we are. That's to say, I do know only the general area. We're in southern Italy."

Akhan thought for a moment. "We spent one, maybe two hours in the jeep. But I have no idea which direction we came from." As Akhan said this, a burning question arose within him.

"Do you know what's going on in Europe?" he asked Rita.

Rita looked at the men in amazement. "You don't know what's going on?"

Akhan remembered Rita didn't know anything about them yet, so he briefly recounted their journey to her. She was clearly impressed by their adventures.

Rita's look betrayed she had important but disappointing news for the men.

"You can forget your dream," Rita said. "It all started a little while ago. As a bolt from the blue, hundreds of caliphates were simultaneously established all across Western Europe. It was a terrible fight, as if a civil war had erupted."

Akhan and Tarpi looked at each other in amazement.

"Caliphates?"

"Yes, they declared over the radio they would claim their rights, that the West should be punished for their selfishness, depravity, and materialism. After having exploited others for hundreds of years, it had now become their turn to be exploited, and so forth. They communicated via social media, internet, cell phones, and radio and it looked pretty coordinated. It turned out they had a lot of weapons and so they were well prepared. Within hours, armed extremists controlled most parts of major cities.

"In Spain, where I lived, all non-Muslims had to stay indoors. The occupiers drove their cars through the streets, all the while shouting battle cries and shooting in the air. In some cities, police officers and the army fought back. But the problem was that many military bases were soon taken over. The extremists had planned everything really well, and many strategic locations were soon overrun by them.

Drafted Spanish soldiers couldn't even reach their equipment in the bases. I heard later that many soldiers had regrouped and were being supplied with weapons from America, but those were all rumors. Nothing was certain. The cell phone networks and the internet were switched off, so those sources of information couldn't be used any more. Several parties, however, had radio stations in the air. At one point, these were the only sources of information, but the messages they broadcast were contradictory. They brought more confusion than clarity.

"There were even Muslims that fought against the extremists. It was all very confusing. People who resisted were shot on the spot. Panic broke out, and in some neighborhoods, people resorted to plundering stores and supermarkets. Others made use of the situation to rape women and break into houses. It was one big chaos.

"Armed men were standing or walking everywhere. They wore a black or green headband. They arrested everyone who ventured outside and questioned them. Some were allowed to pass, others abused and sent back to their houses. Our freedom had evaporated overnight. Everyone was terribly afraid, and nobody knew what to do.

"There was all sorts of resistance. Many men, I think street gangs and vigilantes, but also people who simply owned a gun, took on the extremists. That resulted in veritable battle-grounds in some places.

"Some resistance fighters used windows from which to shoot at the men with the green and black headbands, but most people, of course, didn't possess firearms and couldn't do a thing. The men with the headbands had the numbers and they were well-organized. This was probably the result of months of planning. They had quickly secured our city.

"The radio brought us messages of hope. The Army had been mobilized and the Air Force and Navy had already gotten into combat. But their options were limited.

"The only thing they could do was bomb everything from a distance. The jets that flew overhead yesterday were probably with the Italian Air Force."

Akhan and Tarpi hadn't expected this. The paradise-like free Europe was divided into caliphates?

"Now I understand why that Italian battleship blasted our boat to smithereens," Tarpi remarked.

"The caliphates aren't all of one accord," Rita said. "It's as if a great number of city-states have arisen, which pursue the same goals up to a point, but also fight each other. At least, that's what the radio told us. And the conquest doesn't seem to have been complete. Some areas are still in the hands of the European governments.

"From there, they try to take the fight to the caliphates and other groups that've declared independence. Besides the caliphates, organized gangs hold entire neighborhoods in their grips. It's simply chaos. There were no safe places, and all commodities were scarce, because the entire economy had ground to a halt. In the cities, they beat each other's brains out over a piece of bread."

Rita choked back a lump and looked at them with big eyes.

"Unbelievable," Akhan said. His quiet hope of a peaceful existence had been shattered by these reports. "Europe in flames . . . rich Europe. The continent of promise, where we had hoped to build a life of rest and prosperity . . . " He was somewhat disillusioned.

"There is other news," Rita said comfortingly.

The men looked at her.

"A world leader has come. His name is Grandego. I've heard him speak on the radio. This man promises world peace, economic prosperity, and the destruction of corruption.

"He has become hugely popular and very powerful in a short time. He's a Jewish Islamite with a Catholic upbringing. Can you believe that? The man claims to be all sorts of things, but he is humanity's hope. There appear to be large problems all over the word: economic crisis, poverty, scarcity of commodities, famines, and natural disasters. This man claims to be the solution. He says he can bring back peace and prosperity. He has the support of the western countries and the Arab world. And there's a lot of support for him from Asia. He also wishes to negotiate with the caliphates. " She looked at them with a beaming face.

"Well, I hope he succeeds quickly," Akhan said. "One way or another, someone who knows how to find a way always comes drifting up out of hopeless, chaotic situations . . . Perhaps this time, it's Grandego. I hope so."

"If he's a politician," Tarpi said, "this may all be empty words. Hitler and Napoleon also climbed to power because of chaos, I've read—"

"I don't think Grandego is like that," Rita said. "He has already subjected the Americas. With his huge money infusions, he has caused the domestic economies to bloom. The man apparently has thousands of billions, because he seems to have an enormous influence on the international banking system. At least, he puts his words into action. He's *doing* something—"

Just then, the conversation was interrupted by the sound of approaching fighter jets. Before long, they flew into view. It was an impressive sight. Many dozens of jets flew over in tight formations. The penetrating sound they emitted caused the ground to tremble.

"What is going on now?" Akhan sighed.

"I don't know, but it's got something to do with this miserable situation," Rita replied.

"Let's get going." Akhan started to stand. "It's no use staying here. We need to find something to eat and somehow obtain information that will help us determine what to do next."

The company left their hiding place between the dense bushes. In places, the undergrowth was fairly thick, but the ground was hard, so they could move at a fair pace. Through it all, the squadrons of jets kept coming.

Of course, the group wasn't much in shape after all the recent tiring events and the lack of food. Therefore, they often had to stop to catch their breath.

After a while, they saw tall hills rise in front of them. There were many traces of old and new paths through the forest that they could follow up the hills. Some parts were pretty steep.

The heat of the sun became more and more unbearable for the company as well. Their tongues began to stick to their palates. Their stomachs cried for food. Their muscles started to protest.

Tarpi held his left hand over the wound in his right side. His face betrayed a jolt of pain now and then, but the wound didn't bleed.

Physically, Akhan knew Tarpi was used to hardships. At home, he toiled in and around the house and on the fields, that didn't yield much in the way of crops. The entire family slept on a mat on the ground and he could sit in a lotus position for hours without discomfort. He was a sturdy man, who could keep moving as long as he had a single drop of blood in his veins. But even this hardened desert dweller couldn't go on forever without water.

It was all so different than his homeland. He imagined in Europe, a person could arrange for a private sauna, hot tub, or pool, even. But that dream turned out to be a mirage that evaporated in the reality of recent events.

The dream of a free Europe had given them hope for a better future. But where should they put their hopes now? What could he do?

"I'm so sick of this!" Tarpi cried, letting his emotions run free. "I'm sorry, but I'm so tired of it all . . . where are we going? To war?!"

Akhan decided this was a good time for a break. Exhausted, they sat down.

"We don't even know where we're going. There's nothing for us in Europe. It seems we've ended up in a hornets' nest. Where should we go? Russia? The US? And how do we get there?" Downcast, Tarpi looked at the ground. Akhan put a comforting hand on his friend's shoulder.

In order to turn around the sense of defeat, he started to ask Rita some questions about her background.

"I'm Muslim; are you Christian?" he asked straightforwardly.

Rita didn't respond immediately.

"I think so," she eventually responded, carefully probing for words.

"You think so?" Akhan repeated, genuinely curious about how she meant that.

"I was raised a Catholic," she explained. "I used to go to church with my parents. There were annual processions."

She noticed that Akhan didn't understand that word.

"A sort of prayer walk, so to speak," Rita added. "I always liked that, but the Sunday mass, that didn't appeal to me. I never understood what the priest was talking about. As a child, I sometimes prayed to

Jesus and the Holy Father. But when I got older, I frequented church less and less, and eventually I stopped going, altogether. I believe in God, but I don't know how He works in this world. Or why does He allow so much misery?"

Akhan made no attempt to answer that question. Rita didn't seem to expect an answer anyway.

"Despite all the misery I've seen and lived through, I have somehow always gotten out alive."

Rita squeezed her eyes to fight back the tears that were welling up.

"I'm sorry, I . . . " Akhan began, but Rita interrupted him.

"It's not you, it's everything I've been going through. And I fear for my children, I may never see them again. But what I want to say, I think, is that deep inside of me there's always something that's thankful to God. I don't understand it with my mind, but I still believe in love."

Akhan frowned when he heard that last word. He thought about his own loved ones. He loved his parents, his father most of all, despite the fact the impatient man had hit him a couple of times. Akhan respected him and was proud of him. When his father gave him a compliment, he always felt himself becoming strong, even when he was an adult himself. There was nothing that could destroy their relationship. Akhan would always respect his father. When he'd grow old, Akhan would take care of him. At least, that was the plan.

But it wasn't meant to be, because it all went south. Now, Akhan was here, and his father was unreachably far away from him.

But Akhan knew what love was. A very strong, invisible bond of warmth. Something that lifts you above the daily, material world, stronger than the suffering you go through in this world. Love gave you dreams that gave you hope. It gave strength to continue when the going was tough. No man could live without it.

Or could they . . . ? Were there people who didn't know love?

Perhaps people who had been raised with hatred. He had heard once psychopaths were formed by traumatic experiences, but Akhan wasn't a psychologist. He wasn't sure.

He did know, however, that moments of love were short and scarce, and that you had to make do with those few moments.

Akhan felt like he was about to sink into melancholy. To put his mind elsewhere, he suggested they continue. Tarpi let out a moan as he got up. Rita smiled at the wounded man to encourage him.

They were still in a forested area.

After a while, they reached the top of a hill and they could turn around to view the beautiful panorama. There was nothing but forest in the direction they came from, save a scorched place here and there and a column of smoke in the distance. Akhan thought that was the site of the extremists' camp, but he couldn't be sure. In front of them, the forest became less dense and there were more open spaces.

Step by step they continued, until the trees stood farther apart. Akhan, who was going first, suddenly stopped and motioned the others to do the same. He turned around and held his index finger in front of his lips, calling upon them to be quiet. Then, he gestured them to lie down, hidden between the bushes. Akhan himself quietly crawled on.

Further ahead, a man was sitting with his back against a tree. It looked like he was sleeping. A gun stood against the tree. The man wore a camouflaged suit, but Akhan didn't see any insignia. He couldn't make out which party the stranger was fighting for.

Akhan crawled nearer and reached his hand for the weapon.

"Hey!" the man cried, suddenly jolting awake. In a split-second, he was up on his feet.

Tarpi had jumped up as well and ran, despite his wound, towards Akhan to help him. Akhan, quick as lightning, had grasped the gun and assumed an attack position, his finger on the trigger and the barrel aimed at the man's chest.

The man stood as though nailed to the floor with a look of terror on his face. He immediately held up his hands as a sign of surrender.

"Sit down!" Akhan reinforced his words with his gun ready to shoot. The man immediately did as was asked of him.

Rita had arrived and took a jerrycan that stood on the ground. She twisted loose the cap, sniffed the contents and immediately put the container against her lips to let the delicious water glide through her throat with great gulps. She choked and started to cough. As she caught her breath, Tarpi took the can and drank his fill. Akhan handed the gun to Tarpi before he started to drink.

Tarpi gave the gun back to Akhan and lay down. While Rita started to clean Tarpi's wound, Akhan questioned the man.

"Who are you and are you a soldier? For which army do you fight?" Akhan waved the gun around to intimidate the man. He was about forty and clearly nervous.

"I'm with the HG."

"With the HG? Explain!" Akhan ordered.

The man apparently didn't mind telling, because a gleam of pride entered his eyes.

"The Heaven Groups," he answered.

Akhan smiled because of this silly name.

"You don't exactly look like an angel with your unshaven face. Come, explain yourself, and speak truthfully," Akhan said sternly.

"We are the spiritual resistance. Haven't you heard about us?" the soldier asked with a surprised look on his face.

Akhan now looked at him warily.

"The resistance? You mean you fight against the caliphates? Are you with this Grandego?" Akhan asked, sounding interested.

"We're not with Grandego's government forces, nor with the caliphates, nor with the Russians, Chinese, or Arabs. There are people from all those factions in our Heaven Groups, but as friends, not as enemies."

Akhan noticed the man seemed rather proud of his Heaven Groups and was very loose-lipped as well.

Akhan analyzed him once more. Was this man a very good liar? No, he seemed rather sincere. That meant he was either a very professional liar or he was simply telling the truth.

Akhan sat down a few feet away from him to study him carefully. He wanted to be sure of himself, their lives could depend upon it.

In the meantime, Rita had cleaned out Tarpi's wound with water. She'd torn off a piece of the hem of her dress as a bandage for the open wound. Tarpi still grimaced because of the pain the wound caused him, but it had been cleaned and the chance of infections was now greatly reduced.

"Let's turn this into a nice get-together," Akhan said to his fellow travelers.

"I suppose," Tarpi admitted.

"You look hungry," the soldier said. "There's bread in my bag. Please, take it."

Rita discovered the packaged bread and let out a cry of joy.

"Yes, this is our lucky day!" She spontaneously passed along the slices of bread, which were garnished with some sort of cheese. She made sure not to skip the soldier.

"Thanks for your generosity," the soldier said to Rita with a careful smile.

Even though the suspicion about the man's intentions wasn't gone, the atmosphere relaxed. Akhan still held the gun pointed at him.

When they'd had something to eat, the soldier took the initiative to tell his story.

"My name is Georgi Bonetti and I'm a stonecutter. My grandfather started a family business in producing ornamental marble." The Italian's voice was filled with pride. "My sister is a painter and she decorates villas in classical styles."

Akhan looked at Georgi, surprised by his talkativeness.

"All right, spare us your life's story. What are you doing here?"

"Oh, I was keeping watch," Georgi said a bit naively. The three travelers looked at each other and burst out in a fit of laughter because of the sleeping guardsman and his silly remark. The tension of the past days came out, the guffaw increased, and it became an outlet for the emotions that had lately been held back.

Tarpi put his hand on his wound.

The Italian was now embarrassed.

Akhan was bent double with laughter, but he could still keep an eye on Georgi, so he couldn't take advantage of this moment of wild emotions.

"On guard, he was on guard . . . !" Akhan snorted. "You were looking out for dreams, then . . . "

Georgi now also saw the irony of the situation.

"I'd been out here for fourteen hours straight." Georgi defended himself.

"Straight to sleep," Tarpi said, as he gasped for breath. This caused Rita to burst out again, and this time Georgi joined in. After a good few minutes, everyone had recovered, and Georgi was able to continue his story.

"What we're doing here isn't that simple, and it's no laughing matter either. We just defend ourselves . . . against that crazy High Master Grandego who wants to see us exterminated!"

Akhan, Tarpi, and Rita immediately fell quiet and looked at the man with big eyes.

"I'm sorry, continue. What do you mean? Grandego is doing a great job, isn't he?" Akhan said. Georgi was surprised at his captors' emotional change.

"Yes, that man is incredible. He can do things that have not been seen before in the history of mankind. But he's very dominant and demands everyone to have a 'strangle chip' implanted in their bodies. At least, we call it 'strangle chip'. It's what replaces bank cards."

"That isn't too bad, is it?" Tarpi said. Georgi's face fell at this remark.

"Like I said, it's complicated. The chip is more than a bank card. It's implanted in your hand. On the chip is your bank account number, which can be scanned remotely. This way, you can pay with a single swipe of your hand. Very handy, but all your other personal details are also incorporated into the chip. Your medical history, and your criminal record, if you have one. There's also a tracking device included, so they always know where you are. And the worst is," a shiver of fear entered Georgi's voice, "the worst is that the strangle chip is grafted onto a nerve. The minute battery is constantly recharged by body warmth and never runs out. Through that battery, the chip can send electric pulses through the nerve system. That hurts a lot! The pulses can be given remotely, so whoever holds the remote has you in their power. They can force you to do the most horrible things."

Akhan, Tarpi and Rita were startled by this story.

"Who does something like that?" Tarpi said, outraged.

"You can ask yourself that question, but we of the Heaven Groups believe he is the Antichrist predicted by the Bible. This is the fulfillment of Revelation thirteen!"

Georgi looked at them meaningfully. Chips? Biblical prophecies? The Antichrist? This was hard for them to grasp. It was all new. The soldier continued with his tale.

"I haven't told you the most devious part yet. You're forced to take the chip, because otherwise, you'll be a pariah and cannot take part in the economy. They're working on introducing a universal, digital world currency, which would mean you can buy or sell using only the chip. If you don't comply, you're even persecuted as a terrorist, because you're resisting the New World Order.

"But if you want the chip, you must kneel before a strange idol that consists of symbols of the major religions. It's like a Buddha, with a necklace of the Islamic crescent. His arm is in his lap and he's holding an upside-down cross. It can speak and change its facial expression. People say that from a certain angle, it looks like Grandego.

"My aunt did it, the poor, sweet soul. She told me how she, after having received the chip, was led into the special hall of the idol. In the background she heard, to her amazement, her favorite music. When she knelt before the idol, it spoke! It said her name, with the friendly voice of her deceased mother. Then she knelt before it and read the declaration of dedication. When she came home, there was a blush on her face. She couldn't stop talking about that wonderful experience.

"She was full of praise and said we also had to get chipped. She even got angry and threatening if we wouldn't, completely against her nature. After this outburst, she again became dreamy and kept telling us cheerfully how nice the experience had been for her.

"She brought home a declaration of dedication on a 'certificate of service'. The gist of it was that you have to swear off all religions and say a prayer of dedication to the One World Faith. This is terrible! It goes against every form of freedom of religion and freedom of speech. The HG actively refuses to do this."

Georgi looked at his audience with a gaze of rebellion.

"Our chairman says a small amount of ecstasy has been included in the chip, so that after implantation, you'll have a moment of euphoria."

"What is the meaning of this all? It's like a science fiction movie," Tarpi mumbled.

"Is this the same all over Europe?" Akhan asked Georgi.

"As far as we know," he replied. "There are groups, both armed and unarmed, who resist this course of affairs. There is some contact between the different groups to exchange information, but that's minimal, because the high-tech monitoring tools of the government are extremely effective. The Christian Heaven Groups are for non-violent resistance, but there are also Hindu groups, liberals, antiglobalists, Muslim communities, and other factions that refuse to be chipped or bow down to an idol.

"Many people have gone into hiding or have united in resistance groups. Besides, persecution of Christians had started before and became more pronounced after the Global Preaching Event. In those days, thousands of Christians went into the streets to preach and warn people not to take part in Grandego's plans, but they have all been arrested without mercy and brought to prison camps. It's whispered they've been killed in cold blood and cremated, but nobody knows for sure.

"People who refuse the chip or who won't bow to the idol are branded as terrible terrorists by Grandego, no matter who they are: hardworking people, freethinkers, conscientious objectors, or religious. The punishment is execution, because, in his eyes, they don't cooperate with the necessary restructuring of the world. That man has gained almost total control and absolute power, presumably to solve the global catastrophic problems. International terrorism has greatly influenced people to hand him such far-reaching jurisdiction. The people want to shop, travel and enjoy in peace, without the threat of terrorism. They don't care if it's a Hitler who gives it to them. Meanwhile, this comes at the cost of freedoms of speech, press, gathering, religion, expression, morality, and justice, so that every detail of their lives can be determined and controlled from above. People are made into robots in the service of the super elite. They minimize their own lives to a smartphone-experience, in which nothing has meaning or eternal value. Everything has gotten a morbid tone. Slavery and death are suggested as a solution for problems. It's clear they develop psychological disorders because of such a simplistic philosophy. The pharmaceutical companies thrive, and end-of-life clinics get more and more customers . . . "

The group became quiet. With each sentence, their illusions were punctured. But how did they know if Georgi was right? His story sounded incredible, but he didn't seem to be a madman with a runaway imagination or someone who was tripping on LSD. Georgi himself looked as if he was fully convinced of his story.

Tarpi lifted the jerrycan, took a few big gulps and passed it along.

After a few minutes, Georgi suggested to the group to come with him to the camp of the resistance and rest there. Other brothers could then further answer their questions, he said.

"You're free to come because you aren't chipped," he added.

"How do you know we're not chipped?" Akhan growled, as he bent towards Georgi with an angry face.

Georgi backed down in fear, which caused Akhan to laugh loudly. The others could appreciate Akhan's practical joke after all those frightening reports and laughed. Georgi relaxed visibly.

The suggestion to come along to the camp of the "brothers" wasn't that bad. Besides, where else would they go?

They followed Georgi toward his camp.

14

GRANDEGO

IN A VILLA IN THE Kenyan coastal town of Mombasa, Mnaba was practicing his beloved hobby. With his dark-brown hands covered in glue, he molded papier-mâché into rugged mountain peaks.

His steam locomotives on the Hornby model track were ready to depart from the train yard of an impressive railway station. The model trains, and all the accessories, fascinated Mnaba. He could spend days working on it. His model landscape covered over 600 square feet and was the largest in East-Africa.

He enjoyed talking about the details of the tracks to the many curious visitors who came from far and wide to admire his project. He reveled in the admiration in children's eyes when the trains made their rounds, crisscrossing through tunnels and over crossings.

Mnaba was a descendent of one of the leaders of the Mau Mau resistance group, who had fought the imperialist British in Kenya's war of independence. The Mnaba family brought forth a remarkable number of snipers in those days. The secrets of this trade were passed on from generation to generation. His great-great-grandfather had taken over a coffee plantation from a European. This ancestor had been very successful and employed many Indians.

Mnaba Khenius' family had, as a result of having many children, grown out to an influential tribe. With a strong sense of political activism, they used their influence to advocate their own interests. The family was part of both the national and the international high society. Mnaba was the youngest son of a large family with eleven brothers.

His power to influence the family's policy was, as youngest brother, very limited. His elder brothers held the reigns firmly. That's why he had specialized in the armed branch of the family, abbreviated to 'Mau'. He usually just did all sorts of jobs on the plantations, but occasionally led the armed forces of the family to, as they called it, "intervene." Because the economic and political elite of the land were corrupt, and fraud and intrigue were daily business, an intervention was needed from time to time. This encompassed intimidation, threatening and even murder. Mnaba had been proficient with the sniper rifle from a young age. His eagle-eyed sight combined with perfect motor control resulted in his execution of a precision shot at a great distance. That was of course nice when hunting, but Mnaba had expensive hobbies and was a thrill-seeker.

His extensive network provided plenty of jobs for the "Black Panther," as his hunting buddies called him. Mnaba was expensive and couldn't be bought for just any job. The victim could only be someone who was despicable in his eyes. In this, his ideals and business interests flowed together, as was his motto. He had, for example, eliminated several traders in illegal ivory. Poachers and traders in protected indigenous wildlife could also get a bullet, as far as he was concerned. And corrupt politicians, who wanted to squander the environment or the wellbeing of Kenyan citizens to captains of industry, risked execution as well.

Mnaba loved the jungle, the wild the untamed nature, his wife, his children and his model trains.

Mnaba had been called up for a conversation about an intervention and arrived at the designated place in the forest.

His contact was standing with his back towards him, admiring the orchid plants in the trees. The two men never looked each other in the face, for security reasons.

"Well?" Mnaba said when he was close enough to his contact to hear him.

"The big prize," the broad-shouldered man said with a deep, singing voice.

"Oh, what?" Mnaba enjoyed the tension those few words cased.

"Six million dollars for a non-lethal headshot . . . ," the contact said.

Mnaba was pleasantly surprised. "The highest bid ever."

"Yes, it's complicated. There are two bidders. One party wants him dead, and the other wants him only mortally wounded, because his recovery should contribute to mythologizing the victim; he has to become an unreachable hero. The latter party pays five million, the former one million. We split it fifty-fifty—if you take the deal and don't mind the target."

Mnaba frowned.

"So, it's a political intervention?" he asked.

"Yes," his contact said. "Grandego."

"What! Grandego, the great Grandego, who's coming to Nairobi next week?" Mnaba said with an amazed, high-pitched voice.

"Yes, he himself is the five million party, so all you have to do is fire a nonlethal shot and you'll get three million. Am I your man, or not?"

"You're my man," Mnaba said excitedly. Three million was a lot of money, even for Mnaba. His jet needed a thorough check-up in the US . . .

"Have they specified an exact location where I should hit him?" he asked.

"Well, I think it's clear you shouldn't cause any permanent damage. Only a nice scar, of course. People love scars, they impress. His medical personnel are already on stand-by in the hospital, they'll make a nice scar, I think," the contact continued. "So, you'll take care of the details, and I'll make sure the money is delivered to you as usual after the intervention."

"Excellent," Mnaba said, and walked back towards his jeep.

The week before the major event, the city was abuzz to get everything in order for Grandego's visit. Nearly all hotels were fully booked. The World Defense Force had entrenched themselves in every nook and cranny and had hermetically secured the entire route Grandego would take with his float. Despite checkpoints, cameras and intensive surveillance in the area, the streets were hectic.

Mnaba had taken up residence in an apartment owned by his family in the center of Nairobi, long before the great day. Early in the morning of that day he had gone to the Haile Selassie Avenue. It was already busy everywhere. Many people had been standing at the barriers for hours to in order to have a good view of the World Emperor when he would pass. The route came from Moi Avenue onto the roundabout, and then took a right turn onto Haile Selassie Avenue towards the Railway Golf Course. There, Grandego would speak with the national political elite and the press, and hand over a cashier's check. The check represented a grant for dozens of millions of dollars, which Kenya received from Grandego to renovate the slums, furnish new One World Faith temples and stimulate the economy by executing large-scale infrastructure improvements.

The effectiveness of the grant would be symbolized by Grandego hitting a golf ball towards a hole five hundred yards away. Cameras along the track would be able to follow the ball. An advanced GPS homing system would insure he couldn't miss. This was all in line with Grandego's PR: he never misses his goal. He never sways to the left or to the right, but hits with a single shot.

Hordes of people had become euphoric, thanks to the inciting media spectacle that was organized to cover the event. The whole world could share in what the great do-gooder would do.

Mnaba went to the enormous headquarters of Kenya Railways, which was adjacent to Haile Selassie Avenue and provided a good vantage point to cover the Moi Avenue roundabout. In the days before the event he had hidden his Beretta in the cabinet of a small, unused office in the northern wing of the building. Because of his endearing personality, family reputation and his famous model railroad, he had many friends in the Railways. He could get into the building unhindered. Doormen always greeted him as a highly-regarded celebrity, almost a national hero. A few hours before the float would pass, he went to the room in the northern wing. From here, he had a clear view of the Haile Selassie Avenue.

Shouts arose when the float entered the roundabout. Several cars and a few dozen motor police had already passed. Several helicopters hung in the air. Confetti from party poppers filled the air with thousands of colorful shreds of paper. Orchestras played familiar national songs as loud as they could. The public enjoyed the moment.

Mnaba felt his adrenaline levels shoot up. He enjoyed the rising tension. This intervention had the benefit it wasn't going to be a true kill. He wouldn't kill but participate in top-level theatre. He had a plastic bullet developed of which the impact force had been calculated. With his gun, the bullet wouldn't penetrate the skull over a distance of 250 yards. Upon impact, red bull's blood would be ejected from the rear end of the bullet, which would make the hit look fatal.

The float now passed, and he could see Grandego standing in a glass encased, open-topped booth. He recognized the man immediately. Bronzed face, broadly smiling and with dark blond flowing hair. He waved at the excited crowd.

A three million dollar shot. Mnaba looked through the scope and centered his cross-hairs. From his high vantage point he could hit his target over the protective glass booth. He knew that, of course, because he had studied the float earlier that week from information obtained through the internet.

In his scope, he saw Grandego occasionally scanning his environment with an investigative look.

The man surely dares to take a huge risk. Who says I don't hate him and blow him up where he stands, the fool.

Mnaba had followed Grandego's developments for years and, with time, had developed a dislike for him. He, as a man with inside information about the Upper Ten, had learned with what kind of ruthless idiot he was dealing. The dictator had long ago made his "ripe for intervention" list. By putting down the dictator for good, he would only do the world a favor. He did bring metal bullets. For a moment, a whiff of grim thoughts passed through his mind. *I could kill him . . .*

But he thought better of it, because his contact, who was a mysterious figure, would know he was the shooter and take revenge. His contact had a reputation to uphold as well, and wouldn't show mercy, even to the Black Panther. *Besides the Upper Ten would just put forward another idiot and you'd be back where you'd started, except for getting yourself into a lot of trouble. The mismanagement would remain the same.*

Mnaba took a deep breath. He shouldered his rifle and aimed at Grandego's vehicle. The scope gave him a strongly magnified view of his target. The magnification was so strong, he could hit the precise point of impact to within a two-millimeter radius. Through his scope, he saw nothing but a part of Grandego's face.

Now. Mnaba held his breath. As his steady hand slowly followed the motion of the moving float, he found the exact spot on Grandego's head where he wanted to hit him. All doubt was gone now. He squeezed.

Mnaba saw Grandego tumble against the glass because of the bullet's impact. Red blood splashed against the windows around him. Bodyguards immediately ran toward Grandego. The crowd backed off and several women started screaming. The float began to slow down and stopped in front of a gas station on the right side of the road.

Mnaba had just started disassembling his Beretta to put it back in its case when an enormous explosion happened. Startled, Mnaba looked up. He saw tongues of flame expanding from the gas station.

People who were standing on that side of the road were consumed, others were hit by flying debris and shattered glass. Panic struck and everyone started running away from the disaster area. Heavy smoke soon blocked the line of sight to the crime scene.

Mnaba saw the float had been blown on its side. Several on-duty personnel with fire extinguishers hurried towards the place where Grandego lay on the street, between other bodies, and isolated him from the flames with their extinguishing agents.

"What kind of nasty trick is this? This is a setup!" Mnaba cried out as he speeded up his effort to package the gun in order to swiftly make himself scarce. A certain doubt made his heart heavy and he noticed he was caught up in a nervous haste, something he wasn't used to of himself, not even after an intervention. The excitement had been replaced by severe apprehension.

There was more to this than met the eye. He knew of another exit in the building, because the planned route, through the front entrance, now probably wasn't his best bet.

Soon, dozens of emergency workers were busy getting the situation under control where Grandego lay. Several secret agents were among them. They caused more chaos by hindering them on purpose.

Meanwhile, the smoke blocked much of the scene. Apparently, this was the moment of a secret mission.

"Inject them at once!" a superior said over secret agents' walkie-talkies. Quickly, the victims of the explosion who were lying on the ground near Grandego were injected with a deadly poison.

Streets around Haile Selassie Avenue were closed off with crime-scene tape and dozens of people were arrested by the police and deported in police cars. Several ambulances were pulling up with blaring sirens. Bold reporters who were filming and taking photographs were held back, but not hindered. Things now moved very fast.

The body of Grandego was moved to the hospital at high speed, together with a dozen other bodies that were scattered around the upturned float.

Outraged responses came from all over the world. The Kenyan authorities were embarrassed and apologized in every possible way that this had to happen when Grandego was visiting *them*!

Molochi flew straight to Nairobi and made it to the hospital that very night. He had the whole wing cordoned and took it upon himself plus the already present medical team to care for Grandego.

Grandego was held in a medically induced coma.

That same night, Molochi held a press conference that was broadcast globally.

The program started with images of a falling Grandego, hit by a bullet.

Blood splattered on the windows of the cabin, after which the terrible explosion and the ensuing chaos followed. The introductory film ended with images from a morgue, where the bodies of the people who died around the float were lying on steel transportable autopsy tables. They were injected in order to remove all doubts about Grandego's death. They were sacrificed to support the lie.

Then the view changed to Grandego. The camera zoomed in on the pallid face of the world leader. The man wasn't breathing, and specialists were busy trying to save him, but it seemed meaningless.

Molochi started his speech with a sad voice.

"People of our Earth, something terrible has happened today. You have seen a few things during the live broadcast this afternoon. Deep sadness has grasped my soul. It's hard for me to announce that all people in and around the float have passed. You see their bodies on the image behind me. But a lump in my throat takes my breath away when I have to mention the name of my and your beloved leader amongst the victims. Grandego is dead!"

Silence ensued.

Molochi took a white handkerchief from his jacket and wiped away his tears.

"I . . . I'll be back later . . . my apologies. We will now broadcast a black screen all over the world for the next couple of minutes to process this enormous blow."

* * *

Which idiot has blown up that gas station. Besides anxiety about what this would mean for Mnaba, he also felt anger. He knew the headquarters of Kenyan Railways like the back of his hand and took a relatively unknown and seldom used route. Due to this disastrous turn of events, he didn't want to risk getting accidentally caught on camera. Cell phone cameras had made his interventions much more difficult the past decades. Everywhere, there was a risk of getting filmed by tourists or other citizens. The number of security cameras had also increased. There was almost no avoiding them.

Mnaba hurried through several narrow hallways. Because he hadn't anticipated these developments, he hadn't brought his disguise kit.

Quickly, he now walked to a door at the end of a narrow hallway. He knew where the key was and opened the low, but sturdy, oaken door, that had been used by kitchen personnel in the old days. He knew the door led to a small park at the back of the building. From here, he could use the dense vegetation of the park to join the traffic, nearly unseen.

He had opened the door, just enough to get through, and poked his head around the corner to see if the coast was clear.

"Please, come on out," he was surprised to hear a voice say in flawless English. He looked up and saw a World Defense Force soldier standing on either side of the door. They looked at him with an ironic smile, the barrels of their machine guns pointed at him.

"Join us, boy. The whole building is surrounded. You've got a few things to explain, haven't you?"

"Er . . . "

"No, don't speak. Hand over that Beretta case and get in our van." The soldier pointed at a dark blue van that was parked across the street. Several soldiers stood around it, smoking their cigarettes.

It's a set-up, they need a perpetrator.

"Walk along calmly," the soldier said. "No tricks, because we'd just shoot you to pieces. Everything's being recorded on public and hidden cameras."

My contact has set me up., Mnaba could hardly believe it. He had worked alongside him for years . . . even though he didn't know exactly who the man was. He had developed blind faith in him and hadn't expected him to play both sides. Three million dollar or six million was of course a big difference, but had it been just about the money, or was the Grandego's faction just too powerful to confront . . . ?

Mnaba was close to despair. This wasn't something he could simply buy his way out of.

* * *

Molochi looked at Grandego in his hospital bed.

Hmm, he won't be pleased with that. He was looking at a face that displayed deep burn wounds on the left side.

"Has the bullet been removed?" he asked the surgeon standing next to him.

"Yes, it was a perfect shot. As per agreement, the bullet didn't penetrate into the brain. Nice piece of work."

"Any complications?" Molochi asked.

"No," the surgeon replied. "I've manipulated the heart monitor, ECG, and other equipment with the computer program and activated both the cardiac arrest and brain dead simulations. Theoretically, the patient has been dead as a doornail, which is confirmed by the graphs and has been described in the medical files.

"We'll keep him in this condition for three days, and then a miracle will happen. Grandego recovers in such a way that he can show himself to the world with some very nice scars. Those burn wounds won't make him any prettier, but they will make him more impressive."

The surgeon snickered boldly as he stood there, hands in his pockets.

"In their amazement, they'll lift him up onto an even higher pedestal. He's invincible and survives where others drop like flies. The expensive protective clothing has worked adequately. My compliments to the manufacturer," the surgeon went on.

"The only thing that could've been fatal, was if the sniper had fired a real bullet. That was the risk, and I find it bizarre Grandego apparently got a euphoric kick out of undergoing this risky attack. Showing himself to the world after his miraculous resurrection will also give him a nice kick. Good times for Grandego, with so much special attention and admiration from the masses," the surgeon concluded dryly.

Molochi, a bit uncertain because of the surgeon's cheeky attitude and the irony in his voice, whispered: "He can't hear anything now, can he?"

"No, don't be afraid," the surgeon laughed freely because of Molochi's sudden fear.

"No, I won't let him come to until tomorrow afternoon, so we're in the clear until then . . . " He winked at the slightly taken-aback Molochi and walked out.

* * *

On the third day after the attack, all television stations were interrupted by Breaking News.

"Grandego lives!" was the buzz.

"Miraculously, World Emperor Grandego is risen!" an excited newsreader exclaimed.

The images showed the academic hospital in Nairobi, which was surrounded by hordes of people. Regiments of security guards and World Defense Force soldiers cleared the way. An armored limousine, escorted by many motorcycle cops, drove up to the hospital's main entrance. Several people had to jump out of the car's way, because it simply ignored everyone. The doors clicked open, and a number of soldiers with raised shields went to offer protection during the brief walk from the main entrance to the car.

Cheers rose when the bystanders saw Grandego.

"Make way, make way, clear a path!" the security guards cried.

Reporters with press badges called for Grandego. Security roughly pushed them aside. But Grandego stopped halfway to the car and beckoned a reporter to come over. Molochi followed Grandego and stood next to him. The side of the Emperor's face was covered with a white bandage. Grandego's almost frightening eyes were as penetrating as before the attack.

"How are you feeling, Emperor?" a reporter shouted.

Grandego ordered his security to let the journalists through, so he could give an interview. The head of security circled with his index finger, to signify he didn't think it safe to do this now.

"Have no fear," Grandego now said straight into the reporters' cameras. "Life was taken from me, but I have taken it back. Who lays it down, and takes it up again? Who has such power? I have, and why then should I be afraid to give an interview?"

Several bystanders laughed; their confident hero was untouchable.

"Long live Grandego!" several people cried.

Grandego waved at them, sporting his familiar, triumphant smile. The public answered with loud cheers.

"How are you feeling, Emperor, are you all right?" the reporter asked again.

"I'm fine, friends of the world. I was, I am, and I will be. One way or the other, I will complete my mission, as I have promised."

Grandego looked around. The people looked at him, admiringly. This lifted his heart. It even seemed to him most were sincere in their devoted admiration.

"I don't blame the Kenyan political leaders or the security services in this matter. The billions donated to Kenya won't be retracted, but the perpetrators will be punished. They will be sorry for this despicable attack. I've heard the central intelligence unit say they've arrested a suspect, thanks to their cunning and professional research. And as it always is with the earth's great, it turned out to be a Judas. A traitor from our own ranks. A man in high places. A very vicious plot, but they will pay! They didn't really know what they were up against!"

With these words, Grandego, followed by Molochi, entered the limousine.

Just a week after the attack, Mnaba was arraigned at Nairobi's Supreme Court. Even his influential family couldn't do anything against Grandego's supremacy. Mnaba was doomed.

"They tricked me. I was asked to fire a harmless shot to increase Grandego's image as a martyr!" Mnaba cried out in front of the packed courtroom in an attempt to defend himself.

"You have probably already seen the images on TV but let us look at them here as well to bring them in as insurmountable evidence, your honor," the Public Prosecutor said.

On a large screen, video images made from a helicopter appeared. When the camera zoomed in, Mnaba was unmistakably recognized, raising his Beretta and pulling the trigger, without any sign of emotion on his face. Then, the images appeared of the impact against

Grandego's head and the blood splattering the surrounding windows. This elicited an excessive response from the courtroom.

"Filthy murderer!" someone shouted.

Next, the images appeared of Mnaba's arrest as he left the Kenya Railways headquarters. The case with the Beretta in it was shown. Medical documents, which clearly showed Grandego was technically dead, were zoomed in upon. The pallid and disfigured face of the Emperor, surrounded by medical staff in a defeated posture, confirmed the view that this seemed the end of Grandego's story.

The video was followed by silence.

"In a miraculous way, Grandego has been given back to the world to complete his mission," the judge continued after the brief silence. "However, that does nothing to diminish the suspect's guilt." The judge looked at Mnaba with disgust. In the whole of Kenya, only one lawyer had been found willing to take up Mnaba Khenius' case.

"Your honor," he interrupted the judge, a bit timidly, "I have asked the detectives investigating the case to study the bullet that was fired. I was refused, which I find strange, because my client claims to have shot plastic ammunition that's unable to cause a fatal wound, because it cannot penetrate the skull from that distance."

"Liar!" someone in the public cried. An usher asked him to quiet down. The judge looked at the lawyer with pity.

"The images, the hospital reports, the arrest of the suspect and his gun. I'm sorry, but the evidence is so compelling in this matter. Your claims and considerations are concerned with futilities like an iron or plastic bullet. Wasn't the splashing blood enough for you? Were you planning on calling the Emperor Grandego himself as a witness?" the judge said to the lawyer, mocking him with his gaze. His remark was met with laughter.

"Perhaps we should investigate Grandego's wounds to see if they are real?"

"Have you not seen the explosion and everything?" the judge cried angrily through the courtroom. He was spontaneously supported by the public.

"Idiot!" someone shouted at the lawyer.

The lawyer recoiled from the judge's outrage and the public's reaction. He immediately thought wiser of putting a lot of effort into the defense. That was, if he wanted to continue his career after this case . . . although, the Khenius family had offered him a very high fee.

The case was decided, and the members of the jury unanimously declared Mnaba guilty. It had been a long time since a public hanging had taken place in Nairobi. Just a week after the trial, Mnaba was, under loud ridicule, cries of hatred, and clenched fists from the large, converged audience, sentenced to a dishonorable end by hanging.

The attack had been avenged. Justice had been done; the perpetrator was punished.

People could rest easy again, and the honor of the country had been largely restored.

15

THE ORDER

FOR THE INTERNATIONAL MEMBER MEETING, the Order had rented the Studio Theatre of the impressive Sydney Opera House. It had also completely booked the highly expensive five-star hotel Intercontinental Sydney. Despite the 240 luxury rooms and apartments, this exquisite hotel had only just enough capacity to house all members with their personnel, amongst which many beautiful young women could be seen. Most members liked to stroke their egos by making their attendance with a "beautiful specimen" on their arm.

The boroughs where these locations were situated had been fenced off and secured days before by the Black Eagles, the elite troops of the World Defense Force.

The meeting began at nine in the evening. For the occasion, an impressive laser show was projected on the roof of the Opera House, tiled with over a million glazed ceramic shingles.

This was a magnificent sight for the heads of the Order, who came driving up during the show. The effect of the life-like, moving images of remarkable natural phenomena was an experience in itself. Hordes of people were admiring the show from the quays as the Order Members' limousines entered the parking lot underneath the building.

After the World Masters, as the Order Members were also known, had taken place in the magnificent meeting room, High Master Scott entered in a dignified manner.

The most remarkable thing about the room was the sculpture of an enormous goat skull, which had been fastened above the lectern with cables from the ceiling. Out of the ominous skull protruded ten large upward pointing horns, which gave it a rather unnatural look. Initiates knew the horns represented the ten zones into which the world was divided by Grandego and Molochi.

In many ways, Grandego had gained a strong influence within the Order. Not everyone was pleased with that. Especially High Master Scott got more and more fed up with him.

During a teleconference, Grandego had called himself "the Goat's Head," the head of all powers. This remark didn't sit well with Master Scott.

Scott was very ambitious and almost always spearheaded the things he was involved in personally. Although he had helped Grandego become the most powerful man on the planet, as far as he was concerned it was only a formal status that was subservient to the Order. To himself.

As usual, the members got up when the president entered.

With a wave of his hand, Scott gave his audience permission to be seated.

"Welcome, honored gentlemen," Scott said at a slightly higher tone than the others were used to of him.

If they looked closely, they would notice High Master Scott was a tad nervous. He was getting on in years, and one shouldn't underestimate the pressure upon a position like his. But he had always been a sportsman. He didn't smoke, but alcohol slid easily down his throat. Despite that, it was safe to assume he was in good shape.

The mysterious demise of Members Johnson, Rositioso, and Wlascow was curious. Was Grandego behind it? Nobody talked about it. And then there was the circus regarding the attack on Grandego. How should they think about that? A little fear for the dictator seemed to be wise. What were they dealing with? What kind of a man was Grandego really? Things escalated too much. Scott usually had no problems with escalations in his work, except when they fell outside of his control and his sphere of influence.

"The items on the agenda have been made known, gentlemen. I'll immediately move forward to the items that are most important to us at this time."

He inspected the room to see if everyone was present. Absence from an Order meeting was a deadly sin.

The red light on the microphone in front of one of the members had lit up.

High Master Scott was annoyed when he noticed it. Was there a question already, before the meeting had even begun? Outrageous!

But because of his considerable talent as far as self-control went, he was able to gesture lightheartedly to the man with the question.

"I'm sure it's a grave question, to demand the floor at this moment, isn't it, World Master Don?" Scott said with a questioning look at the man in the midnight blue suit.

"It certainly is, High Master," Don answered decidedly.

"Your timing is like a bolt from the blue sky, Master Don," Scott said semi-amused, "but hey, let's hear it."

"Have you taken corrective actions against Grandego yet, as decided in the previous meeting?"

The question affected Scott as would a nerve shock. For a moment, he was taken aback. Why bother him with this question so early on in the meeting? The members probably didn't fully realize this wasn't such an easy assignment for the president. It weighed him down as if a millstone had been hanged about his neck. He had quietly hoped the question wouldn't be asked. Scott shivered at the thought of correcting Grandego. The assembly noticed Scott was taken aback, which caused a bit of unrest, for they had never seen weakness in Scott's response before. The mood changed for the worse.

Usually, someone who asked confronting or misplaced questions was immediately silenced with disapproval by the others. This time that wasn't the case, which meant this question was approved of by the members. This was food for thought, and the mood unsettled the chairman even more.

"Umm, I have a schedule . . . and will make that appointment . . . not yet specific, but that, er, will be," Scott mumbled uncertainly.

After having swallowed, he regained his composure and continued.

"I will get back on this later, gentlemen. It's not on the agenda, but I will immediately make an item of it . . . "

Ambivalent feelings overtook the mood in the room. On the one hand, there was a form of euphoria because the president's position had been weakened, a historic moment. On the other hand, there was doubt about the authority Scott, as representative of the Order, held over Grandego. Perhaps Scott needed replacing . . . Perhaps it was time for a stronger leader, who wasn't afraid to act quickly and decisively where it concerned the enforcing of the Order's utmost authority. Was the competition between the members to obtain his position about to start? But who had more authority than this old fox, President Scott? Was it only Grandego himself? If that was the correct answer to this question, the Order was really in trouble. It would demote them to puppets of the absolute ruler. They'd be turned upside down then! People started wondering what power Grandego had that he could afford such boldness.

"First, the most important issue," High Master Scott continued, internally distraught about the demanded agenda item and members' realization of the crisis of authority that had developed around Grandego's leadership.

"Grandego has carried out the public execution of drug addicts, which has been applauded by the public. He has extended the decree to include petty criminals. A person who is caught shoplifting and is reported to a special branch of the World Defense Force can be publicly sentenced within two hours by compelling him to take the lethal Drion pill. The Dutch legal scholar Huub Drion has done us a great service by developing this suicide pill. On a side note, I must say the liberal Dutch politics have brought us much good the past fifty years: the first policy of tolerance of drugs, providing special locations for drug users, the so-called 'coffee shops', grow shops to improve cannabis production, heroin supply programs, rehab facilities that started to allow drugs. In short, creation of a drug epidemic, socially paid prostitution in psychiatric wards, very loose euthanasia laws and end-of-life clinics, legislation of abortion and making fetal tissue available for medical purposes. And I could continue for a while. These Population Reduction Initiatives were pushed through the Dutch parliament by pseudo-scientific backing and from there they were promoted as a standard for the entire world. These policies have now been implemented in large parts of the world.

"Regarding the Population Reduction Program," Scott looked at World Master Kent, who was the initiator and coordinator of this program, "an excellent development. And people, it has had the desired effect. Grandego is hugely popular, especially in the business sector. The middle class is applauding his measures and the common man shows understanding after having suffered for decades by the hands of street terrorism and crime.

"The proposal now is to expand this policy. Drug addicts, bums, the homeless, drug dealers, criminals, unproductive handicapped people, terrorists, and of course enemies of the State, people who refuse to get chipped, will be finished off. Pardon my French, but we have to put things in order, which we can do only with firm measures."

Scott said this last part fully pleased and had reverted to his usual self-confidence by placing his willpower into this statement.

"Eventually, we will remain with a thoroughly reduced, but compliant world population, marching to the beat of our policy. A world population who will even enjoy it, all the days of their earthly existence."

Scott noticed he wanted to lose himself in his beloved, exalted preaching rhetoric, but the incident at the start had made him watchful. His support had been lessened. He knew the proverb, "when words are many, transgression is not lacking," and thus decided to move on to the next item on the agenda.

"Because I see no red lights, I can assume this policy may be developed further and stimulated with financial injections. Having said this, Masters, I would like to continue straight to the next item. The unwanted and stubborn new caliphates in Europe—"

President Scott had hardly said this, when a red light came on. World Master Tarik wanted the floor. The chairman was not amused, because now the subject could move in an undesirable direction. But Scott couldn't ignore a red light after what had happened, and so he allowed Tarik to speak.

"Mister President, I would like to address the chips. We find there's strong resistance against them. People refuse to be chipped, and many national governments in Africa and Asia don't follow our policy in making the chip mandatory. We need to increase the pressure. I also think the bombing of the caliphates in Europe should be executed more selectively. The World Defense Force obliterates large areas with cluster bombs. Many people fall victim. There are caliphates that resist One World Faith because they refuse to bow to the idol, but they will, however, accept the chip. The chip is a sufficient means of control to keep these factions in line, in my opinion. I would like to put forth the motion that exceptions can be made for Muslims and related groups that don't want to bow before the idol, but who are willing to accept the chip. By carrying out this policy we will probably find these groups more willing to integrate into the global community. Perhaps the extremism will diminish and there will be a basis to work together in a more moderate setting."

These words caused quite a stir. The Muslims had become more strongly represented within the Order. The Islamic Members were largely against extremism, because that could also turn against the established Islamic states, but on the other hand, they also sought protection for the extremists. Considerable effort was being made to include the numerous rebel groups within the global community. They were offered promises of prosperity and a certain level of autonomy, as well as a voice in large institutions like the UN, to entice them to follow a more moderate course.

There were, however, many hardliners within the Order who hated to allow for exceptions concerning important policy. World High Priest Molochi wouldn't be amused if the Order were to enact a policy of tolerance to exempt Muslims from bowing before the idol. To him, One World Faith was all for one, and one for all. One holy grail all must drink from. Even the Upper Ten of the superrich had to comply. It was unheard of to give lower ranks in the pyramid of power privileges the upper echelons didn't have.

Silence fell, and High Master Scott was deep in thought. To put forth a motion was a right, but he himself held a veto. Scott racked his brain on how to settle this matter. Eventually, he had the answer.

"Members, listen. We've been able to use humanism's strategy to make extremes accepted by society by regulating them. Just as the sex industry has become a legitimate business sector, for example. Even terrorism and extreme subcultures, in which slavery, amongst other things, is acceptable, can probably be integrated into the global community with the same strategy. An 'acceptable level of violence' could have a place in it, as long as it's orderly and regulated. We could define boundary conditions, so that the caliphates will get in line and be accepted as integrated parts of the global community. But making exceptions on essential conditions, such as submission to the idol? Doesn't that go too far? So, let us put this proposal, about the exclusion of Muslims regarding this point, to the vote."

Internally, Scott was convinced the proposal didn't stand a chance. But World Master Tarik and his powerful Muslim sympathizers had carefully done their homework. Before the meeting, they had done some work on many members. Their powerful lobby had exerted a considerable pressure. They had threatened with far-reaching economic sanctions, which had been enough for most members to give in.

As it turned out, many members were indifferent to the whole issue. What financial gain would bowing before the idol hold for them? None whatsoever. The chip, which was necessary to gain control over people, was extremely important. But bowing before an image . . . that was a monstrous idea, coming from the mind of that twisted Molochi. Secretly, many members thought he was the most sanctimonious sneak on the planet. Contrary to the masses, they knew full well what he was up to in his free time. That maniac was obsessed with all kinds of bizarre sexual acts and eliminated anyone who dared to stand in his way. But his position was untouchable, because he was protected by the head of the Order and by Grandego himself. There was a dark power about the man that could be felt when near him.

Scott was shocked to see the motion was carried with such a large majority. Scott stoically held his emotions under control, but his blood boiled. The feared talk with Grandego had just gotten more complicated.

It also didn't help that Scott thought Muslims had already gained too much power in the world. They were on top of everything to see if there were options to Islamize. According to Scott, Europe had largely fallen prey to this. In the US, this grab for power had been narrowly avoided. Vigilantes and armed civil groups had played an important role. The civil right to bear arms had provided a significant advantage in this fight.

In the chaos of the civil war those extremist factions ignited, Grandego had succeeded in placing a president in the White House who squarely supported the One World Faith ideology and Grandego's politics. The president had placed the mighty American army under the World Defense Force's command, basically handing the army over to Grandego. In the US, the situation was largely under control. And as commander of the World Defense Force, Grandego could now, more than ever, position himself as one of the greatest players in global politics. Perhaps *the* greatest. But he had to beware the Russians, the Chinese and the Islamic powerhouse.

Scott ended the meeting.

"In conclusion, I will soon make an appointment with our honored and successful World Emperor Grandego. As soon as this conversation has taken place, you will receive an evaluation report of this meeting," High Master Scott promised. He stepped down from the podium where the lectern stood and walked to the door with his head held high. Taking a bow, a Black Eagle opened the high door for Scott, and he disappeared from sight. Never before had Scott been so displeased after a member meeting.

* * *

Scott hurried to his hotel room and began pacing in circles. He was a bundle of nerves and he felt his heart pounding in his chest. It took him quite a while to get his nerves under control and was finally able to let himself fall into a comfortable armchair. The magnificent view over the green-blue waters of Botany Bay helped him to relieve the psychological pressure even further.

Eventually, the stress drained from his body and he became his old self again. Doubts about his position and functioning, not to mention his health, started to cause him more worries. Perhaps he should take his wife's advice seriously after all.

The moment he had this thought, his phone rang. Scott took his cell phone out of his shirt pocket and looked at the screen. Unfortunately, it was Grandego.

Immediately, the stress was back, and with trembling fingers, he pressed 'accept'.

"Hello, Grandego," Scott said as optimistically as he could.

"Scott, as President of the Order, I want to share this information with you. King Sadi of Mecca urged me to call the Russian President Stalnov concerning his recent troop movements," Grandego began without interruption or waiting for Scott's reply. "A coalition of Russia, Iran, Turkey, and a number of former Soviet states in the Caucasus has just invaded the Middle East with thousands of armored vehicles. Initially under the pretext of destroying terrorist groups, but the Army is heading straight for Israel. The Saudi's are wary of Iran's desire for expansion and king Sadi has pressed me to use the hotline to ask the Tsar an outright question: 'What does your coalition with Iran and the others plan to do in the region? Take many spoils? Are you after Israel's stored riches, the gigantic Leviathan oil field, the natural gas supplies and the enormous mineral deposits of the Dead Sea?' Stalnov answered it was about a switch in the status quo that would deal a fatal blow to terrorism, cause Israel to step back and thus stabilize the energy market. So, then you know what's behind it—it is indeed a grab for power over resources."

Grandego paused briefly here. Scott didn't know what to say.

"I, er . . ."

"I understand your response," Grandego said, once again taking the initiative. "I have five out of the United State's seven naval fleets stationed in the Middle East, but I'm not interfering. The negative feelings of the world towards Israel are too pronounced, and I also don't want to offend our partners in the Middle East. Israel is on its own, and we'll just see what happens. If Stalnov's coalition takes control, we'll be able to sufficiently influence them through the Saudi's and other stakeholders. The spoils will have to be shared with us as well," Grandego declared threateningly. "I've demanded Stalnov grants me mandate over Jerusalem's Old City when he takes control. This way, we possess the Temple Mount, for that's where I want my inauguration to take place."

"Er . . . yes," Scott stammered. "Of course . . . we absorb this . . . er, as usual it will work to our advantage," Scott answered professionally.

THE CHURCH

HIS EMINENCE THE GRAND MINISTER Bastian had summoned Brother Jones, who had been promoted to Cardinal, from Florida to the Cathedral of La Plata in Argentina. In recent years, Argentina had become a popular place for major church leaders to meet. The country was mostly Christian, and thus a fairly safe place for church leaders. Something that couldn't be said of large parts of the world. Actually, all places on planet Earth had become unsafe. Intensive security had become essential for any event.

The enormous, neogothic cathedral dominated the area around La Plata. This appealed to the Grand Minister. The fantastic architecture and colorful, towering stained glass windows gave the building an exalted feeling, according to the visitors. How much more so if you were presiding over it as Keeper of the Faith, the function Grand Minister Bastian now held.

Bastian couldn't complain in that regard. To him, the cathedral symbolized his personal greatness.

Yet, now he sat before Cardinal Jones with a suffocating fear in his heart.

"Listen, Jones. Isn't there something you could arrange?" Bastian said with trembling voice. "There is nothing I can do against those two self-proclaimed prophets in Jerusalem. How can I then comply with the orders from Molochi and Grandego? You understand, right?"

Jones remained seated and looked with pity upon his colleague.

"I've thought about everything," Bastian continued, defeated. "I've prayed and fasted. I've cursed those prophets and tried to proclaim them away in the powerful name of the Black Madonna. I've invoked the sacred angels of Lourdes, Santiago, and the Vatican to take away their powers. Nothing helped. Eventually, I even asked Yogi Swami Sirini to curse the two prophets in Jerusalem and deal them a crushing blow in the spiritual realm. The man can leave his body and astral travel for hours. His spiritual highness sent me a panicky message after a week that he had tried to contact the prophets spiritually. But during that attempt, he had fallen to his knees before them and he had pronounced blessings instead of curses!"

Jones looked at him with large, unbelieving eyes.

"Sirini said that he had never, in his seventy-year career, encountered such a spiritual power as with these two prophets. They are Elijah and Enoch, was his analysis. During the contact, Sirini said, he had a very humiliating experience, because the fact was revealed to his spirit that his supposed humility had always been conceited haughtiness. It was a shocking revelation. He also discovered all his meditation in trance held no value whatsoever in the eyes of the most-high God, the Yogi said. He, for whom several weeks of fasting and meditation were commonplace, who withheld himself from every form of luxury and always obeyed his spiritual Master to the letter, declared after the confrontation with the two men in Jerusalem, that all his efforts had been nothing but vanity and didn't hold any useful value. He was almost consumed by their spiritual light and immediately fell to his knees to submit to those two."

Silence fell after these words and Jones' eyes penetrated Bastian's even more. Confusing thoughts flashed through Jones' mind. Bastian had condemned himself to death by disappointing Molochi because of the fact he couldn't cause the death of the two prophets. But the information he learned about Sirini had even endangered his own position. If the prophets were truly on a mission from God, wouldn't he, in fighting them and God Himself, ultimately be cast into hell?

In Jerusalem, new incidents had occurred concerning the two prophets. They had, before the rolling cameras of the global press, held a moving sermon about forgiveness, conversion, and the second coming of Jesus Christ. They had also proclaimed a rainless period of one and a half years over different areas of the world, and more of those supernatural things, that actually came true. They did this, according to their own words, to confirm the divine mandate of their calling and to stress the seriousness of their message.

In a secret meeting with Jones and several Grand Cardinals, held to discuss the problem concerning the two prophets, High Priest Molochi had suddenly become very angry and outraged. He had taken a three-foot-tall candlestick from the altar and thrown it through the stained-glass windows of the church. His fit of rage had been so impressive and threatening, the Cardinals feared Molochi would hurt them. Which he could have done physically, had he wanted to.

Molochi was a lot younger than the Cardinals, and extraordinarily strong. In his youth, he had successfully practiced Kung Fu. Besides that, the man could also unleash demonic powers.

"No, dear friend, I am afraid there is nothing I can do for you," Jones answered his Eminence with a sigh. "You have failed, Bastian, to please Molochi, and you have been unable to act against those two prophets."

With his elbows on the solid oak table, Bastian hid his head in his hands.

"What must I do now?"

Bastian sobbed uninhibited.

"Jones, tell me what to do. You plotted the course. I followed you blindly, I believed in you. Come, please . . . " Bastian mumbled, teary-eyed.

Jones felt for him, but he knew this was the end of the career of his Eminence Bastian.

"Bastian," he said with a dark voice, "I find this hard to say, but . . . I have one of Drion's pills, if you want to use it."

Bastian raised his head to study Jones' face.

"Drion's pills? Are you saying this is the only solution?"

Jones sighed deeply.

"I don't know, brother. I mean . . . the situation has run aground. If you appear before the cameras in Jerusalem to try and do something against the prophets against better judgment, you'll be destroyed before the eyes of the world. Our image would be damaged too much, so we can't allow you to do such a thing. But if you take matters into your own hands, I'll make sure you'll get a beautiful tomb. That way, you've saved your honor. I'll say you've succumbed to a chronic illness. You'll be honored as a hero who has served mankind for decades. Your family will be proud of you. Your grandchildren will see your marble tomb and praise themselves for belonging to such an exalted bloodline."

A deep frown appeared on the face of his Eminence Bastian.

He put his head back into his hands and sat silently, indecisive, for a long while.

Cardinal Jones didn't wait for Brother Bastian's decision, but took a pill out of one of the inside pockets of his robe.

Subtly, he pushed the pill, packed air-tight in foil, across the table until it was in front of Bastian.

Bastian raised his head again when he heard this slight noise. He saw the pill. Slowly, his hand moved towards it.

"I'd rather do this alone," he said, without looking at Brother Jones.

Jones slowly got up and stretched out his arms over Bastian.

"Adios," he said, and left the high room which was decorated with arches. Outside the room, two other Grand Cardinals were waiting for him.

"Well?" one whispered.

"Yes, he'll do it," Jones said softly.

A few moments later, they heard a dull thud. Bastian's body had fallen to the floor, dead. Jones beckoned several soldiers, who were waiting further down the hall.

"Follow the instructions I have given you to the letter," Jones commanded, after which he and the other two Cardinals left.

Outside, they entered a dark blue Mercedes GL and told the private driver their destination.

"What can I offer you gentlemen?" Jones asked his colleagues. He pulled down a blind next to him, upon which pictures of all kinds of delicious drinks were printed. The men drank the best wine and enjoyed the sight of the beautiful coast, which was clearly visible from the car.

When they had been driving for half an hour, Cardinal Jones' cell phone rang. He accepted the call, listened for a moment and almost dropped his glass.

"What?" He looked meaningfully at his fellow passengers, who were also very curious. "The two prophets have been killed?"

The Cardinals rejoiced.

"The two prophets have been killed, hurray!" Jones shouted with a cry of victory. "This is good news indeed!"

"Finally, some good news in these days of adversity, excellent!" one of the men now loudly yelled. The mood became more excited.

The driver pushed down on the gas pedal, for now they had gotten wings. The obstacles were cleared and the inauguration of World Emperor Grandego could now be celebrated in style. They would attend as special Cardinals to assist High Priest Molochi, under the watching eyes of all of humanity.

Excitedly, they decided to send all the Bishops a present: a miniature replica of the Idol of Reverence, in honor of Molochi and Grandego. Jones thought he had perhaps sent his Brother Bastian to his death too soon, but this bitter thought was soon forgotten, a psychological skill someone in his position must have. So much didn't fit, and so many people suffered from their ambitious pushing. But they were sacrifices for a higher goal, he told himself to get rid of his negative emotions.

The three euphoric Cardinals decided to stay a few more days in the luxurious Palace Hotel near the coast to enjoy the grand dinners and the magnificent view. When they walked through the streets, they enjoyed the humble greetings and the nods of passersby.

On a 120-inch smart TV in their spacious suite, they could follow the events in Jerusalem, live. For several days now, every hour a live image was broadcast of the two prophets' bodies lying dead on the ground near the Western Wall. These images confirmed their victory. It gave a good feeling of world power to everyone who loved Grandego's and Molochi's politics. They, Cardinals, were with them at the absolute summit of the power on earth and in the entire universe.

On the third day after that victory, the Cardinals had decided to travel on to Rome and they were busy packing their suitcases. His exclusive clothing filled Jones with pride every time. On the TV a nature show about the Amazon was running. The beautiful imagery of colorful birds was complemented by a pan flute orchestra in the background. The surround sound made it feel as if one was amongst nature. While Jones was putting his gleaming shoes in a leather bag, the nature show was rudely interrupted.

Suddenly the TV reported there was breaking news. The Cardinals' full attention was immediately directed toward the television. They saw the Western Wall, and . . . the bodies of the two prophets, moving.

"What . . . ," Jones began, and his mouth fell open and fear came over him.

The two prophets began to stand up and stretched out their arms, upwards to the blue sky. Color came back to their faces, and they started to shine. An enormous energy seemed to emanate from them. Soon, they were radiating pure power and, with looks of gladness on their faces, began to levitate up from the ground. A small cloud in the sky moved toward them, until it formed into a gate and opened. The two saints levitated toward it and disappeared into the cloud. Penetrating trumpet blasts accompanied this scene, until the cloud eventually evaporated into nothingness. On the screen, devastated people were seen pressing their hands against their ears. Some had fallen to their knees. Others had turned their backs and, bent over, walked away from the place. Soldiers had their weapons pointed towards it but didn't fire. Several tanks drove towards the place where the prophets had lain. Dozens of reporters kept filming and taking pictures, against the soldiers' instructions. Some were arrested. The whole world had seen this take place. Jones sat down on his bed in dismay.

"Deception, deception," he stammered. "I'm doomed . . . disillusion, or is it not true . . . ?"

The other Cardinals were also upset.

"We're not the highest power," one stammered.

"This means we serve the wrong god," Jones deduced. "We've made the wrong choice; we've, at some point, taken the wrong path."

His words made Jones realize he had been following his own selfish devices and lust for power. Emotions of despair, sorrow, loss, and anger followed each other in rapid succession. For a moment, he thought he was going insane.

"My pills . . . "

With trembling hands, he took out his toiletry bag, zipped it open in panic and took out the bottle with strong Librium pills. Clumsily, he put a couple in his mouth, walked into the bathroom and drank a few large glasses of water to wash the stuff down. He then lay himself flat on his bed.

I wait, wait for rest . . . away, away with the thoughts and emotions . . . they make a man crazy . . .

It took about ten minutes before he started to feel the effect of the pills. His brain was numbed and eventually, his breathing calmed down and he became more relaxed. Yet the words "I'm doomed" kept resonating through his mind. It wasn't until hours later that Jones recovered himself.

He had made his choices in life. That meant he had to accept the consequences, such as they were. *Let me try to enjoy my last few days.*

"A little while." He had preached long ago on those words about the second coming of Christ. That little while was what he had condemned himself to. No eternal life, but a brief time of worldly riches and then God's judgment . . .

17

PROJECT MOMENTUM

SOMEWHERE, DEEP UNDER THE GROUND beneath Jerusalem, in a secret place that was known only to a small number of initiates, was the GICCB, the General Israeli Crisis Coordination Bunker.

The bunker was soberly furnished but held all supplies to stay there with a group of more than a hundred people for a considerable time. The bunker was seldom used, only during severe crises. Which was now the case.

Authorized personnel were present, except for two. They had been tragically killed by falling bombs on their way to the bunker.

The central control room was staffed by the prime minister and several generals, each one an expert in a different area, along with a communications officer. He was charged with relaying orders and guidelines, which were passed along from the control room to different military divisions.

The Goldstein Companies had developed an ultramodern medium for the control room. It was a special radiation frequency, that had accidentally been discovered when researching laser techniques. Contrary to other frequencies, this one could barely be stopped, interrupted, or influenced by matter. The signal could transport over one hundred terabytes of data over a distance exceeding three thousand miles, enough range to cover the entire Middle East.

A unique decoder was necessary to decrypt and categorize the data. This was inserted as a chip into the body of especially trained agents, the so-called 12th Ground Pointer Platoon. Because each decoder was linked to a specific person, intercepting the data was virtually impossible.

"Men," the prime minister said, "we have to make some difficult decisions and fast. I don't like it, but there's no other way."

Prime Minister Rekavit was brilliant, but his thoughts and communication were so fast he seemed like a speed freak.

He anticipated so quickly with thoughts and situations, that he was often very hard to follow. He seemed like a chess player who could think twelve steps ahead and was able to tell every combination.

In the past, Rekavit had made so many effective decisions his authority was unquestioned, so when he made this statement, the generals looked at the prime minister, expectantly.

"The prognosis is no other powers will add to the enemy coalition of Russia and Iran, where surprisingly, Turkey, or Gog, if you will, also has a role to play. I am not surprised that Ethiopia and Sudan have joined as well. Which weapons system will we deploy?" The Prime Minister put forth the question.

The generals looked at the electronic 3D map of the Middle East. All strategic locations were marked. They knew the geography and features of the landscape like the back of their hand. An array of lighting effects showed the troop movements across the model. They saw a large number of red dots, symbolizing the enemy, moving towards Syria from the north. There wasn't much left of that country;

everything was in ruin after the civil wars and past military actions by world powers.

Although there was nothing to be gained in Syria, it provided an access route to Israel from the north. No other conclusion could be drawn: Israel was the target.

"Goldstein's LaserDoom," Prime Minister Rekavit suggested, answering his own question. "Goldstein's Doom," he said again. "That way, we've got the chance of salvaging military equipment."

"You read my mind," one of the generals dryly confirmed.

"Set out all coordinates, calculate the effect, and when the drones arrive—*boom*, fire the laser shots."

The prime minister and the generals studied the model. Their satellite system *Gad* did an amazing job. It sent real time information about troop movements to the control bunker.

"The weapons system has never yet been used in the field on this scale. Hopefully, the theory will work in practice, otherwise this is the end for Israel, and we can use only the ultimate weapon."

A slight tremble was sent through the bunker. Little clouds of dust came loose from the ceiling and floated to the ground. A large bomb had hit outside, but shock-absorbing layers had been included into the bunker's concrete. The people in the control room looked at each other in concern.

"The defensive laser shield over the city doesn't destroy every projectile," one of the generals said. "That's a bummer."

"We have to make haste," the prime minister urged his staff.

A man had already finished preparations and was already in constant communication with the intelligence services in the field. The Israeli troops had been equipped with synthetic materials.

They bore no metal objects on them, and so could not be felled by the laser pulses.

"Ezekiel thirty-eight," General Moshe suddenly said across the control room. "Two thousand six hundred years ago, the current geo-political power distribution had been written down by the prophet Ezekiel with remarkable precision. And if this prophecy is about to be fulfilled, this is going to be a very brief war. Other powers in the West and China will remain neutral."

The prime minister now lifted his gaze from the model to look meaningfully at Moshe.

"The military maneuvers look suspiciously like it," he answered, obviously impressed. "And Goldstein's LaserDoom weapon," a shiver worked its way up the prime minister's spine, "will ensure a swift but terrible end to this war. A devastating blow, but a regional conflict, and this way it won't grow into a world war."

Rekavit's gaze fell back to the model in front of him. "Is everything set to generate the first charge?" he asked with a penetrating voice.

"Give it a minute. I'll count down, and then you give the order," General Moshe replied.

"Three, two, one . . . "

"Fire!" the prime minister said at once.

This procedure was repeated seven times, activating all laser pulses from the drones. The electronic model showed the effects of the laser weapons, but they didn't display details. A wall monitor, a dozen feet across, however, showed several images from cameras attached to the very same drones. These were sent to the control room via satellite and placed in a geographic perspective by the computer. This way, they could be viewed very lifelike in 3D, but were also very confronting.

They saw large numbers of motor vehicles grind to a halt. Jets whose pilots had been hit seemed to fly in all directions, out of control. Some flew into each other mid-air, causing violent explosions. Others crashed onto the land or into the sea, yet others kept flying straight ahead, without any maneuver or response.

Horrid images of thousands of soldiers collapsing in agony flashed before them. Prime Minister Rekavit grabbed the model for support and the control room was filled with dismay.

From the descriptions of the weapon, the gathered staff knew it was terrible, but now that they saw the actual effect shown larger than life on the screen, they were filled with disgust.

It became deadly quiet in the room. They kept on looking. Eventually, all the pulses had completed their destructive work. General Moshe pointed out several people moving here and there.

"Those fortunate people probably haven't had any metal on their bodies when the pulses were delivered," he informed with a calm voice. "They're healthy as a horse, another advantage LaserDoom has compared to a nuclear weapon, besides the fact there's hardly any material damage."

The monitor, which showed a part of the Golan Heights, displayed several men waving at the drones' cameras.

"Zoom in on that," the general said to the technician. "These are men of the 12th Ground Pointer platoon."

The men in the control room were filled with feelings of triumph.

The people in the bunker were shocked though when they saw images of Jerusalem. The city hadn't been free of damages.

The PC, the Projectile Counter—the system that keeps track of everything that enters Jerusalem's airspace and counts it based on its mass—indicated thirty-nine jets had crashed into the city. Bodies lay torn apart in the streets. People fled from their houses to find a safe refuge in one of the bunkers. They were already overcrowded, causing conflicts. Brave people of the emergency services were already taking care of things. Firefighters and doctors were working in many places.

* * *

For lunch, a buffet was arranged for the gentlemen in the bunker. Falafels, bourekas pastries, ruchelach buns, malabi desserts, and several drinks were invitingly arrayed on the buffet table, but most didn't have much of an appetite.

All afternoon, they had been busy evaluating all actions and their results. At one time, the red light on Prime Minister Rekavit's cell phone began flashing. He looked at it for a moment in surprise, because this signified one of the world leaders using a hotline connection. Just like the Washington-Moscow connection, this one was used only in absolute emergencies.

Rekavit answered.

"Congratulations, Rekavit, for sending the Russians packing. We were sad to see the attack, but you'll understand we have to remain neutral so we don't provoke the Chinese. They forced us to remain out of the conflict so as to not cause a global war. So, we did. My condolences with the victims. Clean up the garbage and build that third Jewish Temple on the Temple Mount."

World Emperor Grandego was speaking at breakneck speed.

"I know all the materials have been manufactured, and I will personally ensure they'll be shipped to you without any problems. I think the Temple can be ready within a few months. A gift from the United States to commemorate your victory! How about that?"

Prime Minister Rekavit nearly fell back in amazement. He had the phone on speaker so the generals could follow the conversation. They looked at him with open mouths.

Without waiting for a reply, Grandego continued. But now he was speaking in a different tone of voice, presidential and fatherly.

"I've decided to hold my inauguration in that new Temple, in the Navel of the World! Yes, you've heard it correctly, Prime Minister. Not only will this be a great feast, but it will also be an enormous honor for the Jewish State to host and organize this event. The inauguration is hugely important for the coming world peace and the One World Faith movement! Immediately after your victory, I have called King Sadi in Mecca. He was relieved the Russians and Iranians, who formed a threat to him as well, have been beaten back for now. Sadi is so relieved, he wants to personally support the Covenant between you and us. He has now become the most powerful leader of the Muslim world. The Great Covenant implies Israel is allowed to build its desired Temple next to the Omar Mosque, meaning my inauguration can take place in two sanctuaries at once! In the Vatican in Rome we'll project a three-dimensional hologram of the event. World High Priest Molochi will conduct the blessings. Excellent! One World Empire, One World Faith, and peace in the Middle East. Isn't that great? This has never been seen before, it's a victory for our generation!"

Grandego sounded very enthusiastic at this point in his mono-logue. In the GICCB, Rekavit and the generals listened with increasing amazement. It felt like their emotions were in a roller coaster. Was this sincere, or another political game of lies, a cunning plan . . . or was it indeed the reward for their victory and the beginning of long desired world peace?

As the phone call went on, the prime minister became more annoyed. Who did this man think he was, to arrange everything himself and impose it on Israel? Then again, building the Temple was a two-thousand-year-old dream of the Jewish people.

There would be nothing for it but to go along with this obligatory policy of the arrogant world leader.

"I have two conditions for your freedom and right to exist under my power," Grandego continued. "To wit: giving me the technology of your LaserDoom weapons system, and integration of the Jewish religion in the One World Faith movement. That's the price you're going to pay, Rekavit. Simply put, you're gaining the Temple and world peace, and you're giving up your laser weapon technology and the illusion your religion is exclusive. As a bonus, I'm giving the Jews back the original Menorah, the Temple candelabrum from Rome. I want your answer within three hours."

With these words, the connection was cut. Astonished, Rekavit looked at his cell phone, but Grandego had indeed disconnected.

The generals didn't try to hide their outrage about this monotonous dictate, but despite that, many fell for Grandego's plan.

"Who does this guy think he is?" asked General Moshe as he paced through the control room with annoyance. "He plainly abandoned us in the fight against the Russian coalition."

"You know his arrogant attitude, a scary, but unavoidable man," another general added.

"Incredible! What a crazy day," Prime Minister Rekavit said, who had regained his equilibrium somewhat. It was quiet for a while in the control room as the men sat down to think. After a while, Rekavit broke the silence.

"It is, in my opinion and under the given circumstances, the wisest to agree to Grandego's bizarre covenant."

"It won't be easy to gain the support of the Chief Rabbinate in this matter," one of the generals remarked.

General Moshe had a worried expression and suddenly dropped a term not regularly used'.

"It's a monster covenant. I don't think this will be the solution for our problems. The world has never kept its word, brothers." Moshe tried to convince the others. But the faces of most men in the control room told him his words didn't gain much of a foothold and seemed to dissolve into nothingness, despite that there were some doubts.

"Giving up the modern weapons system is what worries me the most," one general said, putting words to the thoughts of many.

But Moshe was approaching the matter on a different level. "Isn't it written somewhere in the Torah that trust in the world is as leaning on a reed? After a while, that reed will penetrate right through your hand, after which the wound must be accepted. We shouldn't act out of opportunism, there's a reason for this proposal."

"Yes, it's a risk, but on the other hand, what's the alternative? Declare war on Grandego and the rest of the world?" Rekavit objected to Moshe.

"What's the worst that could happen?" another general asked himself aloud. "Extermination, but that's nothing new. We've been threatened with that for thousands of years, and we've been confronting this monster for so long fear has turned into fighting spirit, which, by the way, has given us the opportunity to become heroes."

"Thousands of years of suffering, for no other reason than being a Jew, now culminating in the development of a final blow," Prime Minister Rekavit added. "An eye for an eye, a tooth for a tooth. For even if we're at a later time attacked by the UN and thus betrayed by the world, we'll have our plan at the ready: the DNA Revenge Weapon. The extermination of the entire world's population, save for us. Perhaps we should make this secret weapon known to the world, for no other reason than the preventative and repelling effect." Rekavit looked around the room, filled with conviction. "We could accept the covenant, but we'll keep an exit strategy."

These words took hold with the majority, which was signified by the agreeing hubbub that filled the control room.

"Besides," Rekavit continued, "we'll get the original Menorah. We'll use it to appease the Rabbinate and entice them to go along with this development."

These optimistic words comforted many men. Another Temple in Jerusalem after over two thousand years, that was something! Prime Minister Rekavit saw the relevance of this momentum.

"Gentlemen, we're going to sign the great covenant! This is a once in a lifetime opportunity, we can't ignore it. I'll convince the House and the Rabbinate."

Sounds of agreement and optimism came forth from the group. Someone walked to the buffet table.

"Let's eat and drink to this—that the future may dawn."

Their appetites had returned and now that the decision had been made, they felt hugely relieved. Deep in their souls, they hoped for the best. Although . . . intuitively, they realized, deep down, that the signing of the covenant would only buy them time. The traumatic past of the Jewish people simply didn't allow them the illusion that a covenant could nullify the monster of immanent destruction, and the ever-present watchfulness for it.

For now, they didn't expect any problems with Grandego and the rest of the world. The prospect of a celebration when the Temple was dedicated would embolden the spirits of the people who had to start repairing the destructions in Jerusalem. A feast . . . yes, they could use that.

18

AKHAN AND TARPI

AKHAN WOKE UP IN A small tent.

His sleeping bag had kept him warm and dry.

They had decided to trust the Italian Georgi Bonetti, who kept talking about his family, and they had followed him to the "brother camp," as he called it.

After a day's journey through the forests, they had arrived at the camp in the evening. There were no lights, so they hadn't seen much of the camp yet.

A brother had taken care of sleeping places. These were very primitive: a plastic tarp with a few sticks that formed a small tent, a sleeping pad, and a sleeping bag. That was all, yet it was enough for people who had nothing themselves.

Akhan had risen early. He crawled out of his tent, rubbed his eyes, and stretched his arms to loosen his muscles. He took in the view. There wasn't much to see. Between the trees, he saw the same green tarps here and there, tents that weren't three feet high and about six feet long.

Near a tall tree some ten yards away, several men were talking.

Tarpi and Rita still slept in their tents, directly adjacent to Akhan's. Tarpi awoke and felt himself blessed for the air mattress that had provided him a comfortable sleep.

"Have you recovered?" he heard Akhan say.

"Yes," he groggily replied.

"Good, time to get up, you old slacker," Akhan teased.

Now, they also heard signs of life from Rita's tent.

The men who had been standing underneath the tree now hurried towards them. Georgi the Italian was amongst them.

"Well rested?" one of the men asked kindly.

"Quite well," Akhan said. "Thanks for the hospitality."

"You're welcome," the man replied. "But I have to say, you are under arrest."

The man, Baris, had a Turkish appearance, was of average height, bronzed, hairy and muscled. A handsome man, but it seemed wiser to not get into a fight with him.

"Arrest?" Akhan asked.

"Yes. This isn't the boy scouts. We're not here in the forest just to have a good time, you understand? We want to know exactly who you are."

Tarpi and Rita had also emerged from their tents.

"Do you have some water?" Tarpi asked, unimpressed, as he rubbed his eyes.

"That would be nice," Rita added.

"Yes, there's water a-plenty," Georgi said. "I'll escort you, and then we'll talk. Agreed, Baris?" Georgi directed this to the Turk.

"Go," he answered, still studying the three newcomers. The third person, a woman, stood watching in silence.

"All right, come along then."

Once again, they followed the Italian, who briskly walked before them. Besides the natural beauty of the forest, nothing much was to be seen. The fresh, oxygen-rich air did them good though.

It was marvelous to have caught up on sleep. They felt at peace in this place. Here and there, people were standing or sitting, busy with all kinds of things. None of them looked threatening. They even waved or wished them a good morning when they passed.

These were people bound by fate, individuals who had found each other through a certain set of circumstances and who helped each other.

There were Western Europeans, Turks, Northern Africans, and even Chinese. Akhan hoped the latter would take care of the evening meal. He loved Chinese food.

"I'll look after your wound," Rita said to Tarpi.

He smiled at her, a bit taken aback. "That's nice," he answered. He wasn't used to women who spoke with him in such a direct and open manner. That was unheard of in his culture, then he remembered this open attitude from European movies. He saw a woman, a beautiful woman even, and in all honesty, couldn't help but look at Rita that way. He noticed he had to force himself not to constantly cast his gaze upon her and those Spanish, deep brown, smiling eyes.

He knew she didn't mean anything by it, but it was difficult for him. After his wife, although the marriage had been arranged, had passed away, he had always been tormented by the empty spot she had left behind in his heart.

"This is Abraham's Well," Georgi proudly pointed out. It wasn't much more than a hole in the ground, filled with clear water.

The water overflowed the hole and fed a small stream that trickled away into the forest.

"Oh," Akhan said, a bit disappointed when he learned such a grand name was given to such a small stream.

"Is this all?"

"Yes, drink, wash yourself and take it along if you have a flask or something, for there's plenty," Georgi advised.

They did and it was a marvelous refreshment.

"This camp isn't that bad," Tarpi said.

Rita lightened up and immersed her feet into the watering hole. Akhan and Tarpi followed suit.

"Why is it called Abraham's Well?" Akhan asked Georgi when they were on their way back.

"Because of Ibrahim the Aqua Man. He's been with the Heaven Groups from the beginning and can trace springs. For our safety, we move every ten days to a different place in the forest, and then he digs a well. He never misses," loose-lipped Georgi revealed.

"He walks around in prayer and starts digging somewhere and *bam*, water! There's always enough for everyone." Georgi got more and more excited. "It's so miraculous how we always have everything to survive. Last week, dozens of chickens came running into the camp. Perhaps they had been fleeing something, I don't know. Either way, they ended up in pots."

He looked very amused.

Rita had gotten more joyful because of the goings on in the camp. It seemed a lot of tension just fell off her.

Tarpi observed it with gladness but couldn't be so relaxed as easily. Caution was always prudent. Danger could come from all sides, and many things could look good from the outside, but in his experience, it was often just appearance.

However, the atmosphere in this camp was special indeed. What was behind it? Why did these people feel so secure, while the world was burning, and they were marked for death?

"Most people here are religious. They were Hindus, Jews, you name it. Many Muslims as well, who've had a dream from Isa or who have met the God of peace one way or another. Everyone has his own story, but we are friends and we experience the Holy Spirit of Jesus, or Isa, as many people call Him over here. No one here wants to have anything to do with violence or governments who oblige you to be injected with that cursed chip and who want people to bow to a dumb idol," Georgi said.

The talk took place between several trees under the blue sky. The newcomers, Georgi, the Turkish leader Baris, and the woman who had introduced herself as Zeorachi, or Zeri for short, were present.

Zeri was the quiet type, with an intelligent, keen look. She had pinned up her hair underneath a green beret and wore a military outfit she could use to move about, nimble and well protected. Her expression was one of impeccable professionalism, sharp and observing, yet friendly. She had a small cross pinned on her lapel, directly beneath an attached walkie-talkie.

Everyone in the camp who was interested in the conversation was free to join and listen to what the three newcomers had to say. As Akhan and Tarpi's story progressed, more people became interested and joined the group.

"Impressive," Baris said after Tarpi had finished his recounting of the turbulent events.

"Are you going to betray us?" Baris suddenly asked.

"We betray you?" Akhan said with a look of insult because of this remark.

"I don't think so, but it would be better if they'd join us," Zeri said to Baris.

"They haven't been chipped and they've been through enough to sincerely accept our cause," Georgi quickly added.

Baris still looked doubtful.

"They handed me back my gun when they arrived in the camp yesterday," Georgi blurted.

"What do you mean?" Baris asked with an edge to his voice, which startled Georgi.

"I'm sorry, but I fell asleep during my watch and they were too quick for me," he said, slightly nervous.

"Oh boy. 'They could not watch with me one hour.' Didn't the Master say something like that?" Zeri remarked as she shook her head at Georgi.

Baris obviously wasn't amused, which reflected his care and responsibility for the Heaven Groups.

"Oh well, it'll turn out all right," Zeri said while she comfortingly patted Baris' shoulder. "I sense no danger in these people," she added decidedly. Zeri's opinion seemed to be important to Baris.

"Well, I guess we have to tell a story ourselves then," Baris said.

He began to explain how the Heaven Groups first formed and how they functioned. During the civil war that had taken Europe by surprise when the caliphates were declared, dictator Grandego had risen through the ranks and his strangle chip, combined with High Priest Molochi's coercive measures to subject humanity to his One World Faith, were for many people reasons to form a resistance.

"Many rebels were arrested. Some were seen again, having accepted the chip.

"I had a written invitation from the World Accept Centre and, as a good citizen, went to that government center to get chipped," Baris said. "Me and many of my brothers were Muslim, but like anyone, we just wanted to build a good life for ourselves and had nothing to do with terrorism. I had to sustain my business, which would be easier with the chip. I saw no harm in it. I even thought the chip was a good idea, because many monetary problems could be solved. Dirty money, laundering of drug money, et cetera . It would all be made impossible, and I supported that cause. I've seen only misery when drugs were involved, and as far as dirty money is concerned, it turns people into killers.

"So, I stepped out of my car and walked towards the center, where several people were standing in line to have the chip injected. As I was walking over, I heard someone call my name. I looked this way and that and saw someone sitting on a bench. I didn't know the man, but he looked friendly and I thought he just wanted to ask me for directions. Perhaps he knew me from my store. When I reached him, he asked me to sit down next to him.

"The moment I sat down, a memory depicting my life flashed before my mind's eyes: my father and mother, brothers and sisters, my childhood, and all kinds of events. I've been into two serious accidents. As a child, I fell from a high roof I climbed up on, and later I was in a heavy car crash. I took a turn while driving too fast and lost control of the wheel. I slammed head-first into a truck. Both times, the doctors were surprised I survived.

"But in my memory, I saw those two events, and the same angel saved my life both times. He did it by catching the blows and tempering the impact of them on my body. When those miraculous flashbacks had finished, I looked into the face of the man next to me on the bench. It was the angel who had saved me. I was speechless, but the man started talking in a friendly but stern manner. He told me that if I would accept the chip and bow before the idol of the One World Faith, I'd be beyond saving by God and would die because of my own sins.

"Bowing in worship to the idol flies in the face of any monotheistic religion. 'This divine intervention was a sign from God,' the man said. He told me I had the choice not to bow before the idol but give God the glory He deserves. Faith without idols, and from the heart. The man radiated such peace, it made me jealous. I wanted to experience that same peace."

Baris' face, handsome but a bit gangster-like, shone as if the very gates of heaven had been opened. He was keen to continue.

"It was as if the man knew what I thought. He said the structural, deeper feeling of unrest every human experiences is because of a spiritual and legal problem. Sin brings separation between God and man. Every person has sinned: stealing, lying, selfishness, coveting, loveless behavior, et cetera. God's Law condemns the people who break it to death. But Jesus has taken that punishment for all mankind upon Himself at the cross, so that everyone who asks for forgiveness will receive it. This way God can be both just and merciful at the same time. Merciful because He forgives us, and just because the legal punishment for sin has been executed when Jesus died in our place upon the cross.

"I didn't fully understand at that time, but the angel asked if I wanted to accept peace and would bear the consequences of refusing to take the chip and to bow down to the idol. I said I wanted that. My soul cried *yes*.

"I saw something move in the sky. I looked a little closer and saw it was a white dove. When I looked back down, the man had vanished. Then, a sharp police whistle disturbed my rest. When I looked up, I saw a man in a black uniform coming my way. 'Get in line for your chip,' he said sternly. When he'd gotten near, he looked very threateningly at me and ordered me to get in line this instant.

"A strange kind of fear got the better of me. This was all new to me, because I usually don't move for anyone.

"'Why are you hesitating? You don't want to betray your own people by refusing, would you?' the policeman reproached me. Overwhelmed by this intimidation, I went to stand in line without saying a word. It'd gotten quite long.

"I saw that a little down the line, a man was casually talking to another man in the row of people. I thought it strange that this was allowed, because the man didn't look like he belonged to the chipping organization. Suddenly, the man was gone and the person he'd been talking to bolted off. A nearby officer responded immediately, spoke into his radio and started the pursuit. They ran along the sidewalk and then crossed the road. Sadly, the policeman didn't pay attention and was hit by a car. He was hit hard. Many people in the line went over to see if they could help him but to me this was the moment to escape. In the confusion, I could get to my car unhindered.

"I went home. I needed to think. My mind worked overtime to make plans and think about what the best course of action in this situation was. Through the window, I saw two cars turn into the street and stop in front of my door. I immediately knew they were after me. And indeed, they came straight to my front door. Quickly I left through the backdoor and fled, using back roads out of the city and into the forest.

"I didn't feel safe. Then I remembered the angel, and I thought, if this was a messenger from God, then I could pray. Which I did. To my dismay, I saw before my mind's eye all the sins I had committed in my life. But I also knew that I could ask forgiveness for them there and then. I saw Jesus' suffering on the cross in my place and I became peaceful.

"It had gotten dark and I kept walking throughout the night. In the end, I arrived at a crossroads where someone suddenly flicked on a torch and shone it in my face. I heard a woman's voice telling me to stay where I was. That woman was Zeri, I later found out. Blinded by the torch I stood there, frozen in place. At that time, I wondered if this was a detective. Had they found me?

"The woman started talking in a cold voice saying, 'You don't want to bow before the idol, right? And you also refused that slave chip in your hand, right?' Somehow, those words captured me, and I felt completely powerless before her. I couldn't lie to her and confessed my civil disobedience. I told her about the encounter and the conversation with the man at the chipping center and my attempt to flee. In hindsight, this was my passport into the Heaven Groups.

"And here I am. Later, they learned of my leadership qualities and put me in charge here. There are hundreds of Heaven Groups, all over the world, and we await Jesus' second coming. The Bible says this will be the next great step in God's plan to total world peace. Many people in this camp have had experiences with angels. They appear to operate all over the world.

"It's God's method in these times to reach people in this world of confusion. You probably remember the chaos right after millions of Christians all over the world mysteriously disappeared. Nobody knew what was going on. It was said aliens kidnapped them. UFO-sightings that had been reported for decades were said to be signs in preparation of this event. Others said it was a Biblical phenomenon. Christians who had been left behind for various reasons were found in a state of dismay and they pointed out Bible verses that seemed to predict the rapture. Other rumors suggested they were members of a sect who had collectively committed suicide.

"Anyhow, there was chaos and there was a large, spiritual void. People became less flexible, more agitated, and more easily offended. Social coherence seemed to have crashed after the disappearances. One World Faith quickly came up and gained in popularity. But it was totalitarian and intolerant. Although many people endorsed it, there were also many who resisted. And despite the persecution awaiting those who refused to bend the knee to the global religion, the number of insurgents grew massively. The angels' preaching of course had an influence on that.

"The test of faith for those who didn't want to accept became more and more horrid. At first, we were excluded from financial services. Everyone who kept refusing the new faith was incarcerated in large prison camps and later it became known beheadings took place there. Those who refused had to pay the ultimate price. It is whispered Molochi himself participated in the sentence rituals; he's really sadistic, that one."

"This is both amazing and bizarre," Akhan said.

"Very curious indeed," Tarpi confirmed.

"Can we ask some questions?" Akhan asked, looking alternatingly at Baris and Zeri.

"Sure, go ahead," Baris said. "There are no grey areas anymore such as there used to be. It's 'do or die', and . . ."

"I'm sorry, friends, but perhaps first a forest pizza?" Georgi interrupted.

"Well, that could be nice," Rita said.

"Forest pizzas, excellent," Baris agreed.

They welcomed the break, because they had a lot to process. "Take a rest; I'll call you when they're done," Georgi said and ran off to prepare the forest pizzas.

They went into their tents to take a rest, but mostly to think about the impressive flood of information they'd gotten that morning. Many questions had arisen. At first glance, these Heaven Groups people seemed trustworthy. But that was usually the case in the beginning. What was behind it all, and was it true what they said?

After a while, they heard Georgi shout "pizza!." They walked out of their tents and Baris and Zeri headed their way.

When they had assembled again, it was Georgi's turn to talk.

"My mother has taught me the recipe for forest pizza. She made the healthiest and most delicious ones in all of southern Italy," he explained.

The men saw the pizzas on a tray.

These forest pizzas consisted of leaves with a mixture of ingredients on top—mushrooms, nuts, blueberries, and chestnuts. Some sort of sauce seemed to have been drizzled over it.

"Voila, five pizzas each!" Georgi said roguishly.

Akhan and Tarpi looked doubtful, but Rita dug in right away.

"Delicious!" she cried and started on her second one. Akhan and Tarpi took a cautious bite and discovered it tasted excellent.

Tarpi asked Georgi what was actually in them.

"Beech leaves, dressed with weeping bolete, and, as you can see, blueberries and chestnuts, with a peppered nettle sauce on top. Very healthy."

They each also got handed a cup of water as Akhan asked Baris, "Do you know something about the Sickle Secret Service?".

"Yes, that's an organization which forced refugees in Europe to work for them. Gathering information and money for them, in the name of a so-called good cause. They did a lot of preparatory work and coordinating for what have now become the caliphates. Here," Baris said, as he pulled a newspaper out of his bag and handed it over to Akhan.

Akhan looked nonplussed, because the newspaper was printed in a language he couldn't understand. Rita, who could read Italian, took the newspaper from Akhan.

When Baris saw that she did, he asked Rita to translate the headline on the front page into English for Akhan and Tarpi.

"Iranian-Russian offensive halted by Israel," Rita cited aloud. Intrigued by the headline, she began to read the rest of the article.

"World Emperor Grandego condemns Israel for deploying a secret ultramodern and highly destructive weapons system against the Russian-Turkish-Iranian coalition. He demands a ban on the further use of it by Israel and is conducting talks to demand a peace treaty. Related to this, he had announced a global day of atonement, which will be crowned with his inauguration in Jerusalem. As part of the deal, the Jewish nation will be allowed to build a temple on the Temple Mount. An American-Jewish organization has already taken preparations decades ago and has gathered all the building materials, which would enable the Temple to be built quickly, following the Thora's directions.

"This amazing political achievement has personally been made possible by Grandego. The fact that the most important Islamic countries agree with this course shows the enormous political influence Grandego has on the international political playing field. The Arabs did put forth the condition that the Ben Gurion International Airport doesn't increase its capacity, so that there will be no mass tourism to Jerusalem. They don't want to see a place of pilgrimage in Israel that's comparable to Mecca.

"Furthermore, this demand has probably a military motive as well. The ever popular Grandego wants to place Israel under UN guardianship and he wants to have inspections carried out by the World Defense Force. Because China and the Arabic nations are fully behind this policy, Israel has no other choice but to go along with this unique peace process. Grandego wants to use the opening of the Temple to lift his position of World Emperor to a higher rank. Which title he will have is an unanswered question at the moment. Speculations abound, but it remains top secret. It will be made known at the opening of the Temple and humanity will recognize and acknowledge Grandego in his new title.

"High Priest Molochi has agreed with this development and will give his blessing. World Emperor Grandego, who is not only Secretary General of the UN but also World Master of the West, which he calls the neo-Roman Empire, has voiced the ambition to globally implement his successful policy.

"This plan is well-supported by the political elite, because they realize the deep-rooted global problems can be resolved only on a global level and with a central base of power. Partly because of this, Grandego has declared all forces who work against his policy to be sects and terror groups. Hundreds of World Defense Force task groups have been mobilized to track down these people and incarcerate them for questioning. The difference between compliant citizens and rebels is easily distinguishable, since the rebels refuse the personal identification chip in their hands and the acknowledgement of One World Faith as the only legitimate religion. A telephone hotline has been established to anonymously report these people. Call the international number 000656565 if you suspect anything.

"World Emperor Grandego's favorite motto, 'mankind destroys, but the Man restores', is showing on millions of billboards all over the world. A quote by Grandego brings hope to mankind: 'He who represents both East and West in his own blood, is the Man who will overcome.' The extremely charismatic Islamic Catholic with a whiff of Jewish blood is loved by large parts of the world's population, partly because of his successful actions. In the districts where he rules, the number of drug addicts and street thugs have been brought back by 70%. With huge financial infusions, he causes economic bloom. The banks seem to follow him like trained dogs, since they give out loans without asking interest.

"After Grandego's speech in Abraham's Colonnade in Mecca, six lightning bolts miraculously lit up the crowds, to their rejoicing.

"The High Priest Molochi . . . Blah, blah, blah, this goes on for three more pages!" Rita cried out, as she leafed through the rest of the newspaper.

"Very tiring language, indeed," Baris said.

"The Bible says we don't fight people, but principalities, powers and evil spirits in the heavenly places," Zeri explained gravely. "These are all lies by dark forces who are driving the masses. That's why we don't fight against people, but pray for them, so that they won't let themselves be taken in by the darkness, but that they may come into the true Light."

This impressive woman was engaging, and when she said something, there was no other choice but to take the time to let it get to you. It was information about spiritual dimensions. About the battle between angels and demons in the invisible world.

Baris steered the conversation back to the present situation.

"You have to make a decision. Tomorrow, you have to say if you want to become aspiring members of the Heaven Groups. Therefore, I will tell you who we are.

"The Heaven Groups have been established by evangelizing angels. They've taught us we're living in the time known as the 'Great Tribulation'. This will last for a few more years. Many of our members will be taken prisoner by the global dictator and beheaded, but we will be a special group with the Heavenly Father. We will become the countless souls before God's throne who are called 'rescued from the Great Tribulation'. The time of suffering is brief, but the joy with God lasts forever.

"The Heaven Groups are close communities. Our relationships are wholly based on trust. The Heaven Groups represent non-violence, we never attack other people, but we will defend ourselves. We refuse to bow to the idol and accept no strangle chip. The Heaven Groups don't fight people or groups with different ideals, religions, or politics. We try to physically and spiritually help people with problems, whomever they may be.

"The Heaven Groups are vulnerable, and they're persecuted by all armed parties and factions, especially the One World Faith. The World Defense Force is tasked to track us down and exterminate us. All means of the heaven groups are applied for communal purposes. We try to obtain foodstuffs and give help to the hungry where we can. And we prayerfully await the second coming of Jesus of Nazareth, as prophesied in the Bible.

"An aspiring member must stay with the group for three months, under observation. In this probationary period, both parties can see if there's complete dedication, or if it's not going to work out after all. Keep in mind that the members have almost all had a personal revelation from the Lord. All have sinned and need Jesus' forgiveness and mercy. That way, you can show that mercy to others as well. We experience the Holy Spirit in our midst, guiding us. We try to have love for each other," Baris explained.

It was strange to hear words of tender love from the mouth of a man who looked like a hardened street fighter. But the sincerity in his eyes was real.

"There, now you know the Heaven Groups' core values," he said finishing his speech.

The three were impressed by this explanation. It intrigued them— as if a force was pulling them to liberating freedom through revelations.

Somehow, it seemed as if an invisible conductor was leading them through all the events of the past few months. The true God was building a personal relationship with them in this way. Everything to do with Him touched the deepest part of them in a way that felt like coming home. A home where they'd never been before. Everything was seen in a new perspective. Even the trees seemed like wondrous creations in a surreal painting. The whistling bird sang about the Artist who had made him and loved him. The ant on the ground was an ingenious and tireless builder, reflecting the Designer's intelligence. The breeze that made the leaves rustle and caressed the face whispered sounds of a Father who rejoiced over his own child. The body had become a finely tuned vehicle of the soul on a journey of discovery. Everything that seemed ordinary and meaningless before, was now valuable and cherished. It seemed almost a shame to tread on another blade of grass.

There was a sense of forgiveness here, of true brotherhood.

On the horizon of humanity's history, dark clouds packed close for a joined attack.

* * *

To Rita, it seemed as if her eyes were opened for the first time.

But in this moment, she was overwhelmed by a warm feeling of compassion. Now she had learned the faith of her youth had content. Hadn't she prayed to Jesus as a little girl with a sincere faith? He had never left her, despite all the misery, and now she was born again. This far outweighed human love. An enormous flow of energy was the result.

They had until the next day to decide, but her choice had already been made. She would join.

Now they were off to find ingredients in the forest. "Yes," Rita cried joyfully, in part to herself, "I'm going to make forest pizzas!"

The men looked up and saw Rita the woman, a flower in their midst.

19

THE ORDER

BY HIS REQUEST, THE HONORED High Master Scott, President of the Order, was granted an audience with World Emperor Grandego in Mecca. Mecca was Grandego's favorite residence. He had built two identical luxurious white marble palaces. One in the Turkish city of Pergamum, near the mount that once housed the temple of Zeus. The other was forty miles from Mecca, near Hadda.

The spiritual and political elite of Saudi Arabia, King Sadi included, accepted Grandego, but he wasn't much loved. They found him too arrogant and power hungry. The spiritual order thought he compromised too much with infidels. One World Faith was nothing to them. They were manipulated in an incredible way, so they had no other option but to join, for the moment at least. They participated, but secretly hoped to gain complete global dominion themselves. Then, Mecca would be the absolute center. Like other powers, the Muslims wanted to become the sole rulers. They felt nothing for a smart politician like Grandego, who held a sanctimonious show for his own gain and to stroke his own ego, in order to become the only ruler, even though he claimed to be a Muslim. But Muslim *and* Catholic *and* Jewish blood? It took a lot to get used to, the postmodernism, the cooperation. Or was he the Mahdi they'd been awaiting for centuries, even though he looked different than they thought? Many Muslims believed that indeed he was the Mahdi, but many spiritual leaders were doubtful. But Grandego was popular with the masses and he enjoyed their hospitality, dedication, and service.

Grandego had multiple motives for residing near Mecca. Grandego really liked the barren desert. Besides, Mecca, the city which, like Rome, was built on seven hills, appealed to him because of the air of wealth and power. Mecca had an enormous influence on the Muslim world, which represented a large part of the global population. They were represented in all layers of civilization and on all continents. They held many positions of power in politics and industry. The Arabs had invested their superfluous oil dollars well. They could make or break stock markets, bankrupt industries or let them flower. Money flowed freely in their direction.

By choosing Mecca as the location for his palace, Grandego demonstrated his preference for this place above the Vatican in Rome, the UN in New York and the Temple Mount in Jerusalem. Although he was a Catholic as well as a Muslim, he didn't care much for the former. Too many crosses in and on the Catholics' buildings, a symbol that annoyed him greatly and made him think back about a traumatic experience in the distant past. For the moment, there was no way around the papacy, otherwise he would have immediately destroyed the Christian symbol wherever he could find it. The One World Faith, that he, together with Molochi, had erected for strategic reasons, was no longer to his liking.

His choice of settling near Mecca was in fact thumbing his nose at Jerusalem, the only central city of the God of Abraham, Isaac, and Jacob in this world, according to the Jews.

Two cities on seven hills and one surrounded by mountains. This was confusing, and confusion should always be fed, according to Grandego.

For centuries, scientists and theologians were searching for the city on the seven hills, called the 'Whore of Babylon' in the Book of Revelation. Which city was it? Confusion about this was important to Grandego.

This city was going to play a major role in the end times. Grandego knew the prophecies from the Bible, Torah, and Quran like no other. That city would be destroyed in a single hour. Of course, Grandego knew like no other it was a collection of false religions. Just to be certain, he lived in Hadda, and not in Rome, Mecca, or the historical city of Babylon in Iraq, and his palace had been equipped with a modern, very luxuriously furnished, subterranean nuclear bunker.

High Master Scott's private jet landed on the landing strip, several miles from the white marble palace. With much ceremony, he was welcomed, and a white limousine stood waiting for him with the engine running.

High Master Scott knew World Emperor Grandego like no other. Scott had personally helped him take control. Still, he knew almost nothing about Grandego's childhood. After a lightning career in the international banking sector, he had become rich beyond measure, and wealth screams for power, as it had with Grandego. That power seemed to fit him as easily as money had, and because he had joined the Order when still young, nothing had stood in his way. Then, the Order had recognized him as the big man, the Number One. Time seemed ripe and everything was in place to make a grab for the absolute world power.

"Wonderful to have you here," Grandego said.

"Good to see you again," Scott replied as he shook Grandego's hand.

The hall where the bellhop had brought him was decorated like a throne room. Intricate pillars with Corinthian capitals added to the stately feel. Large Persian tapestries and eighteenth century European furniture decorated the hall. A golden throne with lion heads on the ends of the armrests was in the center of the throne room, illuminated by candles in ivory candle stands.

They sat together in a homely furnished corner with chesterfields. A pot of English tea was waiting, and Grandego served them both.

"Belgian chocolates, enjoy," Grandego said with an inviting gesture to the bowl of delicacies. Then, he immediately got down to business.

"We're well on schedule," Grandego said with a self-satisfied smile.

High Master Scott wasn't easily taken aback, but he noticed he was pretty nervous now. He still hadn't gotten over the reprimand he had received at the latest Order meeting. His task to reign in Grandego, although he felt it had to be done, had been giving him a very disquieting feeling for a long time.

His wife had suggested that maybe it was time for him to step back, to hand over the presidency of the Order to someone else and enjoy his riches. This way, he could leave the risky talk with Grandego to his successor, but Scott was addicted to power games, and he enjoyed the tension that came with kneading the situation into what he wanted.

"You're not feeling well, are you?" Grandego noticed.

"Yes, I'm getting older," Scott answered nimbly.

"You don't feel as well in an old body," he said jokingly. Grandego smiled.

"I'm going to push forward, Scott. It's time. I'm fed up with this facade. The religious folk are the worst. Those pale Catholics with their silly incense, and those air callers from the minarets, the Buddhists with their fat god, and those floating Hindus . . . I've made it all up, but I'm through." Grandego got up and paced through the hall.

This didn't bode well for Scott, because if the Emperor was in this mood, he had to watch his words. And he had some unpleasant words for Grandego, indeed.

Scott didn't fully understand what he meant with his expressions. One World Faith had been convincing enough to reach their goals, hadn't it?

"Those Russians and Iranians have been beaten up, the Chinese and the Middle East follow me, so it's time I reveal myself as *the* central Man. I'm the Man, Scott. Me!"

Grandego had stopped right in front of Scott's chair and looked at him with flaming eyes, his finger pointed at himself.

"Yes," Scott said, "I know, buddy, but we're on the right track, what else do you desire? But can I ask you to sit down for a moment, please? The Order has asked me to give you a message."

Scott said it as calmly as he could, but that didn't help much.

"A message? The Order? What?" Grandego frowned.

"Listen, Gran," Scott continued as calmly as possible. "The Order has been working towards this for centuries. She has put you in this position. She sees you as the Number One, and you get incredible privileges and power. That's good for you, and for us. But keep in mind, Gran, that you must respect and execute the Order's decisions. They want you to have your position and power, but some are complaining. You've extorted money from members, so I'm giving you this correction. You're not above the Order, but below us. You serve the Order and the members."

There, it had been said. And for a moment, Scott was relieved. Grandego silently took a step back and now looked at Scott as if he'd been struck by lightning. Grandego's response made Scott shiver and he quickly felt sorry for starting this corrective talk in the first place. He saw a man before him whose face had changed completely and who looked at him in a humiliating way. His eyes became evil. Mockingly, Grandego repeated Scott's words.

"What did you say? I'm below you? *Below?* You dare use that word for *me*? As if you're talking to a laborer in a factory? Below . . . " A harsh laugh erupted from him. "If anyone is a subject, it's you, Scotty-boy."

Grandego's laughter increased.

"Oh, now you've entered my pleasure center, Scotty-boy!" Grandego hissed. "You know, Scotty, I've been thinking to replace you for a while."

Grandego's voice took a more and more satanic tone. Scott felt a shiver go down his spine when he realized Grandego wasn't who he'd always thought he was. That he and the Order were evil, he could accept. But this man seemed the devil himself, so much hatred . . . This was a man, who, once he'd obtained power, didn't care about anyone else anymore . . .

But . . . that this was the monster he had created himself, flashed through Scott's mind. The logical capstone of the pyramid they had been building for so long, Scott realized with a shiver.

Hissing, Grandego paced through the hall, spewing hatred and bitterness.

"Man, what a sickening little creature. Powerless worms, so easily tempted with a little sex, money or so-called power," Grandego growled. "I'll squish them, especially those stupid enough to sell their souls to me, because they wanted to obtain a nice, eternal position for themselves! The sea of fire is their reward! How I enjoy their surprised mugs when they discover their crucial mistake after their death, when they get dealt the true consequences of their rewards! The master they served personally showering them with worms who eat them to the bone. I enjoy their squirming squeals of pain!"

The air was filled with a terrible sewer smell. The nauseating smell got to Scott and he cowered in his seat.

This voice . . . He recognized it from the satanic rites he had performed with the inner circle of Order Members. The same inhuman sound, just as penetrating. A searing noise even the most hardened Satanist couldn't get used to. The sound that brought a fear something terrible could turn against you at any moment.

Grandego came at Scott with a scream. He grabbed him by the throat. White with fear, Scott tried to wrestle himself free from Grandego, but he was no match whatsoever for Grandego's enormous physical strength. Scott's eyes bulged; his throat was in a vice-like grip.

"*I*, your Satan, that you served so faithfully, have put you in your position!" Grandego hissed, as he looked at Scott with penetrating eyes full of hatred. "Not you, idiot. Before Pharaoh, *I* was. Before Caesar, Napoleon, Hitler, Stalin, and Mao, *I* was. The great city of Babylon was and is mine! *I* make the plans for this world. It's *me* who divides people into groups, plays them against each other and lets them wage their filthy wars. *I* rule this petty, silly planet I've been cast on. *Me*! *I* have used your petty life and the Order to do my dirty work, with money. And I push that money to whom *I* want. First East, then West, and now East again." Vile laughter sprayed spittle into Scott's face. "I have made the plans, the Order, One World Faith, the political parties, imperialism, the dollar power of the super-rich, the double standard of the humanists, jihad, Israel's revenge. All that violence for my goals is *my* doing. Soon, I will reveal myself in my full splendor to the world, and they must follow, serve, and worship!"

Scott gasped for breath and heard his vertebrae crack. His brow was covered in sweat and he was losing consciousness.

"And now, *I* will send Scotty to hell, where he belongs," Grandego screamed into Scott's ear. "*I* will now destroy the One World Faith, *I* will exterminate those super-rich worms, *I* will raze all religions to the ground, as easily as I erected them. The people will worship *me*! But you, you won't see it anymore."

Scott used his last bit of energy to look into the bloodshot eyes of a madman, eyes full of hate. There was no shred of compassion in them, which evaporated Scott's last bit of hope for escape. Those eyes, penetrating as though millions of dead people screamed like zombies from the realm of the dead for liberation of searing pains.

Scott heard and felt nothing anymore. Only his thoughts were with him.

What had he done? What kind of idiotic, self-centered killer had he been? To what stupid chasing of foolish delusions had he given over his life? The darkness seemed to soak up his thoughts. His inner voice sounded softer and softer, and seemed to echo away, flowing away into an all-encompassing nothingness.

Far, far above him, he distinguished a sort of light, as though a scuba diver looking at the sun on the water from great depth.

But the glint faded. He wasn't going there; he was sinking further away from it . . .

Scott slid away to the sounds of the zombies he'd seen in Grandego's ice-cold eyes, towards the destination he had chosen with his self-centered ambitions, without realizing the emptiness of it. He heard the echoes of screaming demons. His bizarre welcoming committee . . .

* * *

Several minutes after Scott's death, Grandego's voice rang through the phone.

"No, the man has had a heart attack or something. Take him out of here. You know how to handle it, everything neat and clean. And call Tarik and tell him he has to contact me. He will be Scott's honorable successor and I'll allow him to make a huge career step. He'll be glad for it, because he will become the new High Master of the Order." Grandego finished the conversation.

20

AKHAN AND TARPI

"MY DECISION HAS BEEN MADE, I'm staying here," Rita said happily.

They had eaten forest pizzas that morning from "Rita's Pizza Place," which tasted excellent. She'd added crushed hazelnut and walnut pieces to Georgi's ingredients. The pizzas soon bore the name "PizzaRitas."

"You've decided rather quickly," Tarpi said, still not sure about his decision. Rita seemed to have taken a spiritual fast track.

Akhan and Tarpi were pleasantly surprised by their discovery of this camp and the inhabitants' motivations. The stories about the outside world disturbed them, of course, but they couldn't accept that information without doubt. They read the newspaper articles, but who could say how trustworthy they were?

Baris and Zeri looked at the men.

"What are your plans?" they asked inquiringly.

Tarpi didn't want to say goodbye to Rita and hinted at preferring to stay, but Akhan had different plans.

"I truly appreciate your work and your hospitality," he said, "but I need time to find out what's going on. I'll be leaving tomorrow, if that's allowed, to check things out for myself."

"Then I'll come as well," Tarpi said suddenly. It didn't come easy to him saying farewell to Rita, but abandoning his friend in these dangerous times . . . that he couldn't do.

"The two of us will be all right," Tarpi said.

Rita looked wistfully at the men with her beautiful brown eyes.

"I'll miss you, but I'm sure we'll see each other again someday. I will pray for you," she promised.

"That's settled then," Baris said.

"Stay away from the grey poles," Zeri advised gravely.

They heard a soft *beep* and Baris looked at his watch.

"Into your tents, quickly!" he cried as he ran away.

Something in his voice made Rita, Akhan, and Tarpi obey immediately. Zeri stood near a tree. Several campers ran toward Baris. They carried a sturdy tripod, which they deployed on a small open area between the trees. They mounted a pretty large, green painted device on the tripod. Baris operated some switches and buttons on the device, and the men dove for cover under the trees. Baris took a remote control out of his pocket and peeked upward.

They had barely completed this when a dozen black drones with swirling cameras zoomed across the area.

Baris didn't hesitate for a second and pushed the button of his remote. Promptly, a high, piercing tone filled the air. The green box on the tripod sent forth hundreds of flashing light pulses. Immediately, heavy explosions followed. In an impressive fireworks display, thousands of burning pieces of shot-up drones fell gracefully down, tracing smoke. As soon as they touched down, several campers moved in to put out the smoldering remains. But as they did, some of them were hit by the burning wreckage. Immediately, a trained group of first aiders lent the appropriate care. Two of the victims didn't get up. The first responders began to bury their bodies where they lay. Bizarre, but it seemed there was no other option under these conditions.

The men surrounding Baris had risen after the first explosion and started packing the absolute necessities.

The weapon was taken apart and packed in a crate for transport.

Baris ran to Akhan and his friends. As he was running, he loudly blew a whistle twice.

"Here," Baris shouted at the three newcomers as he tossed them green backpacks.

"Pack your stuff and then follow the rest."

Everyone burst into motion and the camp was broken up in no time.

Around them, many people were running into the direction Baris had indicated, carrying large green backpacks.

"Hurry, because there's a chance it'll be raining bombs in a little while. The World Defense Force has definitely discovered our counter-fire."

Quickly, they packed and ran with the crowd. About a third of a mile away, just as they were running out of breath, they saw the rest of the group, tightly crowded together. Akhan looked at them curiously.

"Come, come," several men shouted, beckoning them over.

Akhan hesitated for a moment, but then he thought the group would know better what to do in a situation like this and he joined them.

There they stood, as still as possible. A strange experience when considering the size of the group.

Fifteen minutes passed, but it seemed like an hour. Then, there were loud bangs. The ground shook and some people held their breath. In the distance, several trees creaked and fell. Plumes of smoke and jumping tongues of flame provided an impressive show. The changes in air pressure made their hair wave and people grasped each other more tightly.

"Don't be afraid," a brother shouted at Rita, who was clearly very afraid. "Holding each other tightly is the best way to limit damages. Close together in one place, under the Father's umbrella. They never expect it. They bomb a few areas around the place where they've located us and hope to take down many of our number."

Rita looked at the man in shock.

"If a bomb falls here, we're all dead," she responded doubtfully.

"In that case," the man said, pointing his finger towards the sky, "we'll have a reunion up there, with the Lord."

The sky had grown darker and it started to rain. Several people took out dark plastic ponchos.

"Much can be achieved with few," Akhan said soberly. "Say what you want about the campers, but they're not stupid."

Meanwhile, Georgi had made his way over to them.

"You guys all right?" he asked smiling.

"Sure," Akhan said. "What kind of weapon was that you used earlier?"

"That's the Lasertick," Georgi answered proudly. "Those things are very expensive but work perfectly. No drone escapes, take it from me. We were able to buy one from an emir in Naples. He had acquired several when raiding a large weapon's depot of the World Defense Force. They just sat there, brand new in their boxes, straight from Israel."

Georgi laughed in his hand to mute the sound.

"Those guys will do anything for money. It cost us nearly eighteen pounds of gold, but it's highly effective. You won't find many people among us wearing golden rings or necklaces. Gold is the new money. But the Lord provides—a week ago, a brother found a dead Bouvier somewhere in the forest. It wore a golden necklace of at least two pounds. The dog probably belonged to a World Master; they've got money to spare. Either way, we always see doors opened to us and we're provided for."

A woman in the group started crying when she realized one of the victims of the falling pieces of drones had been a loved one of hers. Their protocol was to bury the dead immediately and without ceremony in an emergency so the body was already gone. Sadness came over the group. They occasionally lost people, and although they knew they would see them again in Heaven, there was grief. Someone started humming a tune. Others took it up, until the entire group sang a hymn.

As the words rang out around them, Akhan and Tarpi sensed something they had never experienced before, the Holy Spirit came over them. They experienced a moment in which they felt one hundred percent safe.

"You are my hiding-place . . . You always fill my heart . . . With songs of deliverance . . . Whenever we are afraid, we will trust in You . . . "

A soothing feeling washed over them that sparkled with reviving power. It was as though God Himself had come down in their midst to embrace and comfort His children.

After about two hours, Baris gave the sign for the group to move on. The people were glad for it, but the heavy journey would last at least a few days and wouldn't be without danger.

* * *

Despite the attack, Akhan kept to his decision to leave the group. The next day, he and Tarpi readied to leave the group and its leaders with many thanks.

"Watch out for the grey poles," Baris warned once more. "They detect people and notice if they're chipped. If not, they automatically fire an invisible marker ink. A satellite can detect the ink on your clothing and will alert the authorities to your location."

Rita warmly embraced the men and Tarpi found it very hard to let her go.

What a magnificent woman, he thought, and he failed to fight back his tears.

21

GRANDEGO

"THE GREAT DAY," MOLOCHI SAID cynically to the extravagantly dressed Grandego.

"Yes, the great day is here," Grandego said. "Finally, Molochi, many centuries we've been working to this moment. And now it's finally time I will be revealed to humanity. I can remember the valley of Babylon. My image, tall as a house, the music sounding, the oven was fired up to the highest possible temperature and they bowed before me, deeply impressed. All eyes were fixed upon me, remember? Each of my graceful movements, each gesture was enchanting and powerful. Fifty thousand young women on the right flank, desolate and swooning before their master. Those were the great days, and they're about to return. Without intermediate religions, animism, sects or places, and idols of worship. Just a plain worship of the god of this world. Everywhere, my image will be at the center!"

As though in a trance, Grandego paced the throne room of his white palace with his hands in the air. A hyper modern, noiseless helicopter had been designed especially for this occasion and was at the ready to fly him to Jerusalem. The *Chameleon*, as this milestone of technology was called, was fully transparent, save for the chromium coated engine parts. The integrated LED lights took on the colors of its environment, making it almost invisible.

This effect heightened the contrast with the gold-clad man. The masses would see him descend from heaven as if he was walking on thin air.

Molochi plucked some specks of dust from Grandego's robes.

"You shine like never before, Lightbearer," he piously said.

Grandego smiled and walked over to a solid meranti table. The long table had one straight edge, about three feet wide. On that side was an ornate chair, decorated with wood carvings in the shape of a crown that adorned the center of the backrest. The long sides of the table curved towards a tip over a length of thirty feet. Thirteen ornate chairs were set up on both sides, but these didn't have a crown.

"Look at what's happening," Grandego said to Molochi. Five round stones in different colors were on the table.

"It's like a group of twenty-two people. You give a blue shirt to eleven of them and a red shirt to the others. Then you say: 'Red, the blues are your opponents.' And to those in blue: 'The red are your opponents. I am the arbiter and I make the rules. Whoever wins gets a wreath.' You give them a ball or a machine gun, it doesn't matter which, because they will fight each other to the death. We are the spectators and enjoy their downfall. Our plan always prevails, because they fight each other instead of their true enemy. Their ignorance is our power."

The stones started moving together of their own accord. When they touched, they merged into each other and formed a three-foot-high statuette in the likeness of Grandego.

"A pretty holographic animation of our plan. You are the spitting image of their own egocentric souls," Molochi said. "The people get the king they want: the man in the center, and we, well, we deftly make use of it."

They were laughing as they left the throne room.

"Have you gone over the positions and instructions for this day with Bel and Beelzebub? It's surgical precision now. I will not tolerate a single mistake," Grandego hissed fanatically as they walked through the marble hallway towards the *Chameleon*.

"Yes. They have reproached the demons more than usual," Molochi answered.

"It won't be the first time the enemy has humiliated me on one of my days of glory," Grandego said. "I want dozens of millions of demons at minimum around the city, to foil possible angelic interventions. And enough spirits to keep the mood of the public at an optimum. Let the two demons posing as aliens from Andromeda look as impressive as possible. They must appear beside me and tell everyone to listen to me. And it's important there are crippling spirits in the Temple, at the moment I reveal myself. There will certainly be people who want to rebel against me or my words. They need to be crippled, so that they keep watching intrigued and remain passive. Keep disillusionment and revelations from the light at bay with all your power!"

"I know, your majesty, I know. We've gone over this scenario hundreds of times," Molochi soothed. He didn't want his boss in a bad mood, so he did his very best to keep his emotions positive, but Grandego continued.

"Yes, I remember my good friend Antiochus Epiphanes, may he rot in hell, who sacrificed a pig in the Jewish Temple, two thousand and two hundred years ago. After that, we were dealt a huge blow from the Maccabees. Not to mention the trouble with Elijah who destroyed my priests of Baal . . . "

Grandego visibly shivered at the most terrible memory of them all, the supposed death of the Crucified Who rose from the dead. The deception!

Molochi quickly interrupted before Grandego had a complete breakdown.

"Yes, yes, we all have traumatic experiences, Grandego. Let it go. Your future is great! We have also gained many victories, remember?"

"I can't forget it, Molochi. The pain stays, the hatred, the gnawing of teeth when I think back on the Nazarene Who humiliated me before my subjects in hades . . . " Grandego now growled with an unnatural deep voice.

"In the distance, I see smoke rising from a lake of fire, Molochi," Grandego mumbled, back in contemplation.

"Look at your great power on earth!" Molochi encouraged Grandego, helping him to steer clear of a fit of rage. Molochi knew these moods all too well. In a sullen mood Grandego was no pleasurable companion—angry, sad, violent or blaming himself in hours of talking to himself, cursing, and shaking his fist at the Most High in heaven.

"Today is the day, Grandego," Molochi soothed. "The victory is at hand. You are the ultimate victor. The future is ours and that's what it's all about, our victory!"

These words calmed down Grandego, bringing him back into his beloved mood of delusions of grandeur.

"Yes, eventually, the future is ours . . . "

He loved living in his dream, but excruciating aches in his soul and doubts occasionally took away the fun of his made-up ideals.

"You are right, Molochi. I will descend from heaven. I am the Envoy, the Number One . . . " he said aloud to himself. As he proclaimed this, his expectations for the coming inauguration rose. Grandego saw the open worship of the masses before his mind's eye. This vision filled him and made his pains disappear into the background. With renewed strength, he boarded the *Chameleon*. His day was today, and there was nothing that could take it away from him.

22

AKHAN AND TARPI

"OW," TARPI YELLED. HE LOOKED at the sole of his foot and noticed a shard of glass.

"Hurry, Tarpi!" Akhan called. They ran over the harbor's industrial park. When Akhan looked over his shoulder he saw Tarpi holding still and plucking at his heel. Quickly, he ran back and loaded Tarpi across his shoulders with a single deft move.

"Taxi," Tarpi said playfully.

"Yes, go ahead, joke about it," Akhan said. As fast as he could, he ran to a place where hundreds of shipping containers stood waiting.

It should be safe between the containers, but just as they were standing in their shadows, Akhan saw several black drones coming in the distance. Feverishly, he looked around, his thoughts lightning fast.

"Come, into the containers. We'll be completely surrounded by steel and they can't detect us," he said loudly.

They walked between the containers that were stacked three stories high and tried to open several. Eventually, they found one that opened. They went inside and closed the door.

* * *

After Akhan and Tarpi had left the Heaven Groups behind, they had wandered through several areas for a couple of months. They discovered each of these areas were home to a different faction, all fighting each other.

A few times they witnessed a World Defense Forces air force bombing raid. Grey pillars stood in unexpected places, immediately firing an invisible substance at them.

This meant running and taking off and burying the soiled top clothes. Several times, they would "borrow" clothes from laundry lines at night, but it was crazy traveling this way. In practice, they had to check every few steps if there wasn't a grey pole waiting for them, or a booby trap, or a roadside bomb, or an airborne drone, or anything.

Akhan and Tarpi took time to rest up in the container.

It appeared they had outwitted the drones, because there were no further signs of their presence to be detected.

The distinguishing zooming sound was usually clearly heard by someone with sharp ears. Akhan had those. By keeping the door ajar, there was enough light to discover the container was filled with boxes, attached to the walls with belts.

They were lucky. They opened a few boxes and had cookies, chocolate and licorice aplenty!

"Made in Holland," Tarpi read. They emptied a few boxes and used the cardboard for a mattress. The cookies tasted delicious, after eating only forest pizzas for weeks. The pizzas were nurturing, but after a while, they lost their taste. The men laid down to rest and eventually, they were tired enough to sleep like a rock.

* * *

"Whoooohh!" Tarpi shouted suddenly, and his hands caught the container's door. Akhan was immediately wide awake and grabbed on to Tarpi's legs. The door swung open and Tarpi's upper body swerved dangerously far outside the container. He saw he was at least sixty feet up in the air! Fortunately, the other door was locked, so that Akhan, holding Tarpi's legs, could use it for support.

The container soared like a carnival ride, but after a little while, it hung still and started going down. This allowed Tarpi to swing back inside and regain control of the door. Now, he could look through the gap in the door and see what was happening.

"We're being loaded onto a ship," he said sadly. Akhan looked at him wide-eyed.

"I hope it's not heading back to Northern Africa," Akhan said sarcastically. He could remain sober under all circumstances. At first, Tarpi looked at his friend in fear, but then he started to laugh.

"Who knows, we might be going to South America, that's where everyone goes who's running from something," Tarpi said.

"Can we get out?" Akhan asked.

Tarpi looked at his surroundings through the gap in the door.

"Even if you get off this ship, there's a dock full of workers. We probably can not get past them unseen. Perhaps tonight, when it's dark."

"Unbelievable," Akhan said. He sat back down and made himself comfortable. "We have food for months, but only enough water in our canteen for two, maybe three days. There's nothing to do but to wait for an opportunity to escape."

In fact, the two days and nights they spent on the ship as stowaways were luxury compared to the months before. They could catch up on sleep and there was plenty of time to look after Tarpi's foot.

He'd had to bury his shoes after they had been hit from behind by a marker shot from a grey pole they had missed.

For the first time in their lives, they ate licorice. Good stuff, they decided.

In the container, they also found toast and boxes of dried fruit.

Two days later, the container ship moored in a dock and they took another trip through the air. By opening one of the doors a bit, they could see what was going on. A crane unloaded their container onto a truck.

The truck appeared to be part of a convoy with a single destination, because they kept driving one after the other.

"We're in Israel," Tarpi called out. "We just passed a sign saying 'Haifa'."

"Israel?" Akhan repeated. "What are we doing here?"

"Yes, this is bad news," Tarpi said after he had closed the door and reclined on his cardboard sofa once more.

"Israel—" Akhan said again.

"You know," Tarpi interrupted, "I'm beginning to wonder who's guiding our destiny. But I'm afraid we can never have a normal, quiet life again. Where in the world can you get that?"

This humbling emotion stuck. All previous events ran through their minds. It wasn't easy for the men to accept the fact that, apparently, they had no control over their destiny whatsoever.

It was Akhan who eventually broke the silence. "Then all we have left is to seek out the truth and prepare ourselves for eternity in the right way. All earthly plans for the future, ambitions and goals, all human securities have vanished like the morning dew."

The truck started reducing speed. Tarpi immediately took up his position near the door again to glance at the outside world.

"We are going through a gate and then onto an enclosed area. There are as lot of coaches here . . . it looks like a central coach station," he reported.

As they slowly made their way forward and the truck was doing all sorts of parking maneuvers, Tarpi saw the area was fenced off on one side and enclosed with a rising cliff on the other. The cliff was quite steep and had erratic forms. Male voices shouted instructions to each other.

The trucks parked and the drivers gathered near the exit of the area and talked between themselves while enjoying a cup of coffee, which was doled out by women in uniforms. Outside the fences, soldiers in black uniforms stood around the perimeter.

"Lucky us," Tarpi said. "We're trapped."

He explained the situation to Akhan.

"They've even put those annoying grey poles near the fences and the entrance. We better not try anything tonight."

Akhan was quiet for a moment.

"Could we climb those rocks?" he asked.

Tarpi studied the cliff face.

"Perhaps, but not without risk. The cliff *is* steep, but also rough with plenty of ledges and cracks. We won't make it in the dark. It would be best to attempt it early in the evening or morning."

When Akhan studied the cliff again, he saw three deep holes. They made the wrinkly cliff face look like a grinning skull.

"Let's go tonight then, just before dark," Akhan decided.

* * *

Early in the evening, the men climbed out of the container and snuck between the containers towards the cliff face.

"If you fall from there, you won't make it," Tarpi said, as he looked up.

"Let's hope the fall kills you then, because I don't like the prospect of falling into the hands of those soldiers," Akhan answered sarcastically, nodding his head towards the soldiers at the entrance.

The approaching dusk changed the color of the cliff a little bit—a good thing, because that would mean they wouldn't easily be spotted from a distance. For Tarpi, it was a perilous climb, because he had to do it without shoes. Well, he had folded some layers of cardboard around his feet. The wound under his foot had healed up rather well and the cardboard would offer some protection from the sharp edges.

The containers were stacked almost up to the cliff.

Because of this, there was an ideal, two-foot-wide gap between the cliff and the adjoining containers.

The first twenty feet were easy, they just braced themselves between the cliff and the containers.

Then the real climbing began.

Because of the unevenness of the cliff, this was also doable.

Cracks and gaps, protruding rocks and holes allowed them to make good progress. After several minutes, Tarpi looked down. Psychologically speaking, that was a bad decision, because now he realized just how lethal a fall from this height would be. In his imagination, he saw himself crashing onto the containers beneath him and then tumbling into the gap between the rock and the container, onto the concrete floor.

He saw soldiers talking at the entrance to the compound.

Akhan and Tarpi would provide great targets the way they were clinging to the cliff face. He prayed they wouldn't be discovered.

A shiver ran down his back. Using his arms, he pulled himself up a bit further and put his foot on a protruding rock. He saw Akhan above him and to the left. He was having trouble finding a place to grab for his next step.

Tarpi was luckier on that account. There were many possible ways, but those only led further to the left, positioning him partly above Akhan.

The cliff wasn't fully vertical, so they could lean into the rock formation. This was fortunate, because then they could rest after every few steps.

Tarpi saw a good gap above and to the right. It'd give him a good opportunity to lift himself up. When Tarpi put his hand into the gap, a large, brown spider jumped out.

"Ayeee!" Tarpi yelled with fear. The jump had put the spider partly on his hand. Tarpi's reaction caused his left foot to slip from its support.

Akhan jolted as well, but he quickly pressed his right hand against Tarpi's back to press his body against the cliff.

"Hold still, do nothing!" Akhan said.

With Akhan's hand in his back, Tarpi could only just stabilize himself and put his foot back. Tarpi wasn't afraid of spiders, but this one was big, and he didn't know the species. Half-paralyzed, he held his position. As spiders are used to doing, this one also held still in the same place where its jump had brought it.

"Now what?" Tarpi asked.

"Let's wait, perhaps it'll leave. Keep your hand still, or shake that creep off with a quick motion," Akhan suggested.

The tickling of hairy legs on his hand made Tarpi shiver.

"Try shaking him off," Akhan urged.

"I can't, I'm mostly supporting myself with this hand," Tarpi said.

As he was talking, a shadow slid over them. A grey-brown bird swooped down and picked up the spider in the blink of an eye.

"Praise God for birds!" Tarpi exclaimed, pleasantly surprised. He saw the bird flying off with the spider still sticking partly out of its beak.

"It's always something with you, isn't it?" Akhan said as he cast Tarpi a roguish smile.

"Yeah, sure, joke about it. Let's continue." Tarpi smiled.

He turned his gaze upward and realized he would have to put his hand into a number of dark holes.

"God bless my grip." He grinned.

When they had finally reached the top, they hoisted themselves upon the flat rock. They saw small bushes here and there, and lizards darted away.

"Let's tie a few of those bushes to our back to camouflage ourselves," Akhan said.

When they had finished, it had gotten dark. The sky was clear. Crickets provided background music to a magnificent starry spectacle, and the shining moon created a ghostly palette of shadowy colors. The pleasant temperature made it easy for the men to fall asleep.

* * *

Before daybreak, their sleep was cut short by the penetrating noises of engines, coming from the storage yard. When they crawled to the edge of the cliff, they could see the contents of the containers being loaded unto smaller vehicles. Those left the compound in convoys. It was when they tracked the cars with their eyes, that the skyline of Jerusalem came into view with its steeples, the golden dome and the ancient city walls.

"Jerusalem! We're in Jerusalem!" Tarpi exclaimed in amazement.

They had no idea what they had to do now. There was so much movement on the streets below them, which were adorned with ribbons and palm branches, that they concluded something big was about to happen. Military vehicles and troops held all kinds of strategic positions.

"I think we've got front-row seats to the route of some festival parade," Akhan said.

"Well," Tarpi replied, "in that case, let's enjoy ourselves today. It's not like we've got an appointment."

Below them they could clearly make out a coach terminal, temporarily set up as a storage yard to harbor the containers with festival attributes.

"Licorice?" Akhan asked Tarpi. "Licorice made in Holland. Pretty good, that stuff. I also stuffed my pockets with cookies, friend."

Tarpi laughed. "You brought some supplies, smart move."

"Shush, don't talk too loudly. We will need to gather some more bushes around us. I wouldn't be surprised if they deployed drones."

Akhan took out the food he'd smuggled.

"A feast on the rocks. Let's enjoy a beautiful, relaxed day and see what's going to drive by," Akhan said.

As morning turned to noon, the three-lane asphalt road in front of the bus terminal got more crowded.

People gathered behind barriers, until they were several rows deep and pushing to see the parade pass by. Dark blue BMW convertibles drove past with representatives from different countries. National flags waved from the front bumpers. But at the front was the white One World Empire flag, with the moon and the sun on it. The people alongside the road waved at the dignitaries, who enjoyed the attention as they drove past at a slow pace. Riders on horses, adorned with insignias and decorated uniforms of the World Defense Force, rode between the cars.

Orchestras, marching bands and dance groups added luster to the beautiful parade. Floats with special, genetically enhanced animals drove past. One float hauled a cage with a gigantic saber-toothed hyena. Others displayed winged reptiles, and in an enormous terrarium, a large viper with four scaly legs was driven around. It looked around threateningly with its fiery eyes.

There was also a vehicle with a young woman, lavishly dressed and adorned with gold and gems. The religious symbols of all major world religions were at her feet. She herself was seated on a red many-headed dragon. Twelve stars shone above her head. The dragon had a large horn on each head and fire spewed from each mouth.

Birds in all colors of the rainbow flew left and right alongside the parade. These were probably carefully decorated drones. Companies gladly used the parade to show all types of robots to the audience.

After the parade had passed, the spectators fell in behind and went along to the central manifestation.

"It's got to be a very important event," Tarpi said.

"I'm curious at what's to come," Akhan replied. They moved around a bit to flex their muscles.

A vague buzzing sound grew louder, and when they lay back with their faces towards the city, the men saw several blue helicopters approaching in a wide circular formation. A very bright, golden yellow light was at the center of the circle. When the formation came closer and held still over the city, Akhan and Tarpi saw it was two shining people, standing on thin air!

The flying persons raised their arms and slowly moved them back down, as in a gesture of blessing.

When they did, it seemed as if millions of lights in all colors of the rainbow flowed from their hands. All those lights together took the form of a stairway.

The two shining people seemed to walk down that stairway, towards the golden dome and the beautiful Temple building, illuminated with spotlights. A loud cheer rose from the city.

23

GRANDEGO

"RISE!" A WORLD DEFENSE FORCE general called out to the large crowd. In awe, they saw Grandego and Molochi walk down the wondrous light-stairs from apparent nothingness in the sky and eventually set foot on the Temple Square. There, they were greeted with cheers. Dignified, the two men walked toward the colorful entrance to the Temple's Court.

There, the kings, presidents, super rich captains of industry, and everyone who was anyone in the present global politics were seated on thrones. As the hundreds of public figures stood up when Grandego and Molochi entered the Court, a symphony orchestra started playing a piece by Wagner. A hubbub of admiration went through the audience at the sight of Grandego's grandeur, not in the least place because of his lush robes with golden lines and intricately woven crown motifs. His whole appearance radiated power, wealth, and greatness.

He had almost become the sole ruler of the planet. He had turned the economy around. Drug addicts, the homeless, psychiatric patients, and other "useless folk" had been removed from the streets, greatly reducing petty crimes. He had taken care of the judicial powers with their mild punishments and had globally introduced summary judgment and death sentence by beheading. Paper money had been replaced by an entirely digital banking system, which had eliminated money laundering. The personal chip had been implemented, so that no-one could step out of line without being noticed. And what's more, he had brought peace to the Middle East, something that no other political figure in the past had ever managed to accomplish.

While the spirit of personality worship touched the masses, Grandego, enjoying the admiration in this grand moment, strode past the impressive altar with the protruding horns on the corners. Molochi followed at a suitable distance.

Then, he passed the laver, which was also called the "Sea," and next he went towards the colorful, mosaic inlaid gate that gave access to the holy. Here and there, cameras of the global press were broadcasting the event live across the whole world. The colorful gate took him inside the Temple's Holy Place. Inside, the most dedicated Order members were seated on thrones on the left side. There was World Master Hugh, whose job it was to reduce the power of national governments and help despots to power. Master Kent, known for his population reduction programs, and in the middle sat High Master Tarik, tasked with influencing the Muslim world towards the Order's interests, as well as the new president of the most powerful Order in the world.

On the righthand side were rabbis, great imams, the Grand Mufti of Egypt, and cardinals, including Cardinal Jones and Bishop Dant.

World Emperor Grandego said nothing, letting the sounds of the music do its work. He strode past the table of Showbread, across from the well-known Menorah Lampstand.

For a moment, he held still to gaze upon this gold-smithing marvel. They had recovered the Lampstand in Rome's catacombs which were owned by the Vatican. With the destruction of Jerusalem in 70 AD, Roman general Titus had taken the Menorah as spoils to Rome. After that, it had disappeared from history, but there had always been suspicions it had been confiscated by Catholic clergy and kept hidden for centuries.

Grandego grinned when he thought back to the moment the Pope refused to give him the Lampstand. He had immediately relieved him from his duties and with a casual show of power left the Catholics "popeless." He hadn't allowed a new pope to be chosen, but instead placed the entire Roman-Catholic church under the One World Faith and the direct authority of World High Priest Molochi. Because they wanted a pope, that title befell Molochi, although it was meaningless to him. Grandego then issued an investigation of the catacombs, and lo and behold, there they found the Lampstand. Thus, he had gained possession of the illustrious artifact and he had used it to entice the Jews to go along with his plans.

Molochi walked to the middle throne, placed between the rabbis and great imams, and sat down full of dignity.

Then, World Emperor Grandego took place on a raised throne before the Veil, which was the entrance to the innermost part of the Temple, the Holy of Holies. Cherubs were artistically displayed on the Veil.

Next to the golden throne stood the incense altar, from which rose the wonderful smell of frankincense, making one's presence in the exclusive part of the Temple an extraordinary experience. The created ambience was without compare and fitting for such a special event of global importance.

The World Defense Force was represented by an admiral and a general, standing at attention in full dress uniform besides Grandego's throne.

After the World Emperor had sat down on his throne, the general spoke a word of welcome.

"World Emperor Grandego is in our midst! Welcome, let's give him a hand!" All those present in the Holy and the Temple Courts stood and applauded for a long time.

When the applause died down, Grandego started his speech.

"Dearly beloved, kings, businessmen, clergy and invitees. Such a privilege it must be for you to attend here. Welcome, be seated!" He waited for a moment until everyone had sat back down.

"Through my actions, the world underwent a wave of renewing. Those were good advances, which will have a positive effect, but we're not there yet. But today is *the* great day, long awaited. From today, social, civil, and spiritual transformations will begin, which will lead to completeness. Therefore, something grand is going to happen today. Something that will be needed for a world dedicated to me. Today, it will be made possible to take the next evolutionary step. A step that will lead to spectacular possibilities for mankind, that up until now have been seen only in science fiction movies!"

Grandego got to his feet. Others wanted to follow suit out of respect, but the World Emperor motioned them to remain seated. He took a few steps forward. His tone now became pompous.

"The now living generations have the privilege to witness the revolution that has been suggested in the world literature for centuries. The evolutionary revolution that will take place in the coming years, will be led by me, and I will be assisted by specialized alien forces from the Andromeda galaxy. They who have at one time started to colonize our planet, will reveal themselves today!"

The audience couldn't keep quiet after these announcements, and a hubbub filled the rooms and Courts of the Temple. Voices of amazement dominated, but there were several who couldn't suppress their sarcasm.

Grandego gave his audience time to digest all this information As a master demagogue, he had mastered the art of giving room to psychological consequences in order to achieve the desired effect.

"My friends, a lot has been written about them in magazines over the decades, as fiction, and it might take a while getting used to, but they are a reality. In my childhood years, the Andro Masters informed me of my grand identity and revealed to me the New Age Plan. They will appear at this occasion. They represent the gods of the Andromeda galaxy, who have planted life on this planet, sown cultural and scientific seeds in our prehistory, allowing our cultures to develop. They are here to help bring the Plan, to which purpose I was born, to fruition on this earth."

He now stood before his throne and raised his arms.

An excited silence descended upon the Temple. All over the world, billions of people were mesmerized by the live stream. Slowly, two lights started glowing on both sides of Grandego which swelled and got so bright, people in the immediate area had to cover their eyes or put on sunglasses. In the lights, silhouettes appeared of ten-feet-high persons. The shapes became clearer. They wore dark green capes that went down to their knees. A sort of light blue tunic covered their bodies halfway down their thighs. Their loins were girded with a broad, multi-colored belt that covered them tightly and was fastened with buttons. They each wore a sword-like weapon on their hips.

With high brown boots that reached to just below the knees, they stood as soldiers in an "at ease" posture. They had long, dark hair that hung down to their shoulders and rough faces with one blue and one brown eye, which looked dominantly at the audience from beneath thick, dark eyebrows.

"We—yes—we landed on this blue planet and taught the Egyptians and the Babylonians complex architecture, writing, and astronomy. Much has been lost, including much knowledge about natural medicine. But despite that, man has been able to further develop technology. Now, it is time to take the next step. Listen to World Leader Grandego, he will lead you! He has been given to you to complete the preparatory phase, and then," one of the Andros said with a penetrating bass voice as he pointed at Grandego, "then you will take part in the promises. Follow him in all his ways."

Some people warmed up to them, others didn't. Many were deeply impressed, and thought it a privilege to witness this in their lives . . . such a historic moment. Others were skeptical and tried to discover the technical gadgets behind this trick.

Meanwhile, the apparitions faded, and the light fell back to its earlier intensity. Grandego made a slight bow to his left and right, where the Andros had appeared. He spoke once again.

"I will take place on my throne and then enter the Holy of Holies. There will be a complete silence until I return to show my grandeur to the inhabitants of this planet."

The symphony orchestra commenced with background music, and the gigantic Veil, with its depictions of Cherubs, started moving. Slowly, as a curtain, it was pulled left and right, into the walls. The golden throne, with a horned goat's skull on the center of the back rest, started moving backward automatically into the Holiest place. When the golden throne and Grandego had been moved back far enough, the Veil closed again, obscuring Grandego from the crowd.

The moment he had entered the Holy of Holies and the great curtain closed, Grandego took a breath of relief. His moment was upon him. He had been waiting for this for centuries, and he intended to enjoy it fully.

As happy thoughts warmed his insides, a growing light source started shining in front of his face. Grandego was startled, this wasn't part of the day's planning. As the light grew, it started stinging his eyes. Curiously, his body temperature dropped, and he started shivering. The light set a movie in his psyche into motion, showing terrible scenes of his past actions.

"No, no, no!" he began screaming, but no sound came from his mouth. As the light increased, he saw all the bloody, terrible misery he had incited through the centuries. Destructive powers, which he had put into motion through people with his filthy lies, now burned his skin like hot coals.

He saw people being torn apart, babies that were aborted, men murdering each other in hatred, screaming people hurting each other with words, and everything spurred on by his demons.

His own sadistic laughter, that sounded at the sight of people in terrible pain, now cut through his own body like a sharp sword.

"No!" His cries of pain echoed once more as he fled from his throne and tried to take cover in a corner of the Holy Place. He cowered and changed into the shape of a writhing snake, covered with foul-smelling blood.

A terrible scream slid off his forked tongue when he recognized Jesus of Nazareth as the Son of Man in the light. He was clothed in a robe that went down to His feet; His chest girded with a golden girdle. His hair waved as white wool onto His shoulders and His eyes burned like a flame. His feet were like brass, glowing as if straight from an oven, and His voice was the sound of many waters. From His mouth came words that cut like a double-edged sword and His sight was like the sun, shining in all her power. The snake shivered, coiling over itself in the corner, and stared at the Lord of Lords with bloodshot eyes full of hatred and fear.

"You, snake, sower of anger and murderer from the beginning, you've got three and a half years, and then I will cast you into the bottomless pit!" Jesus spoke with full rejection in His voice.

The snake responded as if it had been struck by lightning and screamed in fear.

The light quickly dimmed until it went out. Slowly, the snake morphed back into the now exhausted Grandego, who was wheezing and gasping from the experience. He quickly dragged himself back onto his throne, because the system had been programmed to move it back automatically after a certain time.

He had barely regained his composure before the Veil started opening again. Grandego quickly tried to straighten out his clothes and wiped the cold sweat from his brow and face.

Slowly, the impressive throne slid forward from the Holy of Holies, into the Holy.

Molochi was startled, because he immediately saw Grandego was shaken. This wasn't the Grandego who was going to enjoy this moment. What had transpired? He quickly got up and walked towards the rattled emperor.

When he reached Grandego, he started blessing him.

"I now confirm the divine calling of humanity's leader, and I bless you with all knowledge and revelation necessary to fulfill this grand plan!"

Molochi picked up a cloth which stood on a golden table near the throne and poured scented olive oil on it. He anointed Grandego's face.

Gold dust that had been added to the oil stuck to Grandego's skin, giving him a golden glow. After the blessing and anointment, Molochi turned around and went back to his throne.

The World Emperor took a few deep breaths and gathered his strength to start his previously prepared speech. The blessing had given him time to regain his composure a bit. During the long—to them—break, the people were staring, nearly breathless in expectation at their Emperor. The golden glow had made a deep impact.

"People," Grandego began with a raw voice, "mankind's history is filled with gods, idols, religions and animism. There isn't a people or tribe without its worship and spiritual rituals. Atheism . . . " He stammered a moment.

"The intelligentsia of the past few centuries thought to take refuge in atheism, but that didn't hold with humanity. Why? Because there is a god! Man is a religious being. But all gods, however many there may be, starting today they are finished! They were but the footstool of the truth that is being revealed today."

As Grandego was speaking, he fell more and more into his usual habits. His own words gave him back the feeling of power. This was his moment to shine. After all, it was his inauguration. Nobody could stop him! Yes, *now* is the time.

"Yes!" Grandego exclaimed as he got up. "From today onward, One World Faith is no more! I renounce all our fathers' gods! Religions . . . they are no more!" He shouted even louder, pacing up and down before his throne. A shock went through the audience as they watched him, mesmerized.

"The religions, bundled in the powerful One World Faith, were but the stepping stone to full revelation! I now reveal *myself*! I am the idol to which you bowed when you were honored by being incorporated into the number of service—service to *me*! The unique chip number, without which nothing can be bought or sold, connects you to me. I am the head; you are my body. We are the idol that's worshipped. Calculate it for yourself, because '666' is the universal code to the evolutionary jump. I, man at the center and everything subjected to my image, will lead to the casting off weakness. I, who through perfect policy, take away the problems of the world and humanity! I lead you there, to unity and the total freedom of heart and flesh! Love each other physically, and do not keep your bodies from each other.

"From today, paradise is here, and I am paradise. *Me*. Behold Grandego, your god!"

He stood theatrically; his arms spread wide.

"*Me!*" he exclaimed again.

These words were so powerful that several people fell back at that moment. A shock wave propagated through the rows of people.

Astonishment and surprise were readable on their faces.

Molochi gave a signal, because this was the moment for the paralyzing spirits to fill the air with their inhibitory forces against expressions of rebellion, rejection, aggressive or not, as response to his drastic words.

This had gone too far even for World Master Tarik. He wanted to get up in protest but was pushed back into his throne by the power of the spirits at the scene. It seemed to him he was being strangled. As if stung by a wasp after Grandego's blasphemous words in their own temple, the entire Jewish rabbinate wanted to get up to tackle him and call him names. The demons pushed them back and silenced them.

The large beamer screens showed only positive responses. Images from all continents, showing crowds dancing and shouting and praising Grandego's name.

The Jewish high priest got a humiliating spiritual revelation at that moment. He saw he was being pushed back because of his unconfessed sins. These now were black handles in his soul, which allowed the paralyzing spirits to enforce such great power over him so he couldn't voice his protest. He was shocked to see how he and the masses were misled.

Cardinal Jones and the One World Faith were also dismayed. Why had they sold their soul to the One World Faith movement? Just to satisfy this dictator's hunger for power? And to be rejected and casually cast away afterwards? Anger rose at these thoughts, but they couldn't do a thing.

However, where the captains of industry sat, admiration and respect were the emotions displayed. Grandego, one of them, had made a very extraordinary career step, and that commanded their

respect. Several people left and right fell to their knees and wor-
shiped Grandego. This encouraged him. He continued in a commanding tone.

"I am *the* idol, and I alone. Worship me!"

The screens showed many people immediately did so. Others
doubted and some fled. But then again, there were the images from
the Temple mount, broadcast live. These shots showed only expressions of agreement and worship by prominent attendees.

Grandego raised his arms and pointed his index fingers at the
blue sky. He slowly lowered them until his fingers pointed at the
people in front of him.

"BOW BEFORE YOUR GOD! BOW BEFORE ME, YOUR GOD,
WHO REPRESENTS THE IMAGE OF MAN!"

"OUR GOD, OUR GRANDEGO!" many shouted in unison. Peer
pressure was great and millions of demons all over the world whispered to people to participate in worship.

"Rise, mankind, rise," Grandego continued, arms spread wide,
invitingly. "Celebrate tonight, celebrate exuberantly. Give each other
bodily warmth; give yourself, and my blessing I will give unto you."

With raised arms, he made blessing motions at the delirious
crowd. Through a small microphone in his diamond ring, Molochi
signaled the *Chameleon*'s pilot.

The miraculous stairway of light was unrolled again. Grandego
noticed and walked, with his arms still raised to receive glory, towards Molochi. Molochi got up and bowed before Grandego, who
visibly enjoyed the homage. Especially what was seen on the large
screens. Crowds of people all over the world were shown shouting
his name. Many on their knees and visibly emotional. Both men

now strode to the stairway of light and seemed to be raptured by these images.

Molochi climbed the stairs at a regular pace, but Grandego took his time, looking around and waving, demure as a pope, to the amazed crowds below.

Once in the *Chameleon*, the two conspirators stood theatrically next to each other, with an expression of men with great authority, their faces towards the Temple. Slowly, the helicopter started moving and took the men until they had completely disappeared from sight.

Orchestras and bands started playing at various places across the city, and here and there, entertainers started their shows. A Chinese firework spectacle burst out over the city. Hundreds of waiters and scantily clad waitresses came out and carried trays of drinks and all sorts of delicious dishes. The world was allowed to celebrate. This was a grand day!

24

AKHAN AND TARPI

TARPI AND AKHAN WERE COMPLETELY focused on the events that transpired before their eyes. Breathless, they lay transfixed and saw the two men ascend into the sky on the light stairway from the Temple square.

Fragments of thought about what this all meant fluttered through their minds. After the stairway of light had eventually disappeared and the Chinese fireworks lit up the sky and they still lay recovering from all the confusion, then suddenly they heard a soft voice behind them calling their names.

"Tarpi and Akhan . . . "

Strangely enough, they weren't afraid, because the voice sounded both familiar and very friendly.

As if awaking from a dream they turned towards where they heard the voice, to see who spoke these words. They immediately covered their eyes with their hands, because it seemed as if they were looking directly into the midday sun.

The person walked closer and touched their hands for a moment. The touch felt warm, as when a good father who admires his sons strokes their hair. Their eyes quickly got used to the bright light, after which they discerned the shape of a colorfully dressed, smiling man.

"Akhan and Tarpi," the man said again. "Do you know what this place is where you laid your heads to rest yesterday?"

Akhan and Tarpi looked at each other.

"Yes, in Jerusalem . . . " Akhan replied. "In Jerusalem, sir . . . " he repeated somewhat uncertain.

"That's right, dear friends. On Mount Calvary, to be exact, where I died for your sins," the likable man said.

As these words were spoken, the men saw the film of their lives before their eyes in a split second. They saw their natural life, in which they had done and said lots of things selfishly. They experienced the powerlessness to carry out the good intentions they usually had. They saw the people they had disappointed by that, the lies for their own selfish purposes, the inadequate attention for their loved ones, who yearned for it, the unfulfilled promises.

Above all, Akhan remembered mutilating his brother's murderer as an act of revenge, resulting in his sentence of fifteen years imprisonment. Because of this, he could no longer embrace his beloved wife and children.

Their consciences caused tears of grief and regret to well up in their eyes. Their souls needed rescue. Shame and fear began to overpower them.

"Would You . . . would You forgive us?" stammered Akhan, putting words to the innermost feelings of them both. He raised his bowed head to look upon this unique Man.

Akhan's eyes were wide open when he saw the Man, with a bloodied body, hanging upon a cross. A crown of thorns pierced the skin of His head. His body was mutilated, but His eyes shone with an otherworldly, merciful love.

To his horror, he saw another person on a second cross to the Man's right.

Akhan and Tarpi were shocked to see what followed. The second man started to show a strong comparison to themselves, so that it seemed as if they were hanging there. The crucified man to Jesus' right spoke to the Savior, his voice raw with pain.

"Please remember me, Jesus of Nazareth, when You come into Your Kingdom. I deserve this cross, but You are innocent."

Jesus looked at him as if He had expected this request.

"Today, you shall be with Me in Paradise," He answered with mercy in his voice.

Upon hearing these loving and hopeful words, the eyes of the crucified man shone with joy. At the same time, tears came to his eyes and a blissful stream of mercy flowed to Akhan and Tarpi's souls.

All experiences of fear, shame and sin flowed with it from their bodies. A gloriously refreshing wind seemed to blow through them. The vision faded and the likable Man who had first spoken to them became visible again. His friendly face smiled upon them and Akhan and Tarpi sensed a strong friendship with this Man, Whom they now recognized as Jesus.

"You have received forgiveness, friends. Share My good news with anyone who wants to listen. There will be a difficult time for you in this world, but in the heat of battle, when all seems lost, I will intervene and begin to restore the world. Mankind will understand her origin is with Me, and that through grace, many with Me will transform her to her original state," Jesus explained.

"Proclaim that the Father and mankind, created by Me, will share in infinite love for eternity. Do not be afraid, brothers. I hold all power in heaven and on earth. The complete victory over Satan and all forces of evil is at hand. Keep trusting, and I will lead you to an eternity with Me."

With these words, the Lord of Lords turned around and walked away from them, disappearing from view.

Akhan and Tarpi stayed in the same place for a long time to think about the experience. Somehow, it felt like coming home. The emptiness in the depth of their souls was gone. Their insides seemed to be filled with living water, that welled up like a fountain.

They lay there for at least an hour, until Akhan turned to Tarpi.

"Tarpi," he said. "I thought you were my friend . . . " Tarpi looked at him.

"What do you mean, 'I thought you were my friend', that's what I am, right?" he said, looking at him questioningly.

"No," Akhan said. "You're my brother!"

"Yes, we're brothers and God is our father!" Tarpi exclaimed as well. They jumped up and embraced.

"I can't believe it," Akhan repeated over and over again, amazed by what had happened.

As they reminisced and looked out over the city, Akhan wondered what to do next.

"What do you think we should do now?" he asked Tarpi.

Tarpi looked at him determined. "Do you know what I'm going to do?" he replied. "I'm going to Italy."

Akhan looked at him, curious and surprised.

"What's in Italy?" Akhan asked.

A broad smile came across Tarpi's face.

"Rita."

For more information about

Remko Jorritsma
and
Grand Plans
please visit:

www.grandplans.nl
www.facebook.com/stichting.indevrijheid.9

For more information about
AMBASSADOR INTERNATIONAL
please visit:

www.ambassador-international.com
@AmbassadorIntl
www.facebook.com/AmbassadorIntl

More from Ambassador International

As phenomena escalate, mass hysteria and political tensions begin to mount on a global scale. The world begins to spin out of control, and a former flame reenters Ryan Kates' life, bringing her family along for the ride. The pawns are moved into place, and Ryan must confront the ultimate evil on the world stage, culminating in a supernatural encounter far beyond his wildest dreams.

The Reluctant Disciple

by Jim O'Shea

Author George Rittenhouse combines elements of mystery and adventure in this captivating novel as he follows unlikely hero Randy Grant on a mission of life and death with the fate of the economy on his shoulders.

Blue Dollar

by George Rittenhouse

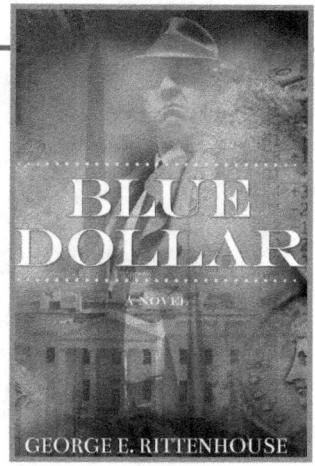

When the dollar collapses, widespread rioting and looting threaten the peace of a family in Zanesville, Ohio. Torn between justice and mercy, with their allies turning against them, their faith is heated in the fire.Will God answer their prayers and deliver them, or must their faith remain blind to facts?

The Reliant

by Dr. Patrick Johnston